©Imrul Islam

Amitava Kumar is the author of *Writing Badly Is Easy*, *The Lovers*, *A Matter of Rats: A Short Biography of Patna*, *Home Products*, which was shortlisted for the Crossword Prize, and *A Foreigner Carrying in the Crook of His Arm a Tiny Bomb*, which received the Page Turner Award. Kumar's writing has appeared in *Caravan*, *Harper's*, *The Guardian*, *New Yorker*, *Vanity Fair*, and the *New York Times*. His essay 'Pyre', first published in *Granta*, was selected by Jonathan Franzen for Best American Essays 2016. He was awarded a Guggenheim Fellowship in 2016. Kumar is Professor of English at Vassar College.

From the acclaimed author of *The Lovers*, a one-of-a-kind novel about fake news, memory, and how truth gives way to fiction.

Satya is an Indian writer living in New York. When he attends a prestigious artists' retreat in Italy, Satya finds the press of the outside world won't let up: a dangerous virus envelopes the globe; Prime Minister Modi wants his citizens to bang plates and pots at 9 p.m.; President Trump continues spreading misinformation online; and the 24-hour news cycle throws fuel on the fire. For the fellows at the retreat, such stories are unbearable distractions, but for Satya, these Orwellian interruptions begin to crystallize into an idea for his new novel, about the lies we tell ourselves and each other. Knitting together accounts of lynching, Trump's tweets, newspaper clippings, childhood memories from Patna, Satya's investigation into a killing near Kolkata, and his tales as husband, father, teacher, *A Time Outside This Time* is a brilliant meditation on life in a post-truth era. Balancing the public and private, the imagined and the real, Amitava Kumar ushers us across time and space in the manner of art and humanity alike, capturing the chaos and dishonesty of the present with intelligence, beauty, and an eye for the uncanny.

Cover Illustration: Amitava Kumar
Cover Design: Bena Sareen

A TIME OUTSIDE THIS TIME

Also by Amitava Kumar

FICTION

The Lovers

Nobody Does the Right Thing

NONFICTION

Writing Badly is Easy

Lunch with a Bigot

A Matter of Rats: A Short Biography of Patna

A Foreigner Carrying in the Crook of His Arm a Tiny Bomb

Husband of a Fanatic

Bombay—London—New York

Passport Photos

POETRY

No Tears for the NRI

{293}

A TIME OUTSIDE THIS TIME

A Novel

AMITAVA KUMAR

ALEPH

ALEPH

ALEPH BOOK COMPANY
An independent publishing firm
promoted by ***Rupa Publications India***

First published in India in 2021
by Aleph Book Company
7/16 Ansari Road, Daryaganj
New Delhi 110 002

ISBN: 978-93-90652-14-3

1 3 5 7 9 10 8 6 4 2

In memoriam
Sonny Mehta (1942–2019)

Every piece of news, any turn of events at all, had this quality: it depressed him utterly. I asked whether his book was done. He said it was. I asked how long it was. "Eight hundred and ninety-seven pages," he said. Then he added, earnestly, "You don't suppose they'll think I wrote it in a fit of pique."

—RENATA ADLER, *Speedboat*

Also, he wanted a book. He was depressed about the political situation and he wanted a book that was either about the political situation or not about the political situation at all.

—SAM LIPSYTE, *Hark*

CONTENTS

CHAPTER I

I'M WRITING A NOVEL, BUT THERE IS THE NEWS

In a little bit, it will be cocktail hour. Our beautiful villa stands on a hill, the sloping ground covered with small olive trees and long lines of tall, angular cypresses; a mansion in the distance is said to be where George and Amal Clooney spend their summers.

I'm on the island for a cushy fellowship, working on a novel. In the week I have been here, this is what I've discovered: one sure way to stop visiting fellows and their spouses from talking to me is to answer them truthfully when they ask what it is I'm doing here. I give my answer and see the light die in their eyes. They nod and look elsewhere—the lake, for instance, which looks lovely at all hours, its color changing constantly. I don't blame anyone. Would you want to talk to someone who says they are studying *models of social acceptance*? (I'm not lying when I say this; I'm just trying to avoid the seductive language of fiction.) What I mean in this utterance is simply that I'm thinking about who in our communities will accept lies and deception. As in all matters, all my projects seeded in guilt, I find myself culpable. But, on this issue, I have certain others in my sights.

If anyone presses, I tell them that my novel is based on an untrue story. In fact, it is based on the *many* untrue stories that surround us and threaten to destroy us. Often, our world comes to us as bad fiction. Toni Morrison read *The New York*

Times every day with pen in hand, making corrections she felt necessary, deleting words or inserting them as she went along. I thought I could start with that idea, a novel about reading the news, but the pencil marks would be found everywhere, not only on the newspaper. Scientific experiments, for instance, or a writer's memoir about writing, and, why not, our relationships and the way we live our everyday life. I'm writing a report from the world of #fakenews.

This evening, while holding my glass of chilled, locally sourced wine, I'd like to be able to tell my interlocutor that the question I'm really asking is this: Who among your neighbors will look the other way when a figure of authority comes to your door and puts a boot in your face?

I wonder what their eyes might do then.

I use what is called real life to craft my fiction. How is it different from fake news? Novelists with a great gift of imagination have invented situations, often quite simple and uncomplicated ones, that you can never rid from your mind: a family undertaking a long, tortuous journey with the corpse of a family member in a coffin to the dead woman's hometown (William Faulkner's *As I Lay Dying*); two men on a train, each one wanting to kill someone, propose that they exchange murders and thereby have an alibi (Patricia Highsmith's *Strangers on a Train*); a woman is on her way to buy flowers for a party she will host that night (Virginia Woolf's *Mrs. Dalloway*); a young man arriving in a city to collect his father's ashes and going on a drug rampage that sends him into a nightmarish spiral (Edward St. Aubyn's *Bad News*). I, however, am unable to invent fictional situations, or maybe they don't interest me that much. Real life, even ordinary life, is what fascinates me, the low road of journalistic observation.

During his last week in office in January 2017, President Barack Obama gave an interview to a book critic from *The New York Times*. Obama told the interviewer that his daughter Malia had read Ernest Hemingway's *A Moveable Feast* and was captivated by the writer describing his goal of writing one true thing every day. ("All you have to do is write one true sentence. Write the truest sentence that you know.") When I read the interview, Trump had been president for two days, and I think the idea for this book was born then.

I began keeping a daily journal, but instead of writing the truest sentence, I noted down a revealing lie. The U.S. president was lying every day but falsehoods, I noted, could be from anywhere in the world. Here's one from my country of birth, India: In the days prior to his retirement from the Rajasthan High Court, Justice Mahesh Chandra Sharma said that the cow should be declared the national animal of India because hundreds of millions of gods and goddesses lived in that sacred animal. The cow is the only creature, the judge opined, that takes in oxygen and also emits oxygen. He also extolled the virtues of cow urine.

The other day a friend posted a few lines from a poem by the radical Hindi poet Gorakh Pandey on Facebook. He was aiming to describe the situation in India under Narendra Modi. I read the extract and that same morning sat down to translate it. In my writing journal, I noted in the margin that this extract could serve as my novel's epigraph:

King said it is night,
Queen said it is night,
Minister said it is night,
Guard said it is night.
This happened right
This morning!

A book made up entirely of rumors. A compilation of fatal falsehoods. That's what I first thought of as my raw material.

What is the opposite of a rumor?

A scientific fact, of course.

But once you start thinking of rumors as stories, which they are, it becomes clear that accounts offered by scientists about their experiments are also stories.

One researcher publishes a study showing that chimps will eat food given to them and not necessarily want to share it with other chimps, and therefore we should conclude that we are born selfish; a different researcher finds that chimps will help other chimps open a door even when they themselves cannot see the bananas strategically placed on the far side. Those inclined to engage in further storytelling go on to say something about the presence or absence of altruism across the species.

We are always telling stories. Because we deal only with stories, in literature, in history, or in science, the simple distinction between truth and lies is a naïve one. Any story ought to be surrounded with other questions. Whose story is it? What ends does it serve? Does it affirm or contradict other stories? My point is that we can change the way we consume stories. And, of course, the way we produce them.

But till that happens I want to ask scientists to clarify one thing.

On the BBC show *Top Gear*, a discussion about driverless cars led to conversation about an experiment that was supposedly about self-preservation. You can watch this episode on YouTube. Jeremy Clarkson, the show's host, says that scientists conducted "an awful experiment" in which they put monkeys and their babies in a box and heated the floor. When the heat became unbearable, all the monkeys picked up their babies and held them in their arms. But when the floor got hotter, "till it was absolutely unbearable," the monkeys put the babies down and stood on them.

I have a few questions.

The main one is: Did it really happen, this experiment?

Where and when?

These are perhaps silly questions. But they remind us that there are many ways to respond to a story. And I haven't yet processed what the uproarious laughter of the studio audience meant when Clarkson was done telling his story about the monkey experiment.

I also want to pose a more important question: Did all the adult monkeys act in unison, picking up or putting down their babies as one body?

Were there those—or, for that matter, just one—that changed their minds?

Or hesitated just a bit, looking at the other monkeys, with bewildered gray-brown eyes? Or, if you allow me to be sentimental for half a second, did an adult monkey, after standing on her baby for maybe a minute, pick it up to offer comfort? And, before putting it down again—if indeed all of this even happened—give the doomed baby a last kiss?

Do you remember the days immediately after Trump took office? The crowd. Loud fans in places such as Cincinnati, Ohio, or Des Moines, Iowa, or Mobile, Alabama, had found the freedom to behave like frat boys on a Friday night. Republicans were greeted with chants of "USA! USA!" There was a spike in assaults against Blacks and Muslims and others who, to Trump loyalists, looked like outsiders. The Women's March took place in Washington, D.C., on January 21, the largest single-day protest in the nation's history. The American Civil Liberties Union (ACLU) declared its readiness to challenge Trump's executive orders and witnessed a spike in membership as well as donations. *The New*

York Times published an ad to highlight the fight over truth, which ended with the words "the truth is more important now than ever." The online Merriam-Webster dictionary also took up the good fight; after Trump aide Kellyanne Conway described false statements as "alternative facts," Merriam-Webster sent out the following tweet: "A fact is a piece of information presented as having objective reality." (On January 22, 2017, when I saw that tweet, it had been liked 55,914 times.)

One of the residents at the villa is a filmmaker from Connecticut. Her name is LeeAnn Wendell. She shared a bit of her work with us last week, and I got from her this quote that came from Pier Paolo Pasolini: "I don't believe we shall ever again have any form of society in which men will be free. One should not hope for it. One should not hope for anything. Hope is invented by politicians to keep the electorate happy." I wrote down Pasolini's words because I imagined my editor asking me a question when I sent in the manuscript. "What's your point?" I plan to quote Pasolini and say, "Point? I don't have a point. No uplifting message certainly. We are fucked."

(The residency was shut down when dire reports began to come of the deaths from a new virus. I left and later learned that one of the staff was an early casualty. I had missed an opportunity. There was a researcher there who chattered gaily in Italian with the waitstaff. Her name was Anna Duranti. Her collaborator was a very polite, very serious Chinese social scientist named Li Qinglian. The duo was examining the carbon footprint of fashion in two cities in China, one on the coast and one inland. Li stayed silent during meals unless addressed directly, to which she responded with a monosyllable and an apologetic smile, but Anna could be heard saying things like "Did you know that in order to produce a cotton shirt, up to 2,700 liters of water are needed?" That is exactly what I overheard her ask and she laughed when I made her repeat it so that I could write it down. Trump would go on to call it the "Chinese virus" and the "kung flu." In India, the Union Minister of State for Health and Family Welfare would say that if people took the step of absorbing the sun's rays for ten to fifteen minutes between 11:00 a.m. and 2:00 p.m., they would build immunity. The Indian newspapers carrying this statement mentioned a BBC report that cited experts who said that exposure to the sun is "completely ineffective" against the virus.)

Apart from my notebooks, which are black and numbered, I have three scrapbooks, their pages fat with newspaper clippings and printouts. Each scrapbook also serves as a journal of sorts. Opening one of the scrapbooks on a random page, I found a review of a book about the war in Bosnia and, on the opposite page, an article about the psychology of self-help books. In the review of the Bosnian war book, a Polish forensic anthropologist is quoted saying to the author: "I love bones, bones speak to me. I can determine nationality by bones. A Muslim's femur is bent into a slight arc, because Muslims squat." The clipping is turning yellow but a red pen mark holds the anthropologist's statement in a quarantined plot of inquiry. The information is to be released once I have confirmed its veracity. The article from the opposite page tells me that while positive self-statements (e.g., "I am a lovable person") can help those with high self-esteem, they actually lead to a greater experience of negativity for those with low self-esteem. In other words, if many readers of self-help books are likely to suffer from low self-esteem, the reading of books that encourage positive self-statements may be worse than useless.

Yesterday, during cocktail hour, my choice of drink was the Aperol spritz. Tonight I am having the local Chardonnay. At first I speak to a British man who's working to solve the water crisis in Gaza, particularly the salinization of the coastal aquifer and the threat this poses to the people living in one of the most densely populated strips of land there. Then I chat with a Black woman from New Jersey who's composing music for a film. Nikki studied violin at Juilliard and went to Stanford for another degree in ethnomusicology. I ask her what Stanford was like and she laughs and says that she once played with Condoleezza Rice. But she's been back in New Jersey for nearly two decades. Nikki is the cofounder of an organization that supports music and the arts. I say I have an odd question for her: Has she ever heard anyone say they saw Arabs in New Jersey celebrating the September 11 attacks?

She says, "Other than Donald Trump? No."

I say that he claims he watched thousands and thousands of people cheering when the Twin Towers fell.

She says, "Lies. He lies."

I sip my Chardonnay. Nikki is drinking red wine. I start her on a new train of thought. She wants to know if I've been living in the United States for long. I tell her I came from India in the early nineties. Nikki says that I probably didn't know about the Central Park Five. In the late eighties a woman who had been jogging in Central Park was badly beaten and raped. She was unconscious for several days and unable to recall any details of the attack. Five Black teenagers who were in the park at the time were wrongly convicted of the crime. Nikki tells me that Trump, back when the news broke, had placed a newspaper ad demanding that the boys be executed. It wasn't until a decade or more later that they received justice when the real rapist confessed in prison and his guilt was confirmed by DNA testing. Another decade would pass before the five, who were grown men now, received a settlement from the city that had imprisoned them as children.

Nikki takes another sip and says, "They received $41 million. Largest settlement in the country's history. But you know what kills me? That here is our president, an accused rapist himself, who was back then buying space for an ad in the *New York Post*. This country hates nothing more than its Black children."

That day, prior to cocktail hour, I looked at entries in journal number four from earlier in the year. On the first page is the following:

The most popular stories on Snopes.com:

Did Eleven U.S. Marines Give Their Lives This Week? [False]

Did a Principal Ban Candy Canes Because They Are Shaped Like *J*s for Jesus? [True]

Did a Brain-Eating Amoeba Kill a Woman Who Rinsed Her Sinuses with Tap Water? [True]

Did Miley Cyrus Tell Fans to Worship Satan if They Want to Be Rich and Famous? [False]

Did Jon Voight Urge Americans to "Fight for Donald Trump"? [True]

The list is fairly ridiculous. It reveals the low stakes in the battle for truth in our culture. In journal number four, I also found a story titled "Is Trump's Face Hidden in Baboon Feces?" *Scientific Reports* had published (on January 31, 2018) a paper entitled "Methylation-Based Enrichment Facilitates Low-Cost Noninvasive Genomic Scale Sequencing of Population from Feces." It appeared that the accompanying illustration had been tweaked by hackers to resemble Forty-Five. A statement had later been appended to the article in *Scientific Reports:* "The editors have become aware of unusual aspects to the 'Extract Fecal DNA' illustration in Figure 1. We are investigating and appropriate action will be taken once the matter is resolved." If there was anything mildly uplifting about the nature of things, it was seeing how other ordinary citizens employed themselves in the same zealous quest for something like truth. My notes reveal that a young man in Los Angeles named Sam Morrison sold ten thousand pairs of flip-flops with Trump's contradictory tweets emblazoned on each pair. To wit: on the right foot, a Trump tweet from 2018 saying "Remember, don't believe 'sources said' by the VERY dishonest media. If they don't name the sources, the sources don't exist"; and, on the left, an earlier Trump tweet, this one from 2012, "An 'extremely credible source' has called my office and told me that @BarackObama's birth certificate is a fraud."

Talking of Trump's tweets: On February 17, 2019, the president tweeted, in all CAPS: "THE RIGGED AND CORRUPT MEDIA IS THE ENEMY OF THE PEOPLE." Sarah Silverman, playing Trump's White House press secretary in the Hulu series *I Love You, America,* said: "Don't be enemies of the people." Journalists have pointed out that Trump's unhinged rants make their jobs not just difficult but also risky; an irrational part of me also thinks that if we all repeated Silverman's injunction, the charge would lose its sting and parody would win over propaganda. I go to sleep thinking about this and I wake up with a definite thought: this book that I'm writing, about fake news and journalistic excavation of truth, will be cheekily titled *Enemies of the People.* Also, I like Sarah Silverman. And Kate McKinnon. And, last but most, Tina Fey. *Oh, Tina Fey.* (Tina Fey, in a cameo on *Saturday Night Live* during the pandemic, invoked Dunning-Kruger! She hadn't taken *his* name but everyone knew who she was talking about—if you were to make a public statement like "He's so stupid" or "He's so full of bullshit," is there any danger that in any town or city in America people wouldn't know who you were talking about? In any case, I felt Tina Fey was talking to me because of what I had already written in my manuscript on Dunning-Kruger. For more on that subject, see p. 120.)

I listened to a podcast once where a writer was discussing his short story about a refugee crisis. He was saying that the

Trump administration had hijacked his genre and he resented this fact. "I used to freely traffic in untruths, mostly with a clear conscience, because there were long-established places one could go to find truth." The current regime has muddied the waters. I heard the writer saying that his home turf—that of fiction—had been usurped. With the rise of "alternative facts," what did "fiction" even mean? I had been asking myself the same question. How to insist on facts or on truth, if so many around us invest their beliefs in fictions spun by Fox News? I was lying on my bed in the dark telling myself that I wanted to write my own fiction that felt as real as the weight of my head on the pillow. But who was I kidding? What I was writing seemed fake to me, not least because nothing I wrote would go viral the way that fake story did about Trump in the White House, watching the gorilla channel each night in his bathrobe. The prankster who dreamed up this story (do I remember this right?) wrote that Trump had complained to his staff that "the gorilla channel was broken." And that the staff had rigged a twenty-four-hour feed from right outside his bedroom. The story described Trump in the early hours of the morning, his face close to the screen. I had enjoyed that detail. False, but funny.

At dinner that night, a woman from Colombia is sitting beside me. The villa staff, dressed in white, serves us our drinks. She says, "Are you Satya? The person who is working on fake news..." I say yes and ask her name. "Isabella," she says, adding that she's working on a conceptual art project about evidence. She moved from Medellín to San Diego two years ago. I want to find out more about her work, but Isabella is already saying that there's so much information in the world today she feels overwhelmed. Even before she finished her sentence, I asked myself if she was going to say *overwhelmed*.

Her use of the familiar wording shows that we all read the same things, she in her home in San Diego, Nikki in New Jersey, myself, wherever I happen to be at any moment, and everyone else everywhere in the world. We're all reading and thinking and saying the same things. Then Isabella makes a comment that surprises me. A few years ago, she came across an unforgettable line in a newspaper article: "Anyone reading this essay will accumulate more knowledge today than Shakespeare did in his entire lifetime." I'm a bit incredulous. However, Isabella is confident and says that I can Google it. (I do later in my room and see that she got the quote right. But, at the time, all I could say was that I doubted whether I knew more than Shakespeare. To begin with, language, and the huge gap between his vocabulary and mine. But Isabella was not bothered by my argument. She said that the sheer amount of information, including fake news, any person had in the Internet age couldn't possibly be rivaled by someone living even twenty years ago. I pondered this.)

Our pistachio ice cream is served in ornate green glass jars. We pay attention to our dessert before Isabella speaks again. She says, "For instance, I read on Twitter this morning that a lioness mates up to a hundred times a day." She adds that she wondered all day, locked up in her studio, if that could even be true. (Of course, I Google this detail too. And a website in Africa confirms Isabella's piece of information.) I laugh, not knowing the right answer, and Isabella says, "Who's the genius who dreams up this nonsense?"

In our world, we are surrounded by lies. And, worse, bad faith.

Is science the answer? Not if scientists don't recognize that they, too, are telling a story—trying to find their truths by setting up situations. The same mixture of fiction and fact.

Which brings me to my wife, Vaani. She is a psychologist and lives in the world of experiments.

Let me now describe a situation.

Vaani and I have a child—her name is Piya. Last year, I grew concerned about the lies Piya was telling. She was eight at that time. I complained to Vaani about her. We were in the car, driving down to New Jersey, to the IKEA store in Paramus because we needed new lamps for our home. Piya was in the back, and, though she was asleep, I felt I needed to lower my voice.

Vaani said, "You are needlessly worried. Among children, lying is a sign of cognitive development."

It irritated me that she was speaking in a loud, normal voice. I glanced back at Piya.

I wanted to say that till only recently Piya's lies were so undisguised that I had seen them as signs of her innocence. *Dad, do you have any more chocolate? I didn't eat the chocolate that was on the table.* But now I felt there was in her lies a quality of deception that involved more calculation, even manipulation. On the other hand, I had also observed that Piya operated in a strict moral economy. If we had planned something, say, going out for ice cream on Saturday night, and then had to change the plan and move the outing to Sunday night, she took this badly. *You lied, Mom, you always lie.* I kept quiet, looking at the scene outside. We were passing a row of car dealerships, shiny cars in the parking lots lining the highway, tight clusters of red, white, and blue balloons holding afloat signs announcing July 4 sales.

Perhaps Vaani felt that she had been abrupt. She said with a smile, "Let's play a game."

She said, "A psychologist was trying to find out what reduces lying among children. She read out two stories to the kids whose behavior had been studied and who were going to be questioned about how they had behaved. One story was 'The Boy Who Cried Wolf.' The boy and the sheep get eaten because of his repeated lies? (I nodded.) The other story was 'George Washington and the Cherry Tree.' You know what happens in that one, right? (I nodded again.) Okay, so tell me, which story reduced lying more?"

I knew the question was a trap. The first story was the one that my own mother had told me in my childhood. In fact, not too many months ago, I had found myself narrating it to little Piya too. It was a frightening story, the wolf eats you up, but I felt that this tale would scare her away from her lies.

I suspected I was giving Vaani the wrong answer.

I said, "The Boy Who Cried Wolf."

"Well, you are not alone in thinking that. Most people make that guess. But they are wrong."

Vaani said that most kids lied more after listening to 'The Boy Who Cried Wolf.' They were afraid of being caught having done any wrong, and were lying to cover up whatever they thought or knew had been a transgression.

" 'George Washington and the Cherry Tree' works differently. It cut down lying among boys by 75 percent and by 50 percent among girls. Do you know why?"

"Because George Washington was the president?"

"No. The test got the same results when the psychologist replaced Washington with a nondescript character."

Vaani explained that the fable about the boy and the wolf teaches the lesson that lying begets punishment. But this isn't news for the children. They already know that. In the second story, after the boy George confesses to his father that he used his new hatchet to strike down the prized cherry tree, the father says, "Son, I'm glad that you cut down the cherry tree after all. Hearing you tell the truth is better than if I had a thousand cherry trees."

Telling the truth had made the parent happy. That is what the child chooses after hearing that story. She doesn't lie because she wants to make you happy.

I remember looking back again at Piya, asleep in the back seat. I had done her wrong by telling her the story about the boy and the wolf.

After dinner, I return to my desk at the villa and search in my journal number three. I find what I'm looking for easily enough. A sonogram. My wife must have brought it home after a visit to the doctor when she was pregnant. In the scatter of blurry gray forms there was already skin and hair and blood and bones. The face I have missed while at this residency during my cherished sabbatical semester; the perky voice bringing me reports from the world outside our door. Even her mistakes alerting me to the magic of language. She was five when we had gone on a trip to Maine. Upon our landing at the airport, her question to me: "Dad, are we now going to get our dental car?"

I don't want to lie. I want to make Vaani and Piya happy.

I want to tell you the truth too, dear reader, and make you happy.

I offer you the stories of my experiments with truth. Truth bends like a twig standing in a glass of water. Neither our leaders nor the mobs of killers hounding protesters on the streets admit the fictionality of our existence. There is no admission of doubt or ambiguity in their judgment—no twig bending in the water.

For good or ill, this is where things are in my head: The world has put us all in a dire situation. What can one write to save a life? And what are you to write after that life that you were trying to save is gone?

Once I heard a human rights lawyer, a woman who has provided aid in the past to writers accused by the Indian government of sedition, say to the thousand protesters gathered in a park: "Keep a record. Don't trust the state. Don't expect the police to document the violence it is raining on your head. You have to do this yourself. Note it down." She was saying that, when this time is over, the records you keep will be vital. The news cycle blindly spins each happening into quick oblivion. As a writer I felt I just needed to note down accurately what I knew so that I could remember.

Words like tombstones? Words like hands raised in prayer? Words naked like knives, like bared teeth?

Or maybe something entirely gentler:

When I was a boy in my hometown and it had been raining for three days, it became so that it was no longer possible to have any consciousness of a time when it wasn't raining. Rain soaked through the walls and slime grew on the inside, in the corners, and even on the ceiling. Phones stopped working. No newspapers came. Birds disappeared from the wet branches of trees. No question of going to school. There was no language outside of "It is raining outside." *Water stood in the distant fields. It rushed down pipes and roared in the gutters. The roads became rivers in which people waded or swam. Brij Bihari brought his cows onto the veranda at the back of our house. Mother would switch on the fans in one room to try to dry the wet clothes. It was all in vain. The snake found in the toilet was proof that the world outside had changed, and the natural order had been turned upside down. Only rain was permanent. You could do nothing but wait. I'm saying all this because that is exactly what has happened to us politically. We cannot imagine—I cannot imagine, sometimes—a time outside this time. The people who are in power must also be deluded enough to believe this. They must think that their power is eternal. That they will sit on the throne forever. And it is this thought that is their failing, because it condemns them to missteps and error. Stay alert. You will hear the rain stop and the wind shift. The powerful will not be waiting for it but that moment will come. It will mark the beginning of their doom, their end.*

CHAPTER 2

MY EXPERIMENTS WITH ANTS

Today, during lunch at the villa, I complimented the chef on the excellent salad. The chef doesn't speak much English. He turned around and picked up two pears from a basket, light-green skin tinged with red. On a wooden board there was a section cut from a pale-yellow wheel of Parmigiano-Reggiano cheese. He pointed to the two items and then to the wall behind him and said, "Emilia-Romagna, Emilia-Romagna," as if he were providing an ecstatic introduction to his beautiful lover. More likely the chef was explaining that these two ingredients, from the region Emilia-Romagna, were responsible for the delight I had experienced. He held the two pears in front of his chest, so that in an unintentional pantomime it looked as if he was holding up his breasts. "Fresh, fresh," he said in English. I opened my hand, palm up, and pointed to the pears. He gave me one. I gestured toward the door. Could I take it away with me? Yes, yes, he was saying in his language. Holding the pear in one hand, a notebook in the other, I walked down the hill to the lake.

I sat down at the water's edge in the shade of an olive tree. There was no one else around. The waves beat against the concrete bulwark. Several yards out in front of me, I thought I saw a water snake silhouetted in a rising wave. My pear tasted delicious. I returned to what had preoccupied me earlier that day. I was taking down notes about what I remembered of my boyhood.

(In childhood, adults take care of you. You are pampered. This residency is a little bit like that. You don't cook; you are fed meals. Your room is cleaned and your bed made by others. People are nice to you. No wonder I was beginning my investigation by writing about being a child.) The image that came to me was of the boy absorbed in the mystery of the lives of ants. Solitary, concentrated on his object of study, the boy was carrying out an experiment. And as I sat beside the lake, looking at the endless waves, another memory surfaced: On the small bookshelf in the living room in the house in which the boy lived at that time, his parents had a slightly damaged copy of Gandhi's *My Experiments with Truth*. The boy hadn't read the book but did he wonder about it sometimes? The young can be unselfconsciously literal: Does the boy see the half-naked fakir clad in a white lab coat producing at the end of his experiments a new compound called *the nation*? Even at that young age, the boy knows about the Salt March. He has heard his mother telling his sister about it. Was that an experiment? Did the great man ever *fail* at his experiments? Or did he only record his successes?

I grew up in India hearing about Mahatma Gandhi and when I think about myths, it is his bald, bespectacled head that comes to mind. This is not to suggest that Gandhi, a bamboo staff in hand, stands at the mouth of the dark cave where all falsehood is stored. No, what I want to convey is my early sense that there are people and events that achieve a certain fictionality. Stories become attached to them. As a writer, this aspect of life is of great interest to me. Here's a fragment from a report that I read in a magazine about the aftermath of Gandhi's assassination on January 30, 1948. It is a story that is so good I haven't tried very hard to find out whether it is true or not; when I first read this account, fifteen or twenty years ago, I copied and pasted it in the pages of my writing journal:

> Manno Devi remembers. "We could not eat. Nobody ate that day and night at all. How could we?" Manno Devi and her husband used to look after the goat which provided the milk that Gandhiji drank. That night, as the dough for rotis lay untouched, the animal wandered into the kitchen and ate up all of it. The goat died at night, its belly swollen, its eyes popping out.

What you are reading now is a memory experiment. I'm looking back at the boy I was. In my mind, that boy doesn't stand out clearly in outline but certain incidents in his young life do. I'm struck by his innocence. There is a confusion in the boy's mind, and it hasn't left me entirely. He is cruel to ants that climb up a wall near the front steps of the house in which he lives; out on the streets of his provincial town, men are being set on fire depending on the stories told by the length of their foreskin. The boy's father works in the government bureaucracy—and the boy perhaps senses that if his father cannot protect everyone, he cannot also protect the boy. Is it this discovery of fear that has made him forget so much in his past? I cannot be certain.

My pear had been eaten, the soft pulpy core tossed in the lake's water. I carried my notebook everywhere I went at the villa. I had to be patient, I told myself, I had to wait for my memories to reveal themselves. My half-forgotten world was precious to me; I somehow felt that the past would protect me from the ravages of the present. The outside world was threatening. At breakfast, there could be discussion, largely based on hearsay, about the possibility of a terrible new disease breaking out in that world outside—but, inside the walls of my study here, I was distant from it all, and, removed from that reality, I felt safe to quietly pierce the cocoon that the years had wrapped around my earliest memories. In this private, even intimate, space I was trying to remember the earliest lies I was told about others and the stories I invented about myself. Opening my notebook, I spent the rest of the afternoon recording in its pages the following story.

My Experiments with Ants

> There are lizards—girgit, thin, brown, scaly—in the small garden.
>
> The boy is scared of the girgit. These reptiles have long tails although their thin bodies are no longer than the span of his palm. Many of them have bloated red sacs under their chins. These creatures scare him, but he also wants to kill them. He often daydreams about catching them unawares with a throw, lifting them from their perches with a sharp stone. As they fall back in the air, he imagines seeing their pale, exposed bellies.
>
> Brij Bihari has told him that the lizards are Muslim.
>
> During the riots that accompanied the partition of India, the Muslims were running scared from the Hindus. If the Hindus found the Muslims, they would kill them. If the Hindus did not kill the Muslims first, the Muslims would kill the Hindus. Or they would take the Hindus to the new country, Pakistan, where they would be converted and become trapped forever.
>
> Once, Brij Bihari said, the Hindus saw a bearded Muslim running away. They caught him and were about to chop off his head. The man was a coward. In order to save his life, he pointed with his beard toward the well where the other Muslims were hiding. Because of this act

of treachery, that man was turned into a reptile with a sac under his chin. That is why when the boy and other Hindus look at these lizards, they bob their heads as if they are pointing toward a well.

The year is 1979. He is four years old.

A crack about an inch and a half high separates the bottom of the bathroom door from the cement floor. When Mother takes her bath, the boy slides his toes under the door and waits. He can hear the water running and the sound of the radio inside.

Whenever Mother notices his feet, she switches off the radio. He hears the clink of her bangles as she comes closer on the other side. He stands with his body pressed against the painted wood, and he can feel his own warm breath on his face. A quiet moment passes. And then Mother sprinkles talcum powder on his toes.

No matter how many times this ritual is repeated, he feels surprised and intensely happy. The slight heat of early spring and the smell of talcum powder will evoke in him years later the memory of his childhood.

The giant aerials of All India Radio stand only two hundred yards from their home. Their house is at the end of a short side street. Outside, on the left, is a small khataal for cows and buffaloes. The milk that is needed for the neighborhood comes from this cowshed. Brij Bihari is the owner of the khataal. He is a milkman because that is his caste. His full name is Brij Bihari Yadav. Brij Bihari does not know how to write, but Mother says that he is very smart. He is from Samastipur, where he goes by train during the Holi festival.

Mother bathes during that long hour of midday, after she has finished cooking. She first washes a few clothes and then she fills the buckets for her bath. After she emerges from the bathroom—the jingles on the radio announcing her return—they wait for Father to come home for lunch.

Today, the boy hears her open the bathroom door. "Satya," she shouts out to him. "Did Father call?"

He shouts back the answer. He hasn't heard the phone ringing. Mother walks into the living room and dials the number for the office. He knows Father is not there because her conversation with Bose Babu at the office goes on longer than is usual. She says, "My daughter is at school. I can't leave her there with this trouble in town."

Father is a magistrate in our small town. He goes to his office in a government car, a white Ambassador, with an old driver named Aziz at the wheel.

The boy asks Mother how his sister, older than he by two years, is allowed to come back early from school.

Instead of answering him Mother asks him to fetch Brij Bihari from the khataal right away.

The two buffaloes are sitting at their assigned places outside the straw enclosure. The boy looks inside. It is dark and cool under the thatched roof. The four cows stand in front of their empty tubs chewing on their cud. But Brij Bihari isn't there. Then the boy sees him outside the gate to the radio station talking to two men. He runs up to say that Mother is calling him.

Brij Bihari nods his head but does not move. The men continue to talk in low voices. One of the men has three metal keys and a penknife hanging from the yellow thread that drops in a diagonal across his torso. This man is sitting on the saddle of his bicycle. Brij Bihari and the third man stand on either side of the bicycle. The conversation proceeds in this preoccupied way for another few minutes.

When they arrive home, Mother is inside, standing at the bathroom door listening to the radio. Brij Bihari says, "There is a storm breaking in the city."

Mother says, "They are not telling us much. But they just announced that there is a curfew."

Brij Bihari says, "Arre, the public when it is angry cannot be controlled by a curfew."

The boy does not know who the public is. He is thinking of the two men he had just seen talking to Brij Bihari. The one sitting on the cycle perhaps cannot be controlled when he is upset. He uses the small knife hanging from his sacred thread to kill the curfew.

Mother is worried. She has not been able to contact Father. But she doesn't want to use the phone. "I am afraid he might be calling us here," she says.

Mother tells Brij Bihari why she has called him. "Please take your bicycle and go to the convent school. Stay there till I am able to send a car. Please do this much for me."

Brij Bihari laughs at Mother's tone and he tries to set her mind at ease by saying, "There is nothing to worry about at the school. The public is looking only for Muslims."

Brij Bihari says to the boy outside, "The Muslims have been making a lot of noise lately. Now the postman is going to come." What can he possibly mean? *The postman?* Brij Bihari puts on his cotton vest over his naked chest because he is going to the convent school. "A few of the bearded ones," he adds mysteriously, "are going to be stamped and mailed today." He points above at the sky. He has a sly look in his eyes, as if he were joking. Then he is off quickly on his bicycle.

When the boy looks out of the window on the ground floor of his home, he can see that the white football an elder cousin, Pappu Bhaiyya, had given him for his last birthday is still where he had kicked it under the bushes. A single lizard is sitting on it, its tail drooping over the curve of the ball. The girgit makes a swallowing gesture, and, for a second, he sees its pink mouth. He wonders whether it has eaten an ant.

The boy likes killing ants. There is a matchstick fallen at the edge of the veranda floor. He squats down near it and uses the matchstick's burnt, black head to slice in half the bodies of the ants that are climbing the yellow wall.

He starts with the ant at the bottom and works his way up quickly. But, by then, a new column of ants has started climbing up again, and he has to hurry back to the beginning of the line. Though this is hard work, it commands his full attention, and gives him pleasure. The ants have no idea what he is doing to them. Now and then, however, they break the line and start scurrying in a curve, like the cars that turn on a detour when there has been a bad accident ahead.

He looks up and sees that the lizard has not moved. He puts three dead ants on a small leaf and begins to walk slowly toward the ball on which it sits. But the lizard disappears on the other side of the football and then he catches sight of it diving into the foliage. He places the leaf carefully on top of the ball, a food offering or a trap for the lizard, and slowly retreats to his place next to the wall. He tells himself that he must practice stealth as a hunter, and, making as little noise as possible, he takes up the matchstick again.

His experiment relies on observation. Once an ant is dead, another ant will eat it. If he keeps at this task near the wall, the boy thinks, he will have killed enough ants to feed the rest of the ant colony. He has seen ants carrying other ants on their backs. They are not taking the dead ants to be cremated. Brij Bihari has told him that the ants will take the dead ones into their homes and eat them like toast when evening comes.

The ants live inside the ground. The boy would like to see their tiny rooms, one bedroom separated from another, and all linked by thin lines that are actually hallways. In each house, there is a living room, where ants sit around and drink tea and eat their dead neighbors whom the boy has killed.

Brij Bihari is a tall, thin man. His mustache hangs over a part of his face. Brij Bihari's voice comes out from deep inside his stomach, which he holds tight when he walks. He is clad, for most of the time, only in a blue lungi wrapped around his waist. Bare-chested, he roams the neighborhood with his cows each morning, selling milk door to door.

For as long as the boy can remember, Brij Bihari has been a part of their household. Brij Bihari uses the bathroom in the servant quarters behind the house, and some of his belongings are stored in the garage. In return, his parents use Brij Bihari's services for a variety of tasks. When guests arrive and cold bottles of Coca-Cola need to be brought from the shops near Vijay Chowk, or the doctor needs to be fetched, like the night when Father started vomiting and the phone wasn't working, or when crackers and big chocolate bombs need to be exploded during Diwali, Mother always summons Brij Bihari.

For a few months, the family had a maidservant who had come from Mother's village. Her name was Bimla. The boy's sister let Bimla oil her hair and then weave it into plaits. There was some problem one morning. Bimla was upset. Mother had the red tooth powder in her hand—she was still in the middle of brushing her teeth—and she was speaking angrily to Brij Bihari. Then Father appeared and asked the boy to go away and play. From the window above, the boy saw Father berating Brij Bihari, who, for hours afterward, could be seen laboring silently in the sun, cutting the maize in the backyard. He was being punished, but for what?

Bimla did not make rotis during lunch that day. The boy looked for her. She was lying down on her thin mattress in the small room at the back. The room was next to the bathroom that Brij Bihari and she shared. He asked Bimla why she was not in the kitchen and she said, "I have a stomachache."

The boy did not believe her although he did not know why.

He said to Bimla, "I want some water." She turned her face to the wall and began sobbing. He saw how her back heaved as she wept, and he left the room quickly because he had made her cry. He did not immediately notice that Bimla had left their house the next day. It was many days later that he heard Mother telling someone that Bimla had returned to her village.

Brij Bihari is very different from Father. Father is a government officer, and people like Brij Bihari call him saheb. Father does not joke with anyone. He travels in the car with Aziz, and he signs files and gives to the people what they need. Aziz, their driver, is a Muslim. The boy imagines Brij Bihari taking the small and dark-skinned Aziz and putting him in a brown-paper parcel. *Stamped and mailed.* This thought troubles him and he is afraid for Aziz and then for himself and then for everyone. He would like Father to come back home. And his elder sister too. They will all be unexpectedly together, sitting down for a surprise lunch.

Tifflin is the term that Brij Bihari uses for lunch. He cannot really speak English; the boy laughs when Brij Bihari uses foreign words. One evening, his parents were sitting down in the living room with some guests. Brij Bihari was asked to bring tea. In the kitchen, he held the tray bearing the teacups in both hands and walked back and forth in the manner of a woman. Periodically, he stopped in front of the boy. A cup appeared in front of him, but, before the boy could take it, Brij Bihari lifted the cup to his own pressed lips. He simpered, and said over and over again, "T.P." The boy laughed but felt guilty about laughing at the guests and, perhaps, at his parents.

He is often amused by the way Brij Bihari speaks to him although he does not always understand what he is being told. Often, Brij Bihari's words are dark and mysterious, like a trapdoor in the floor. From his place in the present, the boy sees himself falling through the trapdoor. He lands in a dark pit and stumbles into a dimly lit tunnel that opens into the future, where, unknown to him, he will struggle to become a writer.

In that distant future, he will find words to describe his childhood. Words will liberate him. But he will also discover a distrust of the promise of language. Words will fail him. He will not be able to undo the confusion around him. One day he will tell himself that he is a writer because the childhood fascination as well as unease with what he is being told has not yet left him. At the place where the trapdoor will finally lead him, people will find words to justify any injustice. People will kill and they will use words to sharpen their knives. Words will join the battle. Faced with the walls blackened by the fires and then the sight of the corpses, he will feel bereft of language.

In the present, however, in the present of his childhood, which he will later think of as being neither happy nor unhappy, he likes talking to Brij Bihari. This is because, unlike his parents, Brij Bihari speaks to the boy as if he were a part of his larger world. The world that Brij Bihari lives in is very exciting to the boy. Mother knows this and does not like it at all. The boy has just begun writing the alphabet in English. When he does not write in his notebook, or acts irresponsibly, the boy hears Mother asking him, "What will you do when you grow up? Just milk cows like Brij Bihari?"

He wants very much to take care of Brij Bihari's cows. He wants to feed them grass and hay mixed together with a little bit of water in the trough. He likes the smell of hay. He does want to milk the cows, binding their hind legs with rope so that they don't kick at him. Fascinated, he has watched Brij Bihari pulling at their udders so that the milk squirts into the bucket held between his knees. He wants to make the milk foam like that. And he wants to sleep in the open like Brij Bihari does, on a string cot at night, with the red light atop the aerial above the radio station glowing in the dark like a star.

A blue Jeep with police written in red on the sides comes to their door and the boy's sister jumps out of it. Brij Bihari is at the back with his bicycle resting on the Jeep's footrest. Mother is delighted. Her voice becomes girlish. Fluttering like a bird on the veranda, she says, "Munni! Munni!" Using her sari, Mother wipes the girl's face, but it is she herself who is crying. This display of emotion from Mother makes the girl burst into tears. She stops only when Mother gives her a glass of water to drink and, as abruptly as she had started crying, the girl says, "I am hungry."

A constable brings the sister's school bag to the door. He is a young man with a steel bangle on his wrist. He says, "Order hai wapas jaane ka." The police Jeep has been ordered to return.

The boy wants the Jeep to stay so that he can admire the red lights and the red and blue flag that droops on its hood. When the Jeep is gone, Brij Bihari begins to tell Mother a story. The public is likely to get interested in Munni's school very soon. The nuns there have begun taking in the Muslim families from the surrounding areas. Brij Bihari has seen this while he waited with his cycle leaning against the giant peepul tree. Women in burkas with children in tow, all being led by groups of intense young men. The main metal gate at the school is locked. But the side gate is open. The Muslims are using that gate. They are all gathering inside the school's walls.

The boy knows those walls that Brij Bihari is talking about. They are tall and have shards of broken glass embedded at the top. The walls are painted gray with a horizontal red line running in the middle. The colors on the walls are the same as those of his sister's uniform.

Munni says, "Mother Superior has a very big heart."

Mother says, "They have dedicated their lives to the poor."

Both Mother and sister look a bit like the nuns when they say this. But, Brij Bihari says, "The Muslims have been building such a big mosque in town for months. Why are these people not hiding there on that roof under the giant loudspeaker?"

Mother listens to Brij Bihari as if he has presented her with a puzzle. The boy and his sister both look at Mother, who must have an answer to the question posed by Brij Bihari. Mother says, "Should the Muslims not have their mosque?"

Brij Bihari is tickled by Mother's question, or maybe by the fact that she knows so little. He is still smirking when Mother says to him, "What are you saying in front of the children? Have you even fed your cows today? Go to them... At least they do not find differences between Hindus and Muslims."

This provides Brij Bihari the opening he needs. He says, "How can you say that, Didi? The cow is our mother. We care for her with our lives, but those Muslims eat cows."

My mother holds her head in her hands. She says, "Oh my dear God! Why do you say such things under my roof?"

Brij Bihari laughs. He says, "Didi! This is the plain truth. We wouldn't have these riots if it wasn't for the Muslims. The knives they use are the same ones—"

Mother doesn't let him finish.

When Brij Bihari leaves, there is a discussion about whether the family should wait longer for Father. Mother feeds the boy while his sister eats by herself. Mother has cooked fish. She removes the bones and the boy mixes the fish with rice. When he eats his food, the boy thinks of the Muslims, who instead of eating mutton or chicken use their knives to slaughter cows.

The phone rings. But it is not Father. It is someone from his office who wants to know if Father has come home. Mother says she has no news. Mother asks the caller what "the situation" is like in the town. She listens to the answer and sighs. Then she returns to the business of feeding the boy.

It is hours before Father comes home. Mother has not eaten. Brij Bihari comes in first with Father's briefcase and the Eagle thermos. When the boy runs out the front door, Father takes his hand and leads him back into the house.

Mother is angry. She will not speak to Father. She puts a plate in front of him when he sits at the table. Father asks the boy's sister, "The Jeep came for you at school, little one?"

The boy's sister nods but doesn't say anything because she knows Mother is upset.

Mother puts fish in the bowl for Father. He begins making balls of rice with his fingers. Mother says, "Was there not a single phone anywhere for you to tell us where you were and when you would come home?"

Father looks up at the boy and his sister. He does not look at Mother or bother to reply. His face becomes stern and he begins to eat more quickly.

Mother goes to the door and asks Brij Bihari, "Does Aziz want tea?"

Now Father breaks his silence. He says, "You want to offer tea to a man whose house is burning?" His tone is not very kind. He is still not looking at Mother. He says, "It was dangerous even to keep Aziz in the car. I went and dropped him in his neighborhood. The police had to open fire. At least twenty-two people dead."

Mother stays silent. The boy does not understand what he is hearing Father say. He is distracted by the drama of his parents' behavior, which he doesn't like at all. In order to break the silence, he asks a question.

"Father, why does Aziz kill cows?"

A dark shadow passes over Father's face. The boy knows immediately that he has said something wrong. Father turns in great fury toward Mother and demands loudly, "What have you been telling him?"

This confuses the boy. He can see it also confuses Mother. There is such immense sadness on her face as she looks for a moment at Father. Standing at the doorway to the kitchen, where she had gone to get her lunch, she holds the edge of the green curtain close to her. She has turned her face slightly as if she has been slapped. The boy walks close to Mother and puts his arms around her waist. His forehead touches her cool stomach. Mother is crying, or he imagines that she is. He presses his nose against his mother's sari and waits for her to gently place her hand on his head.

The police Jeep has returned to take Father back for patrolling. In the rear are the police constables wearing khaki shorts and red berets. They sit like roosters crammed in a bamboo basket. The men are silent. They have dark, sweaty faces and they look at the boy without much curiosity.

The police driver, also in khaki, has a revolver in his belt. The driver is the only one standing outside the Jeep. Father is sipping lemon tea on the patio lined with flowerpots, listening to the small transistor radio on the table. The police driver listens as the boy asks if he can hold his revolver. Then the man pats his holster and points wordlessly at Father. He shakes his head as if to say that Father will be angry.

The boy says, "Are you a Hindu or a Muslim?"

The driver reaches into his shirt and takes out a ragged sacred thread. He asks, "Why do you call me a Muslim?"

"And they?" The boy points toward the constables in the Jeep.

"Woh hamaare hee ladke hain," he says. They are all our boys.

The boy understands that the police are there to protect Father. He believes that Father is invincible. He looks at Father as he sits on a cane chair without his shirt, listening to the news on the radio and sipping tea. The boy asks the driver if Father also has a gun. The man says, "Why does he need a gun if we are there with him?" He uses the English word *command* to tell the boy that the men will use their guns when Father orders them to.

The boy knows now that no one can harm Father. But, in case anyone dares to try, he has decided that this is how the plan will work: if the attackers are Hindu, the policemen will simply tell them that Father is also a Hindu; and if a Muslim rioter threatens my father, the policemen in the Jeep will shoot him down.

His sister is doing homework. Mother has asked the boy to sit down with his own picture book on the sofa. His sister is wearing in her hair the elastic band with shiny plastic stones that Auntie Rani has given her. Such bands are called Love in Tokyo. In the past the boy has asked his sister about the name but she has just shrugged her shoulders.

When the boy goes down to the kitchen, he finds Brij Bihari standing near the front door talking to Mother. He is telling her that a few Muslim families have collected inside the walls of the radio station nearby.

The boy asks him, "Will they attack us?"

Brij Bihari laughs. He says, "They have their tails between their legs."

Maybe the Hindus will set fire to the whole radio station, the boy thinks.

Brij Bihari tells Mother that it is because there is a police party in the radio station that the Muslims have come there.

Mother says, "I am thinking of Aziz… I hope his family is safe."

And then it is morning. The boy comes down the stairs. The sun is out. He remembers the previous night and the troubles of the day only when he sees Brij Bihari once again standing outside the kitchen. Nothing appears to have changed. Mother is inside making tea. Brij Bihari is holding one of his milk cans, which he bounces lightly against the back of his leg.

The boy asks, "Did they burn down the radio station?"

"No, no." Brij Bihari laughs as he says this, and takes the boy by the hand out into the garden to show him the yellow building, which is standing there with its tall aerials, unharmed.

The boy then discovers that Father has already left with the police party. He wants to know when Father is going to come back. Mother says, "He'll come for lunch. Things are returning to normal. But you have to behave."

The boy looks at his sister. She has planted a small sapling in a pot. It has a single leaf that is fresh green in color. His sister is using a small comb to dig the soil in the pot. She then takes water from the sink in her hand and pours it on the dirt around the plant.

When Father comes for lunch, there are no discussions about the riots. When the sister asks Father when her school is going to open, he says, "Monday."

The boy asks them what day it is that day, and his sister says, "He doesn't know anything at all." When Father looks up at her from his plate, the sister says, "Friday."

Next week the boy's sister will go back to school. Mother has told the boy that he will begin school in July. He will be five years old. His sister has told him that his teacher will be a Christian lady from Kerala, Mrs. Thomas.

The boy asks Father, "When I start going to school, will a police Jeep take me there?"

Father smiles at him. His smile shows that he loves both the boy and his sister. He says, "Do you want to go with the police? Can't Aziz take you in our car?"

Is Aziz still alive?

The boy asks, "Is Aziz going to come back?"

Father says, "He has to drive our car. Where will he go?"

The boy's sister speaks up now. She asks Father, "Didn't you say to Mother yesterday that his house was burning?"

Father says, "No… That's not what I said. It is Friday today. He gets the afternoon off for prayers."

The sister says, "Did you see him today?"

Father says, "My dear, today people are still settling down after the troubles in the town last night. I know Aziz is fine. I know the area he lives in… Eat your food."

Aziz doesn't come on Monday, or on the days that follow.

But then one morning, as Father had promised, Aziz is there, passing a cloth over the white Ambassador car. Brij Bihari is nearby, washing down his buffaloes, using a rag dripping with dirty water. The boy goes out to the gate of the house. A few feet to his left, almost within his reach, there is a lizard sitting on the hedge. He does not go any further and calls out to Aziz.

He says, "Aziz, why did you not come all these days?"

Aziz says, "Beta, bahut aafat tha shehar mein." Son, there was a lot of trouble in the town.

The boy watches Aziz working on the car. Then Mother calls out for the thermos to be taken out and the boy hurries inside. When Father steps out with a few files in his hand, Aziz opens the car door for him. They leave. It is then that Brij Bihari, leaning over the gate with a twig in his hand, tells the boy that Aziz spent these last few days at his sister's house. The sister is an attendant in Sister Mary Family Hospital. Her husband had been killed in a riot five or six years ago, and she lives with her daughter near an old mosque in the city.

The boy asks Brij Bihari, "Will Aziz now return to his own house?"

He says, "How can he? The public threw kerosene on it and burnt it to the ground."

Brij Bihari looks serious. But he must be joking! Brij Bihari says strange things all the time. When the boy looks at him, he knows that what he is saying is true. Brij Bihari looks sad too. The boy wonders what his parents will say when they hear this.

"What happened to his clothes? Did they get burnt also?"

Brij Bihari says, "Ek photo tak nahin bacha paaya." He could not even save one photograph.

The boy wants to go inside the house now. It seems to him that it is hot outside. He tells Brij Bihari that he will tell his parents what has happened to Aziz. Brij Bihari laughs his characteristic laugh. He says, "What will you tell them that they don't know? Mother has given him two of Saheb's shirts."

"Really?"

The boy knows he cannot feel angry with his parents for not sharing with him the news about Aziz. Father was not able to save the house of the man who works for him. The boy feels bewildered by this, and is suddenly filled with disappointment. He is sad for Aziz but he also realizes that his father is not who he thinks he is. Father is helpless, he thinks, just like me. It is even possible that he is scared of the lizards that sit on their fence. The boy is a little bit ashamed, and he now wants to cry.

Brij Bihari looks at his khataal. He says, "Aziz has to travel a good distance to come here every morning. I am trying to sell him my bicycle. I will be like the bank. He will pay me a monthly rate." He laughs. And adds, "You have seen how Aziz likes to wash the car every day. I think he will keep the cycle in a good condition."

That evening, the boy watches as Aziz takes Brij Bihari's bicycle out from its place behind the cows. Aziz walks for nearly twenty yards with the bicycle, as if he were holding a child's hand to help it cross a street, and then, seating himself, he slowly begins to pedal away.

That was all there was to remember. I got up from my place under the olive tree and began the hike back to my studio up in a small tower a short distance from the villa. To my right, I could see the afternoon ferry leaving for the far shore, a growing triangle of foam joining the boat to the pier from which it had departed.

In the studio, sitting at my desk, I returned to Orwell's *1984,* which I had just begun reading. "Attention! Your attention, please! A newsflash has this moment arrived from the Malabar front. Our forces in South India have won a glorious victory..." Hearing this, Orwell's protagonist, Winston Smith, correctly surmises that such a triumphant declaration only means that some bad news is in store. And indeed, close on the heels of a bloody description of battle and the fatalities inflicted on the enemy, there is the announcement that, starting the following week, the chocolate ration will be further reduced.

I brought the book with me to the residency because I had come across a report that it suddenly became a bestseller after Trump's election. In Delhi, when I was in college, I had seen others reading it but never had the chance myself. *Big Brother, doublethink, Newspeak*—Orwell's terms have all become a part of the common sense. I have a narrower purpose in picking up the book. I want to see if I will find in it ways to structure the state's fictions. I have only read thirty pages. What has interested me so far in the book is that (1) Winston Smith is keeping a secret diary; and (2) A girl that he is interested in works in the state's "Fiction Department" and probably has "some mechanical job on one of the novel-writing machines."

At night, after dinner, I resume my reading of *1984.* I wonder how many at this residency know that Orwell was born in Motihari in Bihar—the same town where my father was born thirty years later. Orwell's father was an opium agent for the British rulers in India. In my reading after dinner, I come across the line "Winston was dreaming about his mother." After reading a couple more pages, I put the book aside and return to my private memories. I want to add to what I had written in the notebook before. I know a novelist who, in addition to clamping on noise-canceling earphones and physically sealing the ethernet port in his computer, also wore a blindfold as he touch-typed on his keypad. But I don't crave that kind of silence or even stillness. The lake and the pretty trees provide a serene setting for my thoughts. I don't carry the burden of Winston Smith's afflictions, and yet even in my comfort I want to follow his example. Orwell writes that while he is performing the physical exercises mandated and surveilled by the state, Smith's thoughts return to a near-forgotten dream about his parents: "he was struggling to think his way backward into the dim period of his early childhood." That is what I, too, have been doing. Here at the residency, in these beginning days, my greatest wish is to go back and note down how on seemingly mundane days of my childhood the armies of ordinary citizens were being readied for battle and even milkmen carried swords.

CHAPTER 3

BIAS STUDIES

EAT
SO_P
WASH
SO_P

At the residency, I explained this experiment at dinner.

What will you choose to supply as the missing letter in SO_P? Answer: It depends on how you have been primed. Vaani says that is the psychological term for this phenomenon. If you have recently seen or heard the word EAT, it is likely you will say SOUP instead of SOAP. The opposite would happen, of course, if you had just seen WASH.

Which reminds me. Vaani leaves instructions on Post-it notes. In her angular hand, the word she scribbles at the bottom is KISS but I always first read it as KILL.

This can be disturbing, depending on how you have been primed to regard such experiments.

My relationship with my wife is an experiment, in the sense that I often think I'm being tested. As I said, Vaani is a psychologist. This means that what I say to her is always passed through the fiery examination, the agni pariksha, of scientific research. I say to my wife that our daughter, she's nine now and will likely not appear many times in this novel, is more likely to be able to order pizza on the phone than I am.

"Why is this so?" Vaani asks.

"Well, because I have evidence. None of the cheerful young women who answer the phone at the busy corner pizzeria ever seem to understand what I'm saying when I call and say something as simple as 'Hello, I would like a large pizza delivered. Feta cheese, onions, peppers, maybe fine olives if you aren't taking them out of a can. And, one other thing, please, red chili flakes on half of the pizza.' "

Instead of accepting this scientific statement, my wife calmly inquires, "Satya, are you attributing a common motive to all of these individuals—and if so, what is it?"

I say something like "Yes, of course I am. Without even realizing it, at a subconscious level"—and I understand that even as I'm appealing to her discourse I'm also running the risk of exposing my ignorance—"all those white suburban maidens are racists."

Vaani wants to complicate what she must find simplistic and provocative in my thinking. I can read it in her face, the slight flare of her nostrils, the seriousness that never clouds her beauty. She says, "A study done a few years ago showed that Americans distrust those who speak with an accent. But that behavior is linked to something much larger. Whatever is easy to understand is taken as more credible. This is true of humans everywhere. There's a lot of research on this. You remember the sign we see on Indian highways? SPEED THRILLS BUT KILLS. Just because the words are rhymed, people are more likely to believe that the statement is true."

That is how we talk. Vaani is currently on a yearlong fellowship at Harvard's Radcliffe Institute. I, as you know, dear reader, am a writer, but I also teach literature at a small liberal arts college in upstate New York. I put my faith in stories. That the young ladies at the pizzeria would hear my accent on the phone and think I was drunk or confused or annoying is only the beginning of a story. All of the experiments that interest Vaani tell stories; there's a story, too, in what kinds of experiments are of interest to her.

As far as experiments go, my favorite is the psychological study that tells me a story so good that I don't want to verify it. I don't want to lose the story to science. In those instances, I do not question; I'm merely the grateful recipient of Vaani's reports. So, for example, sad people not only buy more, they also pay more. This is because they are desperate for change. They want to change their situation. This is why stores like to pipe out mournful music. There's your explanation for why Walmart plays Céline Dion on a loop.

I have delayed it so far, but this is what I need to say: the writer's job is to reveal where the experiment in living goes wrong. I have come to this residency to write about the state and its experiments with truth. I have my biases: I was primed for it by the global war on terror.

Several years ago, after I published a nonfiction book on terrorism called *A Foreigner Carrying in the Crook of His Arm a Tiny Bomb,* I was doing a reading at a college in Connecticut. I told my audience that just as I was completing the book, an arrest was made in the nearby town of Newburgh, New York. Four men were accused of plotting to bomb synagogues in the Bronx and fire a Stinger missile at a military jet. The accused were felons with some history of crime but they had shown no prior interest in bombings and terror activities. In fact, one of the accused, described by his lawyer as "semi-retarded," was arrested at a crack house where he lived surrounded by bottles containing his urine.

All four accused had been recruited by an informant for the FBI, a Pakistani man code-named Malik, who provided cash and drove the men in his shiny black BMW to a Denny's to talk about jihad while feeding them hamburgers. A familiar strategy of the FBI: a Muslim immigrant caught for, say, credit card fraud was then used as an informant to inveigle men into conspiracies for which they had neither the motives nor the means. The informants were well paid over several years. The war on terror is an industry; like many industries, it has a dubious record. It has benefited immigrants, the ones who were complicit with it as informers, but it has also ruined countless immigrant lives. Malik, whose real name is Shahid Hussain, was caught in the FBI's web after he was convicted of trying to defraud the state's DMV. Such convictions launched the careers of informants interested in evading deportation or long prison sentences. Malik was no different and he profited from it. I had told such stories in my book. I didn't know this then, but, after Malik's successful deceptions in several cases leading to the arrests of a number of Muslim men, he used the money to buy a motel near Saratoga Springs. The motel was also the business address for the Prestige Limousine Company, which he owned. Years later, a Prestige stretch limo that had failed the inspection test, driven by a driver who also lacked the proper license, slammed into a ravine and caused the death of twenty people, the deadliest U.S. transportation disaster since a 2009 plane crash near Buffalo in which fifty people died.

At the college that evening, I was telling the story of the Newburgh arrests when I noticed a slender man leaning against the wall on the left and shyly smiling at me. He approached me after the Q & A was over and from the way he spoke Urdu I knew he was from the tribal areas in northern Pakistan. He had read my book in his class, he said. Even as he was saying this, his professor joined us and said that I should listen to his student's story. I told the man that I'd get in touch with him the following week, when I was going to drive up to Massachusetts. We exchanged numbers, shook hands, and went our separate ways. On the way to dinner, I asked my host if this man was a good student. I was just making conversation. And the professor replied, "No, it's difficult. He works long hours. His wife often comes when he is in my class and asks him to step out because they are fighting." ("Pakistani?" I asked, interrupting. He said, "No, white girl. From West Haven, I think.") "But the reason I wanted you to talk to him was that he was recruited by the FBI."

I'll call this student Khalid Farooq, a name that he himself chose when I first mentioned that I would be writing about him.

It was hot, the middle of June, and I was headed for a weekend in Provincetown. I stopped in the Domino's Pizza where Farooq worked. (Two tables with red-and-white tops and four red chairs—Vaani tells me that red is a color that makes people hungry.) Farooq was the deliveryman. I had arrived at the time he was getting off from work. We went to a nearby Dunkin' Donuts to talk. He asked for green tea with lemon and six bags of sugar. The server knew what he wanted even before he had finished speaking. Farooq told me he often brought his son to this shop for a donut on the way to school.

"Tell me about yourself," I said.

Farooq told me that he was either thirty-three or thirty-four years old, older than the other undergrads in his college. (He used a phrase that a professor had given him to describe himself: *a nontraditional student*.) He had been born in a village near Abbottabad—the town where the previous month, in May 2011, Americans had killed Osama bin Laden. Farooq's family were farmers. People in the region had cultivated opium because it didn't need much water and could be sold at a profit, but the government had been trying for a few decades to discourage this practice. The more popular crops now were lentils, wheat, and mustard. The entire region, he said, was a tribal area and backward.

Farooq had arrived in the United States on September 5,

2001—which meant, although I didn't say anything about it to him, that he had come here at the same time as Vaani. His arrival had been delayed, he had not communicated with the institution that had admitted him, and he had now lost his place at the college. After the September 11 attacks, there was a lot of anxiety in this country about young Muslim men. Farooq was especially suspect, he said, because his records showed that he had served in the Pakistan Air Force. His visa was withdrawn and he was put in detention in Elizabeth, New Jersey. It was there that one night an officer from the FBI visited him and asked him to work for them. He was told to go into a photocopying shop and ask for a Latina woman there. He was to offer her money and find out if he could get a fake license. Farooq did as he was instructed and he received a license that to any ordinary person would look legitimate. The FBI quickly arrested the woman and her accomplices. At this time, Farooq wasn't enrolled in any academic institution; for months, he worked at a Subway and at a gas station owned by a Pakistani man. I asked him where he lived and he said that he didn't have money for an apartment. He needed to pay a lawyer who had filed an appeal for asylum on his behalf. At the gas station, the owner had taken pity on Farooq and allowed him to sleep in the storage room after they shut down for the night. A bench, he said, rather than a bed, with red plastic bottles of Valvoline motor oil stacked underneath.

The hearing that would determine Farooq's future was held in Hartford. After the judge asked only a few preliminary questions of the lawyer and looked over a couple of sheets of paper, the entire process taking seven to ten minutes, the judge denied the appeal. Farooq said that he had spent eight thousand dollars of his hard-earned savings on the case. Around this time, he was again visited by the men from the FBI. This time they were brusque with him. He was asked for help translating a few recordings and it was made clear that if he didn't do the job he would be given a one-way ticket home. Farooq set to work. These were interrogation recordings from the AfPak area; the men being interrogated were speaking in Pashto. Even though Farooq is fluent in that language, he described it as a difficult task. The men whose voices he could hear in the recordings were also being tortured. He wasn't paid for this work, but he was granted a green card with a Z11 stamp on it, attesting that his deportation had been suspended.

While narrating this story, Farooq held a finger against his temple, as if he was in pain. He had finished his tea and I asked him if he wanted more. He said no and that he was coming to the end of his story. Three or four months later, Farooq said, the men from the FBI were back. This time he was asked to travel to Waziristan with the officers of the Joint Terrorism Task Force. He had two supervising officers; one of them, Farooq wanted me to know, was a man of Indian origin named Jagdish. He spent six months on this tour. When Farooq came back to the United States, he was hoping to become a citizen, but he discovered that his green card was canceled after his return. He called the men in the FBI who had hired him, but they said they couldn't help. They had returned to find him at Domino's and offer him money but not citizenship for more work with translations. This time he said no. In Pakistan, he had given up his job in the air force because the government was carrying out bombings against its own people in Balochistan, and he wasn't going to help the Americans with their interrogations during which he had once seen a man's chest being split open.

"What is your status now?" I asked Farooq.

"I'm married to a U.S. citizen. We have a child. So, I have applied for citizenship."

I shared with Farooq what his professor had told me about his marriage. He didn't appear surprised or hurt at this sharing of information; despite the fact that Farooq had only recently met me, he spoke candidly. His wife's name was Julie. Farooq said that Julie often fought with him and that after their troubles began she had humiliated him by going out with a Saudi man.

Did this white American, a Christian, only go out with Muslim men?

He shrugged and stayed silent.

How does it make you feel?

He said it was disheartening, and that odd word, I didn't know whether to call it a nonnative speaker's mistake or neologism, endeared him to me.

Julie was depressed and angry, he said. They had met while both of them were working at Subway. For a while Julie had been employed as a salesclerk at JCPenney but she was now without a job again. Then Farooq told me about their dog. The dog, Simba, was a German shepherd. Farooq had bought him at a high price because Julie wanted a puppy. How much had the dog cost, I asked. Nine hundred dollars. Simba was huge now, over a hundred pounds, and spent much of the day in his crate. Julie spent a lot of time in bed too. When he returned home late from working at Domino's, Farooq said, he would need to empty the tray at the bottom of the dog's crate. When he pulled the tray out and carried it to the bathroom, the dog's urine spilled on his uniform.

Farooq and I met a few days later in an Indian restaurant. Farooq liked that I would write down what he was saying in my black notebook. He said, "You must tell my story." I told him that I would but then found that I didn't have any free time; I was teaching and I was trying to complete a book on writing. Nevertheless, I was interested in Farooq's story and we met a couple more times over the next several months. I should pause here to explain something. I found that Farooq could remember distant events and—a gift for a journalist—he offered details in his stories. He was specific. (He told me the color of the bedsheet and the pillowcase when he was circumcised in his childhood by the village barber, Baz Gul. "Look up at the plane up there," Baz Gul said, and quickly used the razor on Farooq's foreskin, which had been extended over a tender bamboo shoot. "How old were you?" I asked. "Two or two and a half years old," he replied. I didn't know whether I could trust this memory.) I hadn't yet begun to wonder whether his stories were so detailed because they were fiction or because he was a good storyteller with an amazing memory. Or both. But I do remember being dissatisfied. This was because, despite his penchant for details, there were so many turns in Farooq's story that remained hazy to me, the chief one being his account of repeated stays in jail in upstate New York. I wanted to keep talking to him so that I would get to the bottom of his story.

Some months later, when Farooq graduated from college, I was his only guest at the ceremony. Earlier that morning, I had published a short piece about him in the local newspaper. I didn't know how to introduce him, so I decided to be direct. I wrote about what our recent meetings had been about. He will be graduating today, I wrote, but he is not a very good student. His GPA is only 2.7. Once he was even threatened with expulsion because he had been quarreling with his wife and had missed classes. He had surprised me a few days ago, I had added, by saying that he wanted to give a speech at his graduation ceremony. Would I read the draft he had written?

There had been a further surprise. In what he had sent me, there was mention of his incarceration in a federal prison in upstate New York a few months after the events of 9/11. He was suspected of being a terrorist. I had known of this, but so far I had also found him taciturn and secretive about that experience; I was surprised that he was prepared to stand in his blue and gold robes at graduation and read aloud about having been put behind bars.

Over the time that I had known him, Farooq had mentioned his arrests—the first only a few days after the September attacks—but the details I was now reading in his draft were new to me. He had written that one early morning in 2002, he was taken out of his apartment and asked to sit in a car. Then one of the Joint Terrorism Task Force officers came back and pulled Farooq out. He wanted to take pictures of him being handcuffed. Farooq was ordered to hold his head up. He felt he was being treated like a trophy. (This wasn't as grim as the stories we had heard about the prisoners at Guantánamo. But the prison camp at Guantánamo was a part of the war on terror. It is something I thought about here at the residency when, during my reading of *1984,* I came across these lines: "In the vast majority of cases there was no trial, no report of the arrest. People simply disappeared, always during the night.") Aiming for a kind of honesty, I wrote in my piece that my heart sank when I read Farooq's prose because it seemed that each paragraph could arouse the suspicion of those who followed the rules of grammar: "I used to get a quartz of milk, and bread tost for breakfast. Quartz orange juice and rice with chicken and French fries for lunch and same for dinner. After spending six months, I was let free." Why would the young men and women holding office in student government at Farooq's college accept a speech written in faulty English? And yet, I encouraged him to go on writing.

The truth was that Farooq's essay had made me even more curious. Instead of asking him to correct his grammar, I suggested that he share additional details. (I sent him rule no. 16 of Strunk and White: "Use definite, specific, concrete language. Prefer the specific to the general, the definite to the vague, the concrete to the abstract.") There was another reason. I had realized that Farooq was also bringing news from the other side of the class divide. "My dear colleagues, every day once we left our class, you went to library to complete a project or a paper, I drove to

Domino's to deliver pizza. Over the weekend, while driving, I would see many of you having breakfast at the Goldberg's Bakery, in West Hartford. During all this time, I had worked tirelessly, to the brinks of insanity."

I had myself seen him in the pizza store and spoken to his boss, who had told me about Farooq putting in upward of forty hours for him. This part about his hard work I knew was true. A huge gap divided him from the well-heeled students in his graduating class.

When I asked Farooq why he wanted to present the speech, he answered that he wanted his fellow students to know how difficult it had been for him. And then, perhaps realizing that this motive was somehow inadequate or didn't do enough for others, he added that his speech would teach others the virtues of persistence. Sounding very much like an American, he said, "I didn't give up."

Each year there are countless speeches delivered at graduation ceremonies, and most use words like the ones that Farooq had been careful to include in his draft: *ideals, education, struggle, persistence, success.* I wanted him to get the chance to present his story. It didn't happen, however. I got an email from Farooq informing me that the mantra hadn't worked. His speech hadn't been selected. I'm sure he was disappointed, but I hoped Farooq had gotten to lighten his load—of secrecy, but also of injustice—by writing about his imprisonment and his struggle to make ends meet in this new society.

In my piece, I had aimed for a certain pathos. I wrote that I had seen Farooq in his Domino's uniform, which granted him a kind of invisibility, and now I was curious to see how he would look during the graduation ceremony. I pointed out that if Farooq had been given the opportunity of delivering his speech, his audience would have been conscious, I think, of what is left unsaid in many such conventional speeches. And I, listening to him, would have been aware of what he was leaving out of the account he was sharing with his fellow students and teachers. I brought my piece to an end by then mentioning that after his stint in prison, the federal authorities picked Farooq up several times and asked for his help. If he said no, Farooq feared he would be deported. In the fall of 2004, he was taken to Afghanistan for a few months to help U.S. interrogators when they spoke to suspects whose only language was Pashto or Hindko. It was tough work, Farooq said, translating what a man was saying when his nails were being pulled out.

At the villa, I looked over the notebooks where I had recorded parts of our conversations. Farooq's story would perhaps be the opening tale—or maybe the second—in my *Enemies of the People.* But during the lazy hour after lunch, I liked to walk down to the water or take a cup of coffee and sit in the garden reading *1984.* There, among the flowers, the tiny sprinklers, and the darting lizards, I felt I was safely distant from the dark despair of Orwell's dystopia. At the villa, we felt safe even when we heard troubling news coming from the villages just a few miles to the north: people were now dying from the novel coronavirus that was proving to be very infectious.

I was now at the end of my second week at the villa, the end of January, and there was an announcement that flights from China were to be temporarily suspended. Our villa was like an island surrounded by placid water, and it was natural that even the fictional details in the pages of *1984* seemed more pressing or real to me than the scraps of confusing reports I was receiving in a foreign language. I was deep into my journals; I was writing Farooq's story and making notes on another story I wanted to write about a killing in India; there was enough reality to occupy me, and, to be honest, I felt I had a handle on the truth.

On this particular afternoon, my reading was interrupted by

Bev. She was an artist from South Africa, painting ghostly figures, spectral images of victims, over archival group photographs of the apartheid regime. She had come to the villa with her husband, a labor activist; I hadn't talked to him because he had a back problem and was confined to his room. Bev came over to where I was sitting and asked if I'd mind talking to her for a few minutes. I offered to get her coffee but she said no. I saw that she had Indian-style bangles on her arm. Seeing me looking at them, she said she had visited Jaipur with her sister. Then she pointed at the book I was reading. She said, "Did you know that some years back Amazon remotely deleted thousands of copies of *1984* from readers' Kindles?"

I hadn't known that and waited for her to say that the action on Amazon's part was Orwellian. But she didn't and then the moment for the joke had passed. I stayed silent and an awkwardness sprang up between us. What was it that she had wanted to tell me? For a moment, just for a moment, I was afraid Bev was going to say that I had offended her with some remark I had made during dinner. "Your joke, and I know you meant it as a joke, was insensitive, I think." That is what I expected her to say, though there wasn't anything in particular that came to mind. But, instead of that, Bev stretched her bangle-laden arm and touched my hand. A serious note in her voice, she said, "I've not stopped thinking about what you said the other evening while we were having drinks. You said that the question you were working on is how many among your neighbors will look the other way when a figure of authority comes to your door and puts a boot on your face. And I've wanted to ask you, well, what do you think?"

"How many?"

"Yes."

I laughed. And then, feeling that I needed to rise to the occasion, I said, "The answer would be a full 65 percent."

Bev widened her eyes. She said pleasantly, "Could you explain?"

I sat up straight and inhaled deeply. "You know, of course, about the Milgram experiment?"

In the early sixties, in the basement of a building at Yale University, a psychologist named Stanley Milgram wanted to see how far participants would go in accepting instructions from an authority figure and engage in behavior that conflicted with their own conscience. Milgram's experiment was fake in the sense that the pain the participant was inflicting on another person was not real: the participants were administering electric shocks to other people when they gave the wrong answer in a quiz purportedly about memory, but the people in the other room sitting in electric chairs were actors—and there was no real electric machine or electric chair. The main point of the test was to determine to what extent the participant would persist in obeying commands like these:

1. Please *continue.*
2. The experiment requires that you *continue.*
3. It is absolutely essential that you *continue.*
4. You have no other choice, you *must* go on.

Milgram had begun his project only months after the start of the trial of the Nazi war criminal Adolf Eichmann in Jerusalem. His experiment was designed to investigate a question prompted by Eichmann's claim that he was just following orders: Was Eichmann alone in making this claim or would his behavior have a more universal resonance? In Milgram's own words: "I set up a simple experiment at Yale University to test how much pain an ordinary citizen would inflict on another person simply because he was ordered to by an experimental scientist."

I now told Bev that what Milgram found was that 65 percent of the participants were willing to shock their fellow citizens over and over again despite the cries of agony—and, on occasion, subsequent silence. Other participants were often willing to administer the shock in smaller doses. The 65 percent, when encouraged by the authority figure, administered "the experiment's final, massive 450-volt shock." The study's findings scandalized the world and are routinely cited even today to explain human cruelty.

"And yet, if we repeat this figure of 65 percent," I informed Bev, "we would be wrong. That figure is widely cited—but it is wrong."

The point I began to elaborate is essentially what Vaani means when she begins talking about the richness of data. Here the richness lay in the repeated schema Milgram adopted. In other repetitions of the original experiment, he used variants, altering the scenario involving participants, places, et cetera. In one variant, where the "shocker" and "shockee" were in the same room, there was a significant drop in the percentage of people willing to administer the highest voltage. If the experimenter was no longer an authority figure but an ordinary person, the earlier figure of 65 percent fell down to 20 percent. In experiment number 17, if there were other actors who, standing next to the participants, said that they didn't want the experiment to go on, only 10 percent of the participants indicated a desire to persist with the punishment. Also, if there were two experimenters, in other words, two authority figures, and if they started disagreeing with each other, then the percentage of participants willing to go on with the experiment dropped to *zero*.

When I was reciting these details, with sufficient drama, Bev was smiling. I believe she wanted to have hope in the human race.

I explained to her that Milgram's baseline study, the one that achieved the high number of 65 percent of people willing to administer damaging punishment, was accepted as a fable about human depravity. But the additional figures I was quoting to her—those I grasped as a part of a fable too. A fable about redemption. Bev nodded, but I don't think she was interested in any further commentary. She thanked me and said she would let me go back to my reading.

When Bev had returned to the villa, I remembered another detail. Vaani had told me that every time the experimenter used the fourth prod—"You have no other choice, you *must* go on"—the participant said no. In other words, when people were told, rather, when they were *ordered* to go on with an act of cruelty, they refused. This could be reassuring until we realize that, minus the imperative, a mere articulation of higher purpose (science, religion, research, Mother India, sacred cow, the purity of the race) prompts people to inflict pain—on any number of others, and even on themselves.

The lesson I had drawn from the Milgram experiment was simply this: facts can lead you in any direction, it just depends on the kind of story you want to tell. Which brings me back to Farooq.

On the morning of the graduation ceremony, Farooq texted me to say that he had read my article online. He had liked it; he said his friends wanted to meet me that day. But I didn't see him till after the ceremony was over. It was a bright, beautiful day. The pretty setting matched the florid descriptions customarily found in college brochures: green lawns, white tents, summer dresses, sunglasses, blue blazers, balloons, picnic tables, rows of chairs under tall elms with their sun-dappled branches, bright hopes, joy, et cetera. The ceremony started with a prayer, then the singing of the national anthem, and then a stately procession of awards from which, I had always known, Farooq would remain excluded. A graduating senior presented the student commencement speech. This was the student who had won against Farooq; he was funny, and somewhat frivolous, and at the end of his speech when I clapped, I felt that I was betraying my friend.

The commencement speaker was Anne Fadiman, the author of a wonderful work of nonfiction, *The Spirit Catches You and You Fall Down*. Fadiman delivered a speech that was profound and even critical but without robbing the day of its sunshine. She urged the audience to honor difference and to honor commonality. "It's hard to walk a mile in someone else's shoes," Fadiman said, "especially if theirs are size 6 triple-A and yours are size 12—or vice versa. But learning to do so—in other words, learning to honor each other's differences—is one of the most important skills you can master." I was thinking, once again, of Farooq when Fadiman said, "Don't assume that you—you as an individual, or you as an American—stand at the center of the universe. It isn't true, and it never helps."

Later, I wrote a note to Fadiman asking for a copy of her text, from which I have now quoted for you. She thanked me for what I had to say about her speech. She added: "Thank you even more for missing the graduation at your own college in order to make sure that the student you call Khalid Farooq had someone to watch him get his diploma. I read your article with interest, immediately realizing that if you had not been there, his commencement—a time of triumph for any student, but particularly for him—would have felt like one more instance of driving the Domino's truck while his classmates ate breakfast at Goldberg's Bakery. He may not have had a well-dressed contingent of parents and grandparents in the audience, but he had you. That was something important." I felt so too. After the ceremony was over, I took pictures of Farooq in his graduation robe. He wanted to send the pictures to his parents in Pakistan. At one point, he climbed onstage and asked me if I could take a picture of him at the lectern. Did he want to pretend that he had indeed delivered the graduation speech? I didn't ask. Farooq took me to meet another student who had graduated that day. Her name was Frida. She was going to North Carolina to study philosophy. Frida was from the Dominican Republic and I found her warm. She thanked me for being there for Farooq, and then she said that she had enjoyed reading my article about her friend and hoped to see me again. Then I took Farooq in my car to a Nicaraguan restaurant in Hartford for a celebratory lunch. Even though it was a happy occasion, and we were both chatting amiably, a thought nagged at me.

A week earlier, Farooq had asked me to lend him twelve hundred dollars. When he made the request, he explained that he had booked a flight to Pakistan for his wife and son. His boss had promised him an advance to pay for the ticket but then backed out at the last minute. Farooq's professor, the man who had first introduced me to him, advised me not to give the money; it was a large sum and I hardly knew the man. Vaani was firm. We will soon need some money, she said. But Farooq told me that he would return the cash when I came to his town for the graduation ceremony. Also, I knew I was going to write about Farooq, and thought it was only fair that I was running the risk of losing money. So, a few days before his graduation, I stood waiting at a gas station near the highway half an hour away from my home. Farooq was driving to New York City with his family to pick up the tickets from the airline office on the way to the airport. In my hand was the envelope provided by the bank, and for Farooq's son, who was three years old, I had brought cookies and juice. When they pulled up, Farooq got out of the car. The child seated in the back appeared exhausted and weak but accepted my small gift. His wife, Julie, whom I was seeing for the first time, a somewhat pudgy, attractive white woman in her late twenties, was seated in the front. I noticed that she was pregnant. Julie looked straight ahead and didn't acknowledge me.

I felt rebuffed, as if I was doing something wrong, but I also knew that I was helping the family. Still, I wanted my money back, and now, on the day of Farooq's graduation, we were eating grilled skirt steak with green aji sauce and I was wondering whether it would be impolite to remind him of his promise.

I knew Vaani would be disappointed by my reticence. A month earlier, she had wanted me to take her to see her doctor, a gynecologist named Anjali Patel. While Dr. Patel was examining Vaani, I sat out in the waiting room looking at the TV in the corner—it was April 2011, President Obama had just released his long-form birth certificate in response to conspiracy theories. Dr. Patel emerged from a door to my right, a slim woman, stylish in a leather jacket, and said that my wife wanted me to join her inside.

Vaani was lying on her back on a large reclining chair. She said, "We have good news…" And then she choked, her eyes filling with tears. Dr. Patel said, "I will be back in a few minutes." Vaani held her hand out and I took it in mine, and I bent down to kiss her on the lips and then her hair, inhaling her scent. The first thing she said was that the doctor had told her the exact date in January when our baby would arrive. This precise date made the surprise all the more real. Vaani said, "I didn't want to tell you anything till I had confirmed it with the doctor." I kissed her again. I felt a sense of responsibility descending on me, it was almost like a weight, but I also felt a sense of elation that made me feel weightless. I felt I was flying. We held hands till Dr. Patel knocked and came back inside the room.

And that is why when I saw that Julie was pregnant, I thought Vaani would forgive my succumbing to the request for money. I came home from the gas station where I had handed the money to Farooq and said in an exaggeratedly excited way, "Khalid Farooq's wife is pregnant. That must be the reason they needed the money."

Vaani didn't share my excitement. She simply frowned and said, "She is pregnant? Why the hell is she going to Pakistan, where she knows no one?"

I hadn't considered this question. My preoccupation lay elsewhere. I had sought to justify the loan on moral grounds. *A man who delivers pizza is not in a strong economic position, he needs money for his family, how can we refuse? Remember, it is a loan, not a gift. I feel responsible because I'm also writing about him—his condition is clearly dire. I want to be able to help him.* But what I hadn't said to anyone, not even to Vaani, was that I had put myself in a situation. *This had everything to do with the demands of my writing.* A risky request had been made, and I had responded because I wanted to see how it would play out. It would give me material. This was something I was hiding from Vaani, and maybe she suspected this and that is why she was angry. And on hearing her openly question the logic behind a pregnant Julie going to Pakistan, I felt doubly guilty. I was worried about getting my money back, but I had also behaved like the FBI, which had produced some cash for Farooq and forced him to play a role in their narrative.

During that lunch in the Nicaraguan restaurant, after Farooq's graduation, I knew I wasn't going to ask for the money. However, I remembered Vaani's question very clearly and asked Farooq why Julie had gone to Pakistan when she was pregnant. There was an explanation. Of course, there was. He said that Julie had always wanted to be a doctor. She didn't have much of an education. But it was different in Pakistan. There was a quota reserved in medical institutions, but also in government jobs and the military, for people from the tribal areas of the northwest. As Farooq's wife, Julie would be eligible for admission to a medical college in Abbottabad. This was her best chance. She could get admitted before the baby came. If they missed this opportunity, Farooq said, things could get complicated.

Time passed. Not too long, six or seven weeks, maybe even as long as two months. I was worried about the money. I reminded Farooq by text but nothing happened. I had stopped mentioning him to Vaani because doing so irritated her. During this time I had sent Farooq more messages and also called him once or twice at work. When I finally got hold of him on the phone, he told me that he was sorry. He hadn't yet received money from his boss. He said he had received his salary, however, and would be able to return half the amount he had borrowed. I lied to him and said that I would be passing by his town later that week and I'd collect the money on Friday at 10:00 a.m.

Farooq sent me his address and I arrived at his door on time. When I rang his bell there was no answer. I called him on his phone too, but it went straight to messages. I felt disappointed and more than a bit annoyed. Had he made me travel this distance for nothing? I sat in my car and read a Roberto Bolaño novella for class. After half an hour or maybe closer to an hour, I got a text.

Sorry, Farooq said, he had been sleeping. I texted back that I was outside his door.

Fifteen minutes later, his door opened. He came out to the car and we talked for a bit. I waited. He didn't have half the money, he said, but he had four hundred dollars. When he gave me the cash, I felt relieved and happy. I had got a part of my money back and, what was more, I didn't need to doubt Farooq anymore.

I immediately offered to buy him lunch. But he said no, he was fasting.

I said I was probably going to find a Starbucks close by and get some coffee; I explained that the wait in the car had given me a headache. Farooq said he could come with me so that we could talk. But first he needed to change. Would I want to come in for a few minutes so that I didn't have to wait in the car?

A dog was barking.

I said, "Can I meet Simba?"

Farooq led me toward the kitchen at the back. I heard the loud barking before I saw the dog, a large, ferocious animal who rattled the cage with his leaps. I beat a quick retreat to the room that we had first entered.

I was left standing in a room with a broken sofa and some flowers wilting in a plastic soda bottle. Next to it was another, smaller plastic bottle that said LITTLE REMEDIES SALINE SPRAY. The curtain covered the window and gave the room a stale air. A child's car seat leaned against a wall. I noticed that the battery-operated alarm clock on the desk was half an hour ahead. Next to it was a shabby computer. When I sat down on the sofa, it smelled of dog.

There was a succession of beeps on Farooq's phone while he was getting changed. My headache had grown worse. When Farooq came into the room, he checked his phone and said "Oh." Then he said, "Professor, do you mind waiting five minutes? I need to Skype with my father."

I said I didn't mind at all, and could wait in the car. But Farooq said I could keep sitting on the sofa. Maybe, he added with a smile, I would get the chance to say hello to his wife and son.

Farooq's father appeared on the computer screen. He was holding a phone on which he was able to see us. There was a yard behind him, and some hens. Hanging from a nail on the wall, under a sheet of polythene, was an air force uniform with Farooq's name on it. When the phone moved, I could see hills in the distance. It became difficult to see much else in the background because in response to his father's shouts other men crowded around him. These were Farooq's brothers. They were working men, peasants, and all of them appeared happy to be talking to Farooq. I was introduced as a professor who had been helpful, and then Farooq mentioned that I was a writer who was going to tell his story to the world. I was greeted and offered praise and thanks by the father and the oldest brother. There was a touch of formal courtesy mixed with plainness in our exchange.

Farooq inquired about his wife and child.

They were not at home. In fact, it became clear that this Skype conversation could take place only in their absence. Farooq's father had wanted to talk to his son because he had a complaint.

Farooq's boy couldn't eat the meals that were prepared at home. He wanted American food. The father and the brothers were laughing. They had paid eight hundred rupees for a meal brought from a McDonald's in the city. But Julie hadn't liked this. They also paid five hundred rupees for each meal from Olive Green restaurant in another town. This hadn't been satisfactory either. A family doctor, a friend, had been summoned more than once to examine Julie, but she had demanded to be taken to the hospital. Now the men weren't laughing anymore. The father said that a trip to the hospital could cost twenty to thirty thousand rupees. There is nothing like health insurance for us. Farooq said that they should have Julie call him when she returned. He wanted to hang up and began to say goodbye to everyone. The father held up his hand. He said, "You don't go to a hospital for a headache!"

Halfway across the world, Julie had a headache too. I felt sympathy for her. I wondered where she had gone. I put the question to Farooq and he guessed that she had gone to the American embassy in Islamabad. I wouldn't find this out till a few months later but he had guessed correctly. The person who told me this was Julie herself. Most of what she said went against everything that Farooq had told me earlier.

Can I share here with you what Vaani has told me about the research on lying? In a study beginning in the mid-1990s, a social psychologist named Bella DePaulo and fellow researchers at the University of Virginia asked seventy-seven students and seventy people from the community outside the university to keep a record for a week of the lies they told. This anonymous record of lies was classified into categories: self-serving, out of kindness to another, et cetera. The students were telling an average of 2 lies each day, while community members told 1 lie per day. The most prolific liars among the students told an average of 6.6 lies a day, while the average among community members was a bit lower. DePaulo noted that a more recent study of the lies told by one thousand adults in the United States found that people told an average of 1.65 lies every day. A significant detail in those findings is that 60 percent of the respondents reported not telling any lies at all, while the top 5 percent of the liars were responsible for nearly half of the lies. In late 2017, DePaulo authored a comment piece analyzing Donald Trump's lies. *The Washington Post*'s Fact Checker feature had been tracking every false and misleading claim made by Trump: in his first three years in office, Trump has made 16,241 false or misleading claims. DePaulo noted that with 6 daily lies on an average, Trump's record on falsehood was higher than the average in the study she had done at the University of Virginia. (In June 2019, an article on the CNN website said that Trump "is lying more every day than a majority of Americans wash their hands." This ratio, I felt, must have changed with the adoption of hygienic practices during the coronavirus pandemic. The *Post*'s Fact Checker has a new category for the coronavirus. And it notes that although much has changed in our world because of the pandemic, "one thing has remained constant—the president's prolific twisting of the truth.") DePaulo also suggested that Trump's average was likely to be higher because the *Post*'s database only had access to the public record. Also, the following observation: starting in early October 2017, the

Post's tracking showed that the rate of Trump's lies had been accelerating and, as DePaulo put it, he was "outpacing even the biggest liars in our research."

But there is a further point to consider. Wrote DePaulo: "The flood of deceit isn't the most surprising finding about Trump." DePaulo and fellow researchers found out that Trump told 6.6 times more self-serving lies than kind ones, a higher ratio than that of the average participant in the study. The "most stunning way" in which Trump differed from participants in the original study was in the cruelty of his lies: "an astonishing fifty percent of Trump's lies were 'hurtful or disparaging.'"

Trump's lies have had an effect on the general population: fewer than 40 percent of Americans believe he is telling the truth. DePaulo writes that many studies on the detection of deception show that human beings have a tendency to believe that they are being told the truth. This "truth bias" works even when, in psychological studies, participants are explicitly warned that only half of what they are being told is true. DePaulo's assertion is that "by telling so many lies, and so many that are mean-spirited, Trump is violating some of the most fundamental norms of human social interaction and human decency." Which, given my truth bias, I readily believe.

In the car once during my commute, I heard on NPR that a scientific paper had just been published that began with a startling first line: "Most published research findings are false." The authors allowed that the most extreme opinions likely overstate the problems in the scientific literature, but they also cited empirical evidence showing that most published research is neither reproducible nor replicable. I heard the commentary but didn't bring it up with Vaani. I knew she would be impatient, and a bit defensive: *Is the research question matched by the design of the experiment? Are you providing adequate information for duplication?* I imagined her asking those questions before slipping into more arcane territory about data sets and code sharing.

I bring the matter up because, unlike among scientists, among writers there is an openness about admitting bias, but that might well be my own particular bias. We wave it like a flag. "Look, I am guilty! I'm biased but at least I'm honest about it! I hold aloft my diseased heart!" That is what I'm trying to do here with my entangled story about Farooq. How to explain his behavior—or mine?

I don't set much store by experiments. Of course, I value science over superstition, but I don't think a psychological theory can exhaust or even explain an individual's complicated psyche. Still, I remember saying to Vaani that I was puzzled by one aspect of Khalid Farooq's behavior. He was always pleasant, I said, and smiled even when asked uncomfortable questions.

Vaani said, "Here's the science on lying. A liar attempts to censor facial expressions more than hand or foot movement. Do you know why? This is because it is generally assumed that people usually pay more attention to facial expressions than to any other part of the body."

"Okay," I said.

"You need to know that the human face is equipped to lie the most, but it also leaks the most information."

What Vaani was saying made sense, but what I wanted to know was how I was going to recognize and trust the information that Farooq's face was leaking.

Vaani said, "Psychologists who have spent decades studying facial expressions describe twenty kinds of smiles in order to distinguish felt smiles from fake smiles."

Twenty kinds of smiles! That was interesting but not useful. I had tried other strategies too. I would ask Farooq for details.

His descriptions of the detention center in Elizabeth, New Jersey, and then later of the prison in upstate New York, were precise. The color of his clothes, the plastic footwear he was given, the nonhalal food on offer at both places. I also found convincing his stories of travel to the AfPak region with the American forces. His memory was astounding. During my interviews I would cross-check him regarding a date or even a tiny fact I had noted earlier and I found that he was always consistent. All of this came from my training as a journalist. Which means that, much as I love my wife and her theories, instead of scrutinizing Farooq's smile, I began to cross-check his statements in more rigorous ways.

Farooq had told me that before he came to the United States, he had been a pilot in the Pakistan Air Force. He had trained at Sargodha air base and then at the academy in Risalpur. I asked him when he was at Risalpur and he replied that he was there from 1996 to 1999. I sent this information to a journalist in Karachi who had earlier worked for the BBC. He checked the records at Risalpur from those years. Farooq's name was not among the trainees. So, he hadn't been a pilot. An employee at a lower rank, perhaps. That explained why he didn't have better English.

It was also unclear how he had been arrested in Hartford in the first place. Why were his papers not in order? How could he have been arrested for not having a visa if he had been legally admitted into this country as a student? Using the letterhead of an Indian newspaper, I wrote to the office of the judge in Hartford who had handled his asylum case. The office confirmed that Farooq's case had been decided by the honorable judge, but they were not at liberty to answer any further questions.

I decided to go one step further.

It cost me twenty dollars on the Internet to purchase access to a data resource where I could locate Julie's phone number and email address. I was taking a risk. It wouldn't be wrong to assume that Farooq would find out about this. I sent a polite note to Julie with a link to the article that had appeared on the morning of Farooq's graduation. I had presented her husband's story, I wrote to Julie, and would welcome the chance to hear her story, which was possibly different from Farooq's. The response I received from her was a bit deranged. She threatened to contact a lawyer because I had defamed her, and that too, she said, in an article that had national security implications.

As politely as I could, I pointed out that I had used pseudonyms and had changed some identifying information. I included a request in my note. Would she please meet with me at the Dunkin' Donuts near her house at any time convenient to her? I just wanted a few minutes of her time.

The face that Julie presented to me at Dunkin' Donuts was the same one I had encountered in our brief meeting at the gas station many months ago. She was wearing dark glasses and it seemed she didn't even want to look at me. I gestured to the chair opposite me and asked what she would like to drink.

Julie shook her head and asked, "What did you need to know from me?"

I said, "Why don't you sit down for a second?"

She placed herself at the edge of the steel chair.

I felt she wasn't going to give me much time. I said, "Were you going out with a Saudi man when you were with Farooq? That is what he told me."

She said, "You are asking a personal question. I'm not here to answer personal questions."

This stumped me. I pretended to look at my notes. Like a defense lawyer who ignores the prosecutor's objection and plows on with his line of inquiry, I then asked my next question.

"Why did you go to Pakistan?"

"Farooq bought me a ticket to Pakistan," Julie said, her face acquiring color, "so that he could carry on an affair behind my back with his classmate Frida Rodriguez."

I remembered Frida from the graduation celebration. Farooq had spoken to her in low tones and picked fruit from her plate. I had thought they were friends.

"How was your experience in Pakistan?"

"My daughter was born prematurely there," she said. "It was very stressful. I had to ask the American embassy for help to get me back to the U.S."

Julie shifted impatiently in her chair.

I said, "How did you first become friends with Farooq?"

She looked out of the glass wall of Dunkin' Donuts at the passing traffic.

"I was brought up by my father. My mother died when I was little. My father was a truck driver. He drove long distances and he died on the road, near Memphis, from a heart attack. I was working at Subway at that time with Farooq. He was a good friend then."

There was so much to ask. I had written many questions in my notebook. I was looking at my notes when Julie spoke again. She addressed me as if I were a boy who had thrown a tantrum.

"What do you really want from me?"

Her question was a justified one and yet what struck me more was her open hostility. I couldn't see her eyes behind her shades. Her face radiated a kind of hatred that I couldn't remember having experienced recently.

"I had written that piece you read about Farooq. You disliked it, with good reason. It was really only a recounting of the story your husband had told me. I was interested in talking to you so that I could get your side of the story."

"I have told you my side. Can I leave now?"

"Oh, sure," I said quickly. "I didn't mean to keep you. But, before you go, one last question. How did you find out about Farooq's affair?"

Julie was standing now. She said, "My friend told me about an app. I read all the messages he sent out from his phone. I read what he wrote to you too."

She turned and left without saying goodbye.

You have allowed me to share the research on lies; let me now put down a brief note about writers. At Farooq's graduation, the writer Anne Fadiman had delivered the following line as a part of her speech:

> There's a wonderful phrase from the Talmud: "We do not see the world as it is. We see the world as we are." Actually, I'm not sure it's really from the Talmud, since it's also been attributed to Immanuel Kant and Shirley MacLaine. But whoever said it, it's true.

I also didn't know the source of that quote—it was a part of my general confusion—but it made me think that I had not seen Khalid Farooq as he truly was. I hadn't wanted to; I had only wanted to see him as a victim of the war on terror, a noncitizen expected to furnish proofs of belonging to this new nation by displaying complicity in the brutal acts of the state authorities, of being forced even through as innocuous or normal an act as giving a graduation speech to constantly assert *I am* and I had made that my only story. This was my bias. Just the other day, in the small but elegant library at the villa, I came across a mention of a book about a criminal and a writer and a line jumped out at me: "The writer is not the con man's victim, he is his collaborator." If Farooq was a liar, I had become his accomplice.

I saw Khalid Farooq only once again after my meeting with Julie. I asked him whether he was cheating on his wife.

He was honest and immediately said yes. And added, with that characteristic shy smile of his, "You can say that I'm dating Frida." I didn't want to judge him on this. The Americans had nabbed him on a technicality and then thrown him in jail as a terror suspect. It was certain that he had lied to me about some things, and I had now found out that he was also an adulterer, but that didn't make him a terrorist. And nothing, nothing justified the wars that the Americans had waged in Afghanistan and certainly in Iraq. That is what I would say to those who upbraided me for my biases. Now and again, the thought came to me that I should confront Farooq. I imagined the scene. He would be sitting on a chair across from me and I would ask him a question and then another. I would point out the inconsistencies. But then, if I did that, very little would separate me from the figure of the interrogator. Is that the idea of truth I carried in my heart? No, no, it isn't.

I didn't hear anything from Julie. For a while I thought she might email me to ask if I was going to write her story too. I wrote to Frida on Facebook. I tried to get her to say something about Farooq. I wrote to her twice but she never replied. I heard from Farooq once, when his professor posted a picture of me on Facebook: in the photograph, I was standing outside a temple in Gaya, writing in my black notebook. Under the post, Farooq had written, "I miss you, Professor. I miss you and your notebook." Some more months passed, and, to my great surprise, I received at my home a cashier's check. Farooq had sent me the entire remaining amount. He now owed me nothing. In the accompanying note he said that I had rescued his family when they needed help and he was sorry that this issue of money and debt had come between us and strained our friendship. I didn't send him a reply and I didn't hear from him. Then, a year later, after I published an essay about my mother's death, Farooq wrote to offer condolences. I asked him for his news and, after some prodding, he revealed that he was now divorced from Julie.

He was single and bringing up his children in New York City. They were well. He was not young anymore but he had wide experience, he wrote, and he was thinking of entering graduate school to study international relations.

In my book *A Foreigner Carrying in the Crook of His Arm a Tiny Bomb*, the book that had in a way brought Farooq and me together, I had written about a law professor at Seton Hall named Mark Denbeaux. Denbeaux had examined the U.S. government's own declassified documents about its detainees at Guantánamo—the people that Donald Rumsfeld had called "the worst of the worst"—and had found that 55 percent of those detained had not committed any hostile acts against the United States. Only 8 percent were even considered al-Qaeda fighters. A full 86 percent of the detainees had been turned over to the United States by other parties, who had been offered large bounties for the capture of suspected enemies. All of this was depressing; but none of it was surprising. What moved me more in Denbeaux's testimony was his report that one of his students at Seton Hall had asked him after reading his study, "Where are the bad guys?" The student asking this question pointed to the fact that the only charge against one detainee was that he had been a cook's assistant for the Taliban forces in Narim, Afghanistan. This student had said to Denbeaux, "Okay. We have the assistant cook. Where is Mr. Big? Where is the cook?" *Exactly.* The point I am making here is that Farooq's lies didn't amount to much, and neither did my lies to him as a writer, lies that I have just confessed to. So, my question is the same as that of Denbeaux's student: *Where is Mr. Big?* Testifying before the Senate Armed Services Committee, Denbeaux had declared: "Almost everything said by our highest officials about who was detained at Guantánamo and why they were detained was false."

CHAPTER 4

THE FALL OF A SPARROW

My South African artist-friend Bev announced to us that she and her husband were returning to Johannesburg. Her husband, she said, suffered from an immune deficiency disorder. It was risky for them to stick around any longer at the residency. I wondered whether I should be alarmed. Only one case had been reported in Washington State. In Davos, Trump told a reporter, "We have it totally under control. It's one person coming in from China, and we have it under control. It's—going to be just fine." Did I believe Trump? To be honest, I wanted to. I didn't want to panic like Bev. Bev's sister, a doctor in London, had said that the new flu-like virus from China was by now probably everywhere. She was saying that it was already too late. So far, nine people had died in China and the number of those the virus had sickened was around five hundred. The media had reported Trump's statements, and not Bev's sister's, and I wanted to finish writing my stories. The rational part of me understood the danger, and I knew time was short. So, I cut down on my long, leisurely walks among the olive trees and on my sessions at the lake, and pushed on with my story about the time I caught a plane that took me from Kolkata to Siliguri.

In early January 2018, I went to Kolkata for a literary festival. The previous week I had spent time with my father in our old home in Patna, where my younger brother runs a clothing and luggage business. There were new shops in my hometown: a spa had opened nearby, perhaps the first in the whole state, and I went for a massage, except the man climbed on my back to knead me with his knees. It was painful. Politely, urgently, I had to ask him to step off. Change was visible everywhere, tall buildings, more cars, women driving scooters, but something in the heart of the town stayed the same: on the morning I left for Kolkata I read in the newspaper that when two young men were asked to pay for their haircut in a barbershop in Patna, one of them took out a gun and shot the barber in the stomach. The barber's daughter came running out from a small room on the side and the young men pushed her into a car and drove away.

In Kolkata I did a reading from a novel called *The Lovers* that I had recently published, and the next day I participated in a panel discussion on the role of criticism in literature. Only ten people came to the event, but all of them were educated and highly opinionated Bengalis. An angry debate ensued; I didn't need to utter a word. Half an hour later, I was in a hired car headed to the airport: I was flying to Siliguri, a small town only an hour away in the mountains. The man I was going to meet was a professor of English literature at the regional college. He taught five days a week: eighteenth- and nineteenth-century English literature and also the plays and poems of William Shakespeare.

The morning was chilly, and, leaving behind the busy road lined with wholesale shops selling tea leaves, I entered a lane near a Bata shoe store. The scatter and press of the traffic was now behind me. In the lane, there was a public urinal on the left and on the right a half-finished building with a green net hanging down from the roof. A man with a wooden cart crossed in front of me. I kept walking down the empty lane before I came to a two-story house with a jackfruit tree, grenade-shaped green fruit clinging to its branches and trunk. I climbed the stairs and rang the bell. The professor, Biplab Ghosh, middle-aged, bespectacled, opened the door. He had a goatee and wore a blue-and-white sleeveless sweater-vest. The vest gave him a bright air but his eyes conveyed reserve. We sat at a table inside. There were paperbacks packed into metal bookshelves around us and two posters for Brecht's plays adapted into Bengali. Ghosh remained courteous and distant. I repeated the name of a friend, Naveen, who had also been his former student.

"It was Naveen who asked me to meet you," I said.

The professor was puzzled. He could see I had traveled some distance to see him.

"Why?" he asked.

In India, for some reason, people saw me as American: just before one of my readings at the litfest in Kolkata, a writer from Bengaluru leaned over to show me what he was reading on his phone. It was an op-ed from *The New York Times* (January 7, 2018): "Mr. Trump's self-absorption, impulsiveness, lack of empathy, obsessive focus on slights, tenuous grasp of facts and penchant for sometimes far-fetched conspiracy theories have generated endless op-ed columns, magazine articles, books, professional panel discussions and cable television speculation." I read from my novel, but the questions from the audience were about the feeling among writers in America. I didn't know many writers; I could only speak for myself. I said I felt that the rug of reality was being dragged out from under our feet. Twenty times a day, I see something and think, I don't know if this is true. We are awash in fake images, false claims, all manner of deceptions, pointless misinformation, murderous fictions. Language acts are unsteady, surreal. You don't know what you're looking at. But there was also something I did not tell the audience. When I had been visiting my father in Patna, I watched on television a report about a famous insurgent killed by the police near Kolkata the previous year. The television report was sensational and repetitive, but it was also mysterious, the more informative parts revealed only by a man who appeared as a dark silhouette and whose voice had been disguised by the use of a mechanical device. As I listened to the man's voice on the screen I wanted to know more.

This story I now recounted to Professor Ghosh. I said to him that in the United States the news we were getting even during the run-up to the elections had been manufactured by unemployed youth in Macedonia and spread on Facebook. There were reports also of Russian interference. There was such radical uncertainty about every aspect of not just our polity but reality itself. (A reviewer had written in a magazine the previous month: "It's a profound relief, these days, to press our collective feverish forehead against the cold steel of actual information.") What was true of America was true of other places, too. All over India, malicious rumors were being shared on WhatsApp, on our TV screens loud rants competed with lurid accounts of nearly everything happening on the planet, and people everywhere unquestioningly embraced angry, wounding fictions.

I repeated Ghosh's question back to him. I told Ghosh that I wanted to see him because I had been watching the TV report that night in Patna and the thought had come to me: Why don't I write a report on this incident? A well-researched story. Perhaps I could even reach out and find the man who appeared as a silhouette on my screen. I wanted to find the truth—to start with, about the man who had been killed. An insurgent in the wilderness, a guerrilla leader fighting for peasant rights. How had he managed to shake the confidence of the state? In what way had he survived, and under what conditions? How did he die? He was a rebel with a charismatic appeal, but, if we were to believe the man in the shadow on the screen, his death was the result of a popular, well-executed plan.

I had imagined someone addressing a meeting in a forest and then turning up magically in a crowded room in a town late at night to speak to a group of radical students. Everywhere, his audience held spellbound by the look in his eyes and the conviction in his voice. At dawn, he put a towel over his head and melted into the crowd at the town's bus depot. A young woman asleep in a bus, or pretending to sleep, with her head on the shoulder of this man, who looked like an old farmer returning from town with his purchase of new fertilizers. The young woman is the best shot in the entire squad and that is why a revolver is hidden in the jute bag in her lap. But what she doesn't know, despite her intimacy with the man, and I know it only because I stand on the other side of the wall called the past, is that the man who is a leader to so many will soon have his jaw shattered by gunfire.

Ghosh made no indication if my answer was sufficient. The window was open despite the cold. A car passed on the street outside, the engine rattling. I could hear quiet laughter somewhere close and the air carried a whiff of cigarette smoke. I imagined a few youth, maybe even Ghosh's students, sitting and chatting at a chai stall nearby.

I continued and said to the professor, because I knew he taught Shakespeare, that I had listened to the account of how the small army of insurgents battled the state and my mind had gone back to a performance I had watched of *Macbeth* in Central Park. One of the villagers on the TV show had looked at the camera and said that the militia, the Naxalites, was active in the forests; his actual words were "You sometimes feel that the forests are moving." It had reminded me of Macbeth's undoing: his enemies using tree branches from Birnam Wood to camouflage their advance.

Suddenly, Ghosh smiled and said when he thought of a death like that of the peasant leader, he was reminded not of *Macbeth* but of *Hamlet*. He had taught *Hamlet* often because it posed a question for his young students. Leaning back in his chair, he began to talk about Hamlet's stepfather arranging for a fencing match between Hamlet and his friend Laertes. Laertes is sure to feel he has been wronged by Hamlet. Hamlet was responsible for the death of Laertes's father, Polonius. And Ophelia, who went mad and drowned herself as a result of Hamlet's actions, was Laertes's sister. There must be a darker purpose behind the proposal for the fencing match. That is what Hamlet's friend Horatio tells him. He suggests that if there is any suspicion or doubt in Hamlet's mind, he will go ahead and call the whole thing off. He will use the excuse that Hamlet is not fit. And Hamlet's response to this is—and here the professor raised his right hand to declaim, his gesture familiar from what one saw of statues—"Not a whit, we defy augury." Do you understand? Hamlet goes on: "There is special providence in the fall of a sparrow." He raised his eyebrows, paused, and then repeated that line. "There is special providence in the fall of a sparrow." He said he had always liked those lines because they were loaded with fatality. Listen, he said, and then went on. "If it be now, 'tis not to come; if it be not now, yet it will come—the readiness is all. Since no man, of aught of what he leaves knows, what is't to leave betimes?"

"Hamlet," the professor said, "claimed that he didn't believe in omens. Especially for an Indian listener, Hamlet seemed to be asserting individual agency and rationalism. And yet, his whole response was a submission to fate."

The professor acted as if he were in class, pausing to allow me to take notes. He went on talking.

"Surrender or a resolve to be prepared for anything? When I teach that passage," he said, "I often discuss scenes from Hindi cinema. An angry young man is a figure of protest, but larger forces arrayed against him are far too powerful and, in the end, the hero dies a tragic death. His death is tragic but dignified. It's almost as if the hero has willed it. I think that is what students are readily able to see in *Hamlet*."

When Ghosh mentioned the angry young man and Hindi cinema, I saw in my mind not the actor Amitabh Bachchan but the guerrilla leader whose killing had been reported on the television program I had watched. He must have foreseen his death, or not balked when it became inevitable, and when was it not inevitable? I said to Ghosh, perhaps a bit too eagerly, "I could write a long report that would be titled 'The Fall of a Sparrow.' "

"Oh," the professor said, his spectacles shining. "You already have a theory? I thought you were first going to research the story."

We sat alone in silence. There were two bookshelves pushed against the wall on my left. Russian novels, histories of peasant revolt, the broken spine of a green leather volume of the collected works of Shakespeare, a few books of Bengali poetry.

Professor Ghosh saw me looking at the books and asked me if I would like coffee.

I looked at his books while he moved around in the small kitchen—unusual for a remote town in India, I thought, first grinding the coffee beans and then percolating the ground coffee in a hissy machine.

The coffee was excellent. Ghosh asked me, "Did Naveen tell you why he sent you to me?"

I tried to be honest. I told him Naveen had appeared busy when I asked—he had simply sent me the professor's address on WhatsApp and told me to meet him.

Professor Ghosh stayed quiet. I knew a little bit about him from before. His father had been a famous communist leader. He was underground during a long period that outlasted my youth; when I was already in the United States for my studies, I read a news report about the older Ghosh's arrest. Was he tortured in prison? I can't remember. He must have been. I had read about a radical poet from his cohort being picked up from a house in Kolkata and then, only hours later, found shot in the back under a mango tree. The detail that remained in my mind about the man who was sitting in front of me—he had been quite young, a schoolboy, when his father was arrested—was what he had said in an interview. At the time that he was taken to identify his father's corpse he noticed that the soles of his father's feet had turned black in police custody. This observation on the youth's part had moved me and filled me with tenderness. Professor Ghosh's father had long suffered from asthma. The police had denied him his medicines. It was said that he died gasping for air.

"The expert you saw on TV speaking about the well-executed plan," Ghosh said presently, "was once my student. He was a police officer. His name is Ravi Shankar. He is retired now. I can put you in touch with him."

"Thank you," I said. "Where does he live?"

"Kolkata," Professor Ghosh said.

The professor said that he also knew the man who was killed and not just the man responsible for killing him. This was perhaps the reason that Naveen had asked me to meet him. When he said this, with his sense of practiced reserve, I stayed silent, hoping that my silence was what he expected or required of me.

And again, after a lengthy pause, Professor Ghosh said, "The man who was killed was named Avinash. He was a great peasant leader. He is dead and you can't ask him any questions but you can talk to the man who killed him. Ravi Shankar is also from Bihar. For three years, when I was teaching in Kolkata, he was my student. Later, he joined the police service. You can tell him that I gave his name to you, and you can hope that he will talk to you."

On the back of an envelope he copied down information from a small diary. But before giving me the piece of paper he said he wanted me to know something important.

He said, "Did you notice that when you were watching the show on television in Patna, Ravi Shankar's voice sounded different?"

"Yes," I said. "I noticed that it had been disguised."

"No," he said quietly. "It is not a disguise."

Just months after Avinash was executed by the police, Ghosh told me, the Naxalites exploded two bombs under Ravi Shankar's convoy. The attack was seen as an attempt to take revenge for Avinash's death. Some people believed Avinash hadn't been killed in the encounter, only injured, and that he had been brutally tortured afterward. Ghosh said he didn't know the truth. But, in any case, during the bomb attack on the police convoy, the explosion sent shrapnel through Ravi Shankar's jaw and throat. He was in hospital for some time and resigned from the service when he came out.

"He cannot speak without the use of a prosthetic device," Ghosh said. "I felt I should warn you."

Ravi Shankar's home was in an upscale apartment building. At the entrance, a security guard instructed me to enter my name in a register and then he called a phone number on the intercom. I was sent up. Earlier, from my hotel room, I had called the number that Professor Ghosh had given me. A woman had answered and then I heard the voice I had heard on TV, except on the phone, oddly enough, it sounded more grating, even garbled. I told him that I was a professor in the United States—it is always better than saying that I'm a journalist. When I mentioned Professor Ghosh's name, he considered this for a second and then asked me where I was staying. My hotel was actually a posh, pretentious place called the Bengal Club, and the room had been arranged by a writer friend of mine who was a member there. I think the name of the stuffy club with its colonial trappings struck the right chord with Ravi Shankar. He proceeded to give me directions to his house and now there I was.

Ravi Shankar was a tall man, plain, rather ordinary-looking. The air of authority he nevertheless possessed could simply be a result of the fact that I was in his home. Just inside the door, a gleaming silver saber embossed with a police insignia rested in a satin-and-glass box hanging from the wall. There were photographs of Ravi Shankar and a woman. On the coffee table, I saw a book on cricket, and under that, lying facedown, its pages open, was another book, this one by the sociologist Ashis Nandy. When Ravi Shankar spoke, he pressed a finger on an opening at his throat. It wasn't difficult to understand him, but I have to admit that I was unused to this form of communication, and, perhaps because I couldn't escape the thought that I was intruding, I felt ill at ease and nervous.

When I thanked him for allowing me to meet him, Ravi Shankar remained expressionless. He was telling me that it was not his job to make me feel welcome. Unsmiling, he asked me how I knew Professor Ghosh. I said I really didn't know him. I told him the story of having watched in Patna the TV show, and how a journalist friend had mentioned that I should talk to Ghosh. Was I right to mention Naveen's name? He was the next person Ravi Shankar asked me about. I gave him the name of my school in Patna. He had asked the questions in quick succession, his face still frozen.

He said, "Do you know Vishal Kishore?" This time his voice had lost its hostile interrogative edge.

"Yes," I said. I remembered Vishal Kishore from my school days in Patna. I had once accidentally burnt a hole through his blazer in the chemistry lab. How old were we then? Fourteen? Fifteen?

"He is coming today in a couple of hours. Vishal was my batchmate in the police service."

Ravi Shankar got up and I heard him making a call from the next room. He was being a good policeman, I thought, checking my references.

When he came back into the room, he said, "Why don't you stay and have lunch? Vishal will join us."

You have gone on a safari and are hiding with a pair of binoculars near a watering hole. I'm describing a situation. You are sitting there and time crawls by slowly like an ant on the trunk of an old tree. And then, after a difficult wait, you see on the opposite bank a deer delicately climbing down close to the water's surface, its nose now nuzzling its own reflection. Your attention is fully focused. Your wait has been rewarded. But then, surprising you but not—or not yet—the deer drinking water, you see, behind in the bushes, the striped head of a tiger that is perfectly still. *Such luck!* That is what I felt when Ravi Shankar took the name of my old classmate from my high school in Patna. I accepted his invitation to lunch, not suspecting, till some months had passed, that all along it was I who had been that thirsty, unsuspecting deer.

"It was a sort of an experiment," I said to Ravi Shankar. And even as I used that word—*experiment*—I felt a tug in my heart. I thought of Vaani. This is how life pays tribute to love. You imitate your beloved. I was using her vocabulary, but I was at least being sincere. I told Ravi Shankar that with each passing year I felt more out of touch with my birthplace. I found this distance from India intolerable. And then, in recent days, after Trump's election, I had discovered with a new force that I didn't belong in the United States either. "I was watching you speaking from the shadows on the TV screen that day, I didn't know it was you, of course, but I felt this great desire to learn from you. I thought to myself, Let me try and find out more about this event that took place. What really happened? Who was involved? Is there a way to take away the mystery and present the truth?"

Ravi Shankar's face remained expressionless. Then his finger went up to his throat. He asked, "You want to write about it? For whom?"

I said I didn't know. And then, "I would like to write it for myself first. If it felt like a story worth telling, I'd try to get it published."

I told him I had written ten books. Why was I telling him this? A man whom men and women in uniform all over Bengal had saluted when he appeared—why would he care about books? Especially by someone who no longer even lived in India. I was trying to tell him that if he talked to me, his time would not be wasted. His words would live on the page. How do you tell someone that the work you do matters? That is a part of the drama that plays out when two strangers meet. You are making space for the other's humanity, and also for your own, when you crack a joke. And when you are asked about how you earn your living, you are saying this is how I have defined myself in this world. But even as I was telling Ravi Shankar about being a published writer, I secretly thought that I'd like to work hard at my reporting and write a piece for *Granta*. They had published the great Ryszard Kapuścinński's reportage from foreign lands. I was now a foreigner even in India.

Ravi Shankar said, "Okay. What do you want to know?"

I followed a formula I had picked up from a book by V. S. Naipaul about his experience in Iran. Ayatollah Khalkhali, the man that Naipaul was interviewing, had demanded that the writer note down his questions. Naipaul knelt down before him and used a piece of hotel stationery for his questions. "I could think of nothing extraordinary; I decided to be direct." But it hadn't worked for Naipaul. The ayatollah had been a disappointment. "He could be prodded into no narrative, no story of struggle or rise. He had simply lived; experience wasn't something he had reflected on." I had faith in Naipaul's questions if only because they sketched a trajectory—and I loved the surprise at the end. In a prison once I had used the same questions with a prisoner convicted of selling a missile to an undercover policeman. I told Ravi Shankar that I had a few questions written out for him on the pad provided by the club where I was staying. *Where were you born? What made you decide to become a police officer? What did your father do? Where did you study? What was your role in Avinash's death? What was your happiest day?*

Ravi Shankar was born in Begusarai, in Bihar, into a family of prosperous landowners. That is what he said at the start. It was a part of his simplicity that he thought of his family as wealthy. From what he said it became clear that there were few luxuries in his boyhood. He had an aunt, his father's sister, living in what was then called Calcutta; the aunt's husband was a postal employee. They had brought him up. Ravi Shankar's father was a farmer and after the boy had cleared high school it was decided that he could study in Kolkata—and not even Delhi, which would have been more expensive—where he spent his days in the college library and slept at night on a folding cot in his aunt's small house. At the regional college in Kolkata, where he was then employed, Professor Ghosh was Ravi Shankar's teacher. Ghosh taught English literature; Ravi Shankar's own interest was in Hindi. Yet, he was drawn to Ghosh because Ravi Shankar saw himself as an artist and "the language of human expression is universal." He began to name the novels in Hindi he had read by himself while staying at his aunt's house. Dharamvir Bharati's *Gunahon Ka Devta,* Agyeya's *Shekhar: Ek Jeevani,* Vinod Kumar Shukla's *Deevar Mein Ek Khidki Rehti Thi,* the list went on. It struck me that it was also a part of what I was thinking of as his simplicity—

that his reading of twenty novels gave him the sense that he had an affinity for the arts and that, at heart, he was an artist.

In college, Ravi Shankar studied Political Science Honors. He knew of Professor Ghosh's past, how his father had inspired workers and students to fight for the revolution. The movement swept up in its embrace a lot of people, young people had died on the streets of Kolkata, and, in the villages, landless farmers had risen up in revolt and gone after moneylenders with swords and axes. In the end, though, what had stayed with Ravi Shankar was the knowledge that his professor's mother had struggled to keep the household together. After the father's arrest and death, it was Professor Ghosh's mother who brought up the children single-handedly, selling insurance from house to house. Even as a young man, Ravi Shankar decided that he would always be honest but he would also hold legitimate power in his hands. He decided to become a police officer.

I had given him the piece of stationery with my questions. Ravi Shankar looked up at me and said that before he went on to the next query he wanted to say something else. Some years ago, when he was the superintendent of police, he received a call concerning a close friend of his. The friend was the officer in charge of a district in Jharkhand. Earlier that day, the officer's wife, Usha, had been caught shoplifting. She was stealing lingerie. In the afternoon, Ravi Shankar's friend put Usha on a train to Meerut, where her parents lived. And then, when he was alone in his bungalow, he shot himself with his service revolver.

Ravi Shankar said, "Look around you. Everyone is stealing money. There is a scramble for wealth. My own top subordinate, competent in every other way, has bought property in Goa and sent his son to North Carolina for his undergraduate studies. Where did he get this money? When I got the news of my friend's suicide, I sat in my home, drinking for a long time. My friend was dead and I wished Usha had got a crooked businessman to give her a flat in exchange for an illegal building contract. No piece of lingerie was worth my friend's life—and I wasn't going to live, and certainly not die, for something small. I reached the conclusion that I'm so shameless that I could have been a thief. But I'm not. I've never wanted more of material things. I'm so utterly without shame that it has never occurred to me to be embarrassed about what I don't have or to pretend to be what I'm not."

When he was saying these things, I felt that Ravi Shankar was telling me the truth and I was moved by his account. Would Vaani have said that Ravi Shankar was only confirming my bias? Perhaps yes. Vaani had greater faith in tests. Remote or electronic tests for personality traits or aptitude to eliminate in-person conscious or unconscious biases. Also, for more complicated assessments, what she called SJTs (for *situational judgment tests*), which meant that you would have to answer questions like the following:

Choose the most accurate statement below.

A. It is important for me to excel at everything I do.

B. I am good at everything I do.

C. If you want to be successful, you can't always put others' needs first.

As a writer, I was biased in favor of a revealing expression of experience, an experience that was unique to the individual and delivered in an idiom particular to that person. I was happy to hear what Ravi Shankar had told me so far. He sat with his back straight, a finger on his throat, as if this were a custom of oath taking in some obscure tribe, a tribe in an old civilization that had a hundred words for war but had not as of yet needed a word for lies. I sat opposite him on the comfortable sofa taking notes, faithfully recording what he was saying, not interrupting him with questions. I understood that he was allowing me a glimpse into his soul and its solitude.

A slim young man in a white cotton shirt and trousers brought tea and biscuits on a tray.

Ravi Shankar said that Avinash's killing was a routine police operation. It was not too different from so many other things that any police force does. What had helped in this case was a simple strategy that he had adopted ever since he was a junior officer. He said he didn't care too much for ideological battles; his duty was to help everyone who was in need. In this particular case, he had received help from an informer.

The informer was a young man whom he had met two or three years earlier. This youth had been beaten up by a ruling party politician during a village meeting. "When he complained to me during a routine visit to the village," Ravi Shankar said, "I talked to the young man. I told him, 'Forget for a moment what happened to you. Tell me what will make you a happier person.' The youth said he was interested in opening a cycle repair shop. I got him enrolled in a government program that supports village employment schemes. He got help. But I also did something else. I gave him a cheap phone and a bit of cash from my officer's fund. I said to him that he was my eyes and ears in the village. If there was any trouble, he was to just make a short call."

"What was this young man's name?"

"I don't think you should use his name," Ravi Shankar said. "Maybe you can change his name. His real name is Kundan."

While Ravi Shankar was speaking, I took notes. I was also recording his voice on my phone. Later, when I returned to New

York, I heard his strange voice and the morning came alive for me again. There was a small feeling of dread but also the excitement of discovery. I was telling myself that it had been quite easy. I was getting the truth that had not been available to me before.

"I didn't see him again, but every couple of months," Ravi Shankar said, "I would call Kundan on the phone I had given him. I would ask ordinary questions. Was he doing okay? Did his business need help? I had a whole roster of such people. In several thanas, I had started soccer clubs. The village teams got soccer balls and jerseys from us. I had distributed a few phones among those soccer enthusiasts too. I learned many things in this way. Anyway, one day Kundan told me that his business wasn't going well. I told him I could increase his payment if he could help me with the problem we were having with the Naxal insurgency in the area. If he couldn't help, he shouldn't worry. We would look for another job opportunity for him."

Ravi Shankar was explaining his social strategy to me. For the first time, a question came to me. Would he say that he had turned an ordinary young man, poor and unemployed, into a collaborator? But I stayed silent. Ravi Shankar perhaps thought of himself as a farmer who had planted the seeds and I was now going to be told about the harvest.

"Then, two months or so later," he said, "I got a call from Kundan one night. He said he had joined the rebels."

What was Kundan saying to Ravi Shankar? He didn't need to ask him this question. Kundan offered the answer himself, "It's not like you think. Give me a year. I want to be of help to you." And Ravi Shankar said, "No problem."

There were framed felicitations and award medals on the wall behind where Ravi Shankar was sitting. Ravi Shankar in uniform saluting the Indian president, with the latter holding a scroll in his hand. An award for gallantry. The story I was being told was really about how those medals and awards had come to him.

Ravi Shankar said, "Avinash carried out attacks on us with impunity. He would then hold these surprise meetings with selected media in the forest and talk to them about class warfare. To be honest, I wondered if Kundan had been trapped by Avinash's rhetoric. More than a year had passed, closer to two, in fact. Then Kundan called and said that we were to watch a rural railway station the following Tuesday. I posted a couple of plainclothesmen there and they saw a group get down from the train carrying two duffel bags that our men were certain held rifles. I told my team to simply observe and do nothing. A week or ten days later, Kundan called to say that the Naxalites had planned a big meeting the next night in the school in his own village. When I asked him to tell me who would be there, he mentioned Avinash. Are you sure? I asked. He said yes. I asked him if he could give me anything more because this news meant that I would need to mobilize more than my unit. Kundan was speaking in a hushed voice on the phone, but he also sounded very confident. To assure me, he said that he had top secret information because he was a member of the bodyguard squad appointed to protect Avinash."

"Okay, one last thing," Ravi Shankar told Kundan, "if the operation is successful, I'll make announcements on the loudspeaker asking for surrender. What color shirt will you be wearing?"

"Red," Kundan had replied. "And I have a brown cap with a picture of a yellow tractor on it."

When Vishal Kishore arrived for lunch at Ravi Shankar's house, he was as loud as I remembered him from school. Booming laughter at the door. The grand declaration that he had told his wife to give him an old jacket because he was going to meet a school friend from his childhood, one who had tried to maim him with sulfuric acid but only succeeded in burning a hole in his blazer. Vishal was full of such boisterous cheer that I wondered whether he had taken on this role after Ravi Shankar's injury and retirement. He told me that Sushil, another classmate of ours, had died from a heart attack while sitting in the film theater he owned in Patna. Upamanyu had published a novel. Did I remember Tinku? Tirthanker Ray? Sure, I did. He was in a car that got stalled just as he tried to beat a train approaching a railway crossing. Vishal straightened his shoulders and said, "But all the others, as far as I can tell, are still around."

There was both chicken and fish at lunch. I found out that Ravi Shankar's wife was a schoolteacher. She was away at work and we were served by the youth in white I had seen before. At one point, Ravi Shankar asked Vishal if he was busy the rest of the day. Why? Vishal wanted to know.

Ravi Shankar pointed to me. "Perhaps you could take him to the Hatta Camp and show him around."

When lunch was over, I said to Ravi Shankar, "I was hoping you would tell me the rest of the story. What happened that night?"

He pointed to Vishal and said, "He will tell you. He was there too."

"Oh," I said, smiling at Vishal. The lack of curiosity on my old classmate's face revealed that he knew what we were talking about.

I thanked Ravi Shankar for lunch. We were standing near his front door. He shook my hand and pointed at the silver saber on the wall. He said, "As to your last question, my happiest day was the one when I was awarded the best cadet medal at the police academy."

Vishal Kishore took me in his official car, sirens blaring, to the police headquarters. A colonial building with tall pillars, red-brick walls with white trimming. At least thirty police cars crammed next to each other. Tube lights with entrails of dusty cobwebs hung in the corridor and also ceiling fans with long stems. Inside his large office, and this was different from Ravi Shankar's house, there were cricket and golf trophies displayed on the walls. A photograph of Vishal at a sports meet, a medal being put around his neck by an old personage flanked by ceremonial guards. I was asked whether I wanted tea or coffee.

I asked him the question. "How was Avinash killed?"

"You will soon find out," Vishal said. "I'm taking you to a camp. You will meet an interesting person there."

I was given two hefty albums. Inside were photographs of police sports events and medal ceremonies—it occurred to me that I could have been visiting a school, and perhaps Vishal had never really left that place where we had been students together—and then suddenly I was looking at mangled corpses. These were photographs of dead insurgents. Which is to say that, from the opening page to the end, the album displayed trophies. When I was near the end of the album, Vishal came near me and put his finger on a photograph. He said, "That is Avinash. Well, that *was* Avinash." Curly black hair on a head that seemed to be resting on a brick on the ground. Mangled face and blood everywhere.

The camp was a two-hour drive outside the city. We went in two cars. Vishal's official car in the lead followed by a truck that contained constables with the barrels of submachine guns pointing out the windows and back. After we had left behind the suburban homes and even the farms, there were stretches of teak forest. And here and there small tea gardens with a solitary shade tree in the middle. Vishal was only interested in the past, in the memories of school, and he told me how, in recent years, he had gone and presented gifts to our old teachers. Our math teacher had a wife who was an invalid. Vishal had made calls at the local hospital so that the doctors there knew about the teacher. Our lovely English teacher was a widow and she had a son who had run into trouble, and Vishal had given him a stern lecture. He had left some money for the kind lady. The Hindi teacher who had once upon a time readily slipped his hand inside a boy's shorts was now an old man and Vishal had been kind to him too, talking to the old man's landlord and getting him moved to an apartment on the ground floor.

The drive through the countryside filled me with elation. This was what I had come to find. I saw the countryside taking on the characteristics of the city. On gaudily painted signboards the names for new eating places, the mixed-up language of signs for photocopying stores and car repair garages, huge advertisements on the sides of buildings for everything from underwear to cement. Our journey had introduced us to the changes transforming the country. I said as much to Vishal and he embarked on a discourse comparing the delights of train travel with the demands made on us on the road. He favored trains over cars or buses. They took him back to our young days in college, when we took the train from Patna to Delhi. Vishal became lyrical. "To travel on Magadh Express across the broad chest of my motherland is to pick up the thread of a magical story, our daily Ramayana, which binds all our lives together. The train has left Magadh at dusk. Lights vanish in the night's vast darkness. Ram-Sita going into exile, disappearing into the forest. The bride that you see on the platform in Mughalsarai is a young mother in the field by the time the train reaches Etawah. The peacock you saw chained to a tree in Allahabad on the winter evening has, when you get off the train to buy a chai and a sweet bun at Aligarh station, already turned into a splendid adornment for an idol of Saraswati on this lovely day in early spring."

Vishal's orderly turned back in his seat, smiling, to look at us. He was cheering his superior's performance. "Wah-wah, sir," he said, wobbling his head from side to side. I wondered aloud if trapped in the heart of every Indian bureaucrat was a struggling poet, and Vishal pointed outside at the guards standing in pairs on the side of the highway. He said, "We are approaching the camp."

The police we could see by the road, each one armed with a rifle, were standing atop the culverts. This armed presence was the result of a new policy after the explosion that had resulted in Ravi Shankar's injury. These culverts were favored by the rebels, Vishal told me, because they could very easily plant an IED under the brick structures and when the police convoy passed over them, the rebels detonated the high-powered bombs using hacked cellphones.

We entered the camp, which had at its gate the image of a black cobra covered with sequins. Lines of barbed wire all around. Inside, in one corner, officers were playing tennis, their white sneakers covered with red dust. On high watchtowers around us, soldiers with rifles resting on turrets. Three uniformed men stood waiting for Vishal's car and they saluted when the car stopped in front of them. We were taken inside. A large, dark room with portraits of political leaders on the wall and regimental colors. Biscuits arrived with tea.

Vishal said, "Do you want beer instead? This camp has everything."

The men standing at attention around us greeted this with laughter as if Vishal had said the funniest thing.

"Call Kundan here," he ordered.

After a few minutes, a young man came meekly through the door. He was in civilian clothes. He was short; he appeared freshly bathed, his hair oiled. Standing in front of Vishal, he bowed low with folded hands and then, turning toward me, he repeated the gesture.

Vishal said, "This is Kundan. He was Avinash's bodyguard. You can ask him anything you want."

I had not been prepared for this. This was the informer that Ravi Shankar had spoken about. They had placed him in police protection by keeping him in the camp. For the second time during the day I thought of the following questions: *Where were you born? What made you decide to become a police informer? What did your father do? Where did you study? What was your role in Avinash's death? What was your happiest day?*

But this time I decided to take another tack.

"When I was living in the forest, we had to be very alert. We didn't want to walk into a police trap. A lot of our training was about this—how to pick up signs of an ambush, what to do in the event of an ambush, how to operate during an encounter, the steps to take to avoid arrest when visiting the town. And how to be prepared to die fighting."

Kundan was responding to my question about an ordinary day in the forest.

"What do I remember of that time? I remember the seven or eight times I felt I had narrow escapes. I remember the one time I nearly got killed. I remember my rare visits home. I feel what I remember the most is how little sleep we got. We had to keep moving. If we walked, it was possible we could be walking into the mouth of death, but if we stayed in any place too long, we risked certain death."

When Kundan said this, the policemen ringed around us gave nods of satisfaction. I wished to be alone with him but didn't think I could make this request. At the same time, it didn't appear that Kundan was particularly self-conscious or inhibited.

"This possibility of death," he said, "I don't know how else to say it, it was like a hot barrel pointed at us. We saw fire leaping from it, even in our sleep. But, to be honest, my dreams were often quite odd and unconnected to the main dangers of the life I was living."

He stopped and I asked him to go on with his story.

Kundan said, "The most recurrent dream I had in those days was that I was squatting in a room, a pile of fresh shit under me, and my father or mother would appear from nowhere. I would feel alarm, and of course shame, but they did not seem at all surprised."

What an odd thing to say. I wanted to hear more but Vishal spoke up. He said, "You get a chance to read here in the camp. Tell him that."

"Yes," Kundan said. "I'm reading books in the camp library. I'm also writing poetry."

"Poetry?" I must have looked curious. "Can you recite a poem?"

He began to recite in a mournful, singsong voice. The poem was in Bengali and I didn't understand much of it. I understood that the poem was a call for peace and a new life. Dull stuff. While his recitation proceeded, I quickly checked my notes. Hadn't Ravi Shankar told me that Kundan had joined the Naxals only two years before Avinash was killed?

"How long have you written poetry? And when did you go underground?"

"I was very young when I started writing poetry. Maybe ten or twelve. I joined the movement when I was fourteen."

"How old are you now?"

"Nineteen."

I didn't have any reason to doubt this account; perhaps there had been a mistake in Ravi Shankar's understanding.

I next asked him why he had joined the movement.

Kundan was only twelve when the police first came to his house. They surrounded the hut in which his family lived and came in with flashlights, which they pointed at his face. (He used the word *searchlight* but Vishal corrected him.) The men were asking him questions which he didn't even understand. He said to them that he couldn't see anything. In response, the policeman standing closest to him slapped him. Kundan's mother cried out and stepped out of the darkness to cover the boy with her arms. She was hit on her shoulder with a rifle. When a cousin who was six years older than him was grabbed by one of the policemen, she screamed like an animal. He remembered her crying out, "Leave me alone, why are you doing this to me?"

None of the policemen said anything, not even Vishal. I asked Kundan what the policemen wanted.

He said that they were rounding up everyone who was opposing the ruling party candidate in the elections. His father was one of them.

Vishal spoke up now. He said, "They must have been making trouble. Elections are excuses for extortion."

"No, sir," Kundan insisted.

The politician that Kundan's father had opposed was the reason the villagers, many of them illiterate, were losing their land to mining companies. He was a big supporter of a corporation in Mumbai.

I didn't want a debate. I asked Kundan how they got arms in the countryside. "How much did guns cost?"

"A nine-millimeter pistol," he said, "could be acquired for around twenty thousand rupees. Arms were always in plentiful supply, but they were expensive."

"How expensive?" I asked.

"Even a single bullet for an AK47 cost around eight hundred rupees."

"Where did you get money?"

He smiled. "We requested shop owners and traders to give us some of their cash."

The policemen snickered.

Vishal said to me, "He looks like a boy to you. But he was very dangerous. His writ ran over this whole area. More than three hundred villages. Everything was very well organized. The underground party had a political organization, an armed squad in which he was the leader, and a cadre of quiet sympathizers in every village."

I wanted to ask Kundan more about finances but he said that in the past six months, while he had been in this camp, he had written nearly two hundred poems. I didn't want to discuss poetry.

I said, "Were there any qualities you admired in Avinash?"

"Yes," he said, without hesitation. "He was kind and attentive to us. He was also full of energy. If we made a halt and he was sleeping, if you just brushed his foot he would be awake in an instant. He was much older than us but he was quicker and stronger. He also taught us history."

"History?"

Here Kundan slipped into mythology. He said, "If you asked him what happened on any day, like June fifth, 1985, he would tell you. This was many years before I was even born."

We talked for about half an hour. It was an awkward conversation with so many others standing around us. Kundan said that what he missed when he was with the insurgents was his mother's cooking. Rice and duck curry. What did he like to eat when he was on the run with Avinash? He said his favorite food in the forest was hot rotis cooked on a makeshift chulha and then eaten with the sour red ants found inside rotten trees.

I said that I was going to ask him a delicate question. "Did you feel that you had betrayed the trust that Avinash had put in you?"

I was surprised that tears sprang into his eyes. I saw that Kundan had a plain and direct mind. It occurred to me that this sense of honesty must have persuaded Avinash to recruit him as a bodyguard.

Kundan said, "Yes. He treated me like a son. But I thought also of my own parents. And of Ravi Shankar sir, who is like a father to me."

When he spoke Ravi Shankar's name the air shifted in the room. The discussion of Avinash's death hadn't posed a threat or a danger; it had been a triumph for the police and a sign that they were going to win the war. But that feeling vanished the moment Ravi Shankar's name was mentioned. The men around us were suddenly conscious of what had happened to their superior in the bomb blast. Their expressions changed. Perhaps they felt a renewed threat. Or there was a feeling of guilt, of having failed. Someone standing behind the sofa made a sound, a sad clicking with his tongue.

We returned to Kolkata and drank beer at the Bengal Club. Vishal wanted to smoke a cigarillo and we sat outside at a table surrounded by Christmas lights. Ravi Shankar called Vishal and they talked for a while on the phone. I heard Kundan's name being mentioned. Once or twice, Vishal said, "I'll tell you later." I wondered what they were talking about. Then, a large area to our left suddenly went dark. Power outage. Vishal embarked on another one of his lectures. "In foreign countries," he said, "the cherished landscape lies revealed when there is a snowfall on the mountains, and the world is white with nothing but matchstick-like trees stuck to the mountainside. I'm only describing a photograph; I've never gone abroad. In another place, it might be hot-air balloons hanging in the vast open-air vault called the sky. Or colorful boats in narrow canals, the boatmen wearing striped T-shirts and silly hats. Or cherry blossoms. Streets lined with pink petals fallen from cherry trees. But where I have my home"—and he waved his hand in a circle around his head—"the true essence of the land is only revealed during load shedding. The sudden loss of electricity at night and everything that was living and dead disappears into darkness. But only for a while. Life returns here and there. And for me, it is like the return of truth. A match flares in the darkness, someone holds up the light from their phone, a smoky lamp is lit near a window. The sound of a generator comes from a nearby hotel. A policeman holds close a flashlight in front of someone's face. Headlights burn into your retina. Your mother appears with a candle. A neighbor does some voodoo with his car battery and hangs a bright light over the badminton net. Suddenly, the game can resume. Do you understand what I'm saying? The darkness is very real, and you don't know how long it will last, but you are never without hope."

Vishal turned his face skyward and blew smoke into the air above him. When I applauded, he laughed loudly and for a long time. I asked him about Kundan and his future, and Vishal grew unusually somber and meditative. He said, "We are conducting some inquiries. We are in the process of finding out more."

I asked him to elaborate but he just shrugged his shoulders. When he spoke again he said that Ravi Shankar was fond of Kundan. Both men, Vishal said, assuming again his pedantic air, had gone against their immediate mentors. Ravi Shankar had become a police officer, acting against the leftist ideals of Professor Ghosh, whom he had worshipped in his youth. And Kundan, having been given responsibilities and prominence by the guerrilla leader Avinash, was the direct cause of the man's death.

A plate of kebabs arrived. I said to Vishal that fate had brought us together again. I was going to write a piece, I said, entitled "The Fall of a Sparrow." He asked me to explain the title. I did and, in an echo of what I had heard Ravi Shankar say on TV, Vishal said that it was not fate, it was planning that led to Avinash's killing.

Ravi Shankar had called Vishal immediately after getting a call from Kundan. At that time, both men were the top police officers in charge of adjoining districts. As had been decided previously, if Avinash or other members of the party were meeting in the vicinity, Kundan was to say "There is water in the canal now." That is what he had done, and, as I heard Vishal say this, I imagined water flooding a canal in my grandfather's village during my childhood. Dark water, cool, life-giving, glinting in the moonlight like mercury. But now Vishal was saying something else. If the police needed to retreat for any reason, Kundan was to call and say "Chowdhury's nephew has been bitten by a snake. Please call the doctor." The police plan had been kept secret even during the mobilization of units. By 3:00 a.m., Ravi Shankar and Vishal had moved their forces into the area from two different directions and, in the silence of the night, with the engines of the vehicles cut and lights doused two miles away, they began to cordon the area off on foot.

"How were you yourself armed?" I asked.

"I had my service revolver and a 7.62 Belgian light machine gun. I was wearing a bulletproof vest and a helmet. Our boys were very well armed. We had AK47s, of course, but we also had several carbine machines, half a dozen grenade launchers. My own unit had two fifty-one-millimeter mortar guns."

Vishal's narration was detailed and precise. I was recording the conversation. While he was speaking, I wondered whether he would have been so generous if I wasn't a former classmate of his. I had asked Kundan if he felt he had betrayed Avinash, and now, taking my notes, I asked myself if I was doing the right thing in writing about my friends. Later, when I made other discoveries about the case, it troubled me to think that Ravi Shankar and Vishal probably regretted allowing me entry into their stories. But I had told them I was a journalist interested in finding out what really happened. I had hidden nothing. What is the truth but the story we tell about it? So, this is my story. My friend was talking and a question came to me, a moral question, about truth and betrayal. What would Vaani think about what I was doing? Once she had told me that children as young as two or three tell themselves stories in order to make sense of the real world. All the imaginary friends that young children always have are means to an end: children learn how to interpret and understand the real world and real people by interacting with these invisible friends. Autistic children, Vaani had said, have no imaginary friends and are unable to engage in pretend play. On the tape you can hear Vishal talking and there is no evidence there of my own thoughts, but I was thinking that I was using my real friend to imagine or understand what had been so far invisible or utterly imaginary to me.

"We encircled the school and the row of huts around it. Our men were also positioned in a wider circle. We sent up flares and Ravi Shankar made an announcement on the megaphone asking the rebels to surrender. My heart was in my mouth. What if the information was wrong? Nothing happened for a few minutes. And then six figures filed out of the school, led by a woman. Kundan was not among them. And, of course, no Avinash. We separated the six who had come out. They were all handcuffed and taken away. These were villagers who had been sleeping in the school when the armed cadre had arrived. Ravi Shankar interrogated them briefly and he was now certain that Avinash was indeed inside."

While Vishal was talking about the darkness, power returned to the area to our left. A cheer went up. A giant neon billboard showed a blue fish swimming in the dark night. Vishal went on with his narration.

"Ravi Shankar made further announcements. More flares. We decided to wait till daybreak but, in the meantime, we used the grenade launcher to send a couple of grenades clattering against the wall of the school. We didn't want any bloodshed; yet we wanted them to know that we would use force. Our men opened fire when they saw or heard movement behind the school. We shouted for the militants to stop resisting. We sent up a flare, and a white flag appeared at a window. Three figures came out. Kundan and two others. We learned that they had been sent out by Avinash to see if an escape was possible under the cover of darkness. They were to make birdcalls if they saw any chance of escape. Kundan saw this as an opportunity. It gave him an excuse to surrender."

Avinash had kept an AK47 with him. He didn't want to surrender. The police had found this out from Kundan, who also told them that there was no food or water in the school. Ravi Shankar and Vishal had to wait a long time, maybe three hours, because they didn't want any of their men to die. Their men kept firing. Their grenade launchers could send in grenades from great distances. Only seventy or eighty meters of barren land separated the school from the shrubs and trees behind which the police were hiding. They launched a dozen grenades. After three hours, they used the mortar gun to knock down a whole wall.

Vishal said, "There was a fighter called Suchitra, who was with Avinash. She was younger than him, but in a town studio we had found a photograph of the two of them; the owner of the studio had brought it to us. In the photograph, Avinash had his arm around Suchitra's shoulder.

"At one point, a rag was raised on a stick and then Suchitra's head appeared over the remains of a wall. She said Avinash had been injured and she wanted us to help him. Ravi Shankar asked her to come out with her arms up. She was herself injured but not seriously; she is now at the same camp as Kundan. Her desire is to be a constable. Anyway, she stepped out and came to us, arms raised. She told us that shrapnel had hurt Avinash in his left thigh and stomach. We asked about his AK47 and she said he still had it. Now, you must understand that our men are from families as poor as those of the men or women they were shooting at. Avinash spoke publicly about inequality in our society. He would say that the police were there not to protect people but to protect property. It is natural for our men to occasionally have doubts about what they are doing. They wouldn't mention it to Ravi Shankar, but he saw it in their eyes and in their actions. Only the idea of death worked. You had to tell them that the old woman they had earlier passed in the village had given shelter, perhaps only the previous night, to a man who wouldn't hesitate even for a second when planting bombs that would blow up the police barracks. That the young woman they were looking at lustily had received training and would know how to point a rifle at their groins and blow their dicks off. The chicken near the pond, the goat tied to the door, the cow at the back, they were our enemies too. Avinash was the leader of their enemies. I'm not exaggerating. Once they understand this, the brutality unleashed by our men, their passion born partly out of self-loathing, is incredible and even frightening."

After a pause, Vishal told me that when he tries to remember that morning he can hear a cow nearby calling for its calf. He was irritable. What are they doing in the village? Bring the bloody calf to its mother. "Until about three days earlier, I had been suffering from the flu. I wasn't myself yet," Vishal said. He then quickly concluded his story: "Over the next half hour or so, more announcements were made asking for his surrender but no word or gesture from Avinash. We didn't want to wait any longer. Direct mortar fire and we had destroyed the school. He was hiding behind a mound of rubble, we could see him and we asked our sniper to take aim. The first shot blew his face away. It was a great day."

I noted all this down while Vishal smiled, and neither he nor I had any reason to suspect that this would be our last conversation.

The piece in *Granta* is available on the web. Here at the villa, it appears that only Nikki has read it. I don't mind; everyone is starting to become obsessed with just one thing. The novel coronavirus. In Wuhan, more than 11 million people are under strict lockdown. Fifteen people have died in China, but they must be anticipating a real crisis because a time-lapse video of a hospital appeared on my Twitter feed yesterday: a hospital near Wuhan with hundreds of beds has been built in just ten days. I mentioned this to a fellow here, Jimi Adeola, who is a doctor in Nigeria. He smiled and said, "Yes, that is Huoshenshan Hospital. An even bigger one, with sixteen hundred beds, has just been built close by too. This one took twelve days." India has one confirmed case. No deaths. The president of the Hindu Mahasabha has said that cow dung and cow urine can be used to treat this virus. How real is the danger? We didn't know whom to trust. The most meaningful discussions here at the villa only happen in intimate conversations involving two or three people. In larger groups, it is better to avoid that topic because we tend to just go in circles.

At dinner, we are usually divided into groups of five or six fellows. On the night I was in the same group as Nikki, she presented the people around our table an elegant outline of my *Granta* piece and said she had enjoyed reading it. The outline was so precise, and even fresh, that I was certain Nikki had Googled my name and read the piece over the last day or two. When she was done, a Canadian man, another musician and a friend of Nikki's but whose name I didn't remember, asked politely, "How was your piece received?"

I had finished my salad and was waiting for the main course. I looked at the faces around me and said, "There is an interesting coda to that story and I still have to write it."

I told them that when "The Fall of a Sparrow" was published in *Granta,* readers liked the portraits I had presented of both Kundan and Avinash's lover, Suchitra. I had interviewed them over two further visits that week. During my private meeting with him, Kundan pointed at my notebook and said that he wanted to add something. In the course of our very first conversation I had asked him what he had liked to eat most, and now he wanted to tell me about what he never liked eating in the forest. "We often ate a raw egg in the morning, and I didn't like it, I couldn't get used to it. But it was always dangerous to light a fire. On more than one occasion, shells came from a clear sky." He also wanted to tell me something else. After a village had been destroyed by the police or the army, if people didn't run away they were put into makeshift refugee camps near the bases. Strangers came to the camps, pretending to be relatives, and took away boys or girls whom they turned into servants or sold to pimps.

Suchitra closed her eyes and said she does this often. She closes her eyes and imagines herself back in the jungle, freer and happier than in any house she has ever lived in. The forest was a place where mosquito bites, bad food, and impure water made her sick, and yet it was home to her. She spoke Hindi with the same lilt as Kundan. I asked her about her family. She said she had once had a younger sister who was mentally disabled. Once, when her sister was bathing in the river, she slipped and was about to drown. Suchitra's mother jumped in but couldn't save the child. After her sister's death, Suchitra's father lost his grip on life and began to drink heavily. One night he didn't return from the railroad construction site where he was working. Her mother now tilled their small piece of land and sometimes took small jobs as a laborer. Both Suchitra and Kundan had become part of the underground to help transform their living conditions. Both had a desire for time to take shape in a way that was different from everything they had experienced so far. Both of them wanted me to understand that they had hoped to change not only their own lives but also the lives of others around them. It hadn't worked out; they had lost loved ones. They had both made peace with the present: they wanted jobs in the police. Had life been hard? I asked Suchitra. She smiled a sad smile. Suchitra said that she had a comrade named Malati, who had been captured by the paramilitary forces. She wasn't killed. She was returned to them covered head to toe in cigarette burns.

I told my dinner companions that each day at the residency I was reading ten or twelve pages of *1984*. The protagonist, Winston Smith, has written in his secret diary this singular line: "If there is hope it lies in the proles." He is talking about the vast majority of the population, "the swarming, disregarded masses." And yet, when he tries to speak to one of them, an old codger who Smith knows had to have been born before the revolution, he can get nothing. The old man's memory is "nothing more than a rubbish heap of details." As I had only read one-third of the book so far, I couldn't say whether Smith's faith in the proles is justified. (No spoilers, please!) But what I had tried to do in the pages of *Granta* was present the proles in the form of Kundan and Suchitra. I hadn't made them heroes; I had been scrupulous, however, about making it clear just how overwhelming were the odds against them.

No one sitting around me at dinner, maybe with the exception of Nikki, knew much about Ravi Shankar and Vishal. So I didn't add that both of them saw themselves as benefactors; they seemed to regard Suchitra and Kundan with benevolence. They had assured me that the two would find employment on the police force. On those remaining two days I had spent in Kolkata, I played tennis with Vishal and then had breakfast with

Ravi Shankar. The conversations with Ravi Shankar had become easier. He showed me the president's medal for gallantry that he was awarded after the explosion that nearly killed him. He also spoke fondly of his old teacher Ghosh, whom he hadn't seen since the days he was a student. He said he thought of Ghosh often and of Ghosh's father, who had advocated violence against the police. His thoughts about Ghosh were not without tenderness. After becoming an officer, Ravi Shankar had looked at the confidential reports. Ghosh and his mother—Ghosh was only a boy then—would be followed when they took a boat across the Hooghly. The police had kept records of a doctor sympathetic to the Naxal cause: this doctor would take the mother and the child in his car to meetings with underground activists who gave them news of the elder Ghosh. The police records also mentioned a morning when Ghosh's father joined the boy and his mother and took the boy to the zoo.

Our dinner had arrived.

I looked at the Canadian composer and said, "My piece for *Granta* was a detailed report on the police operation that ended in the killing of the guerrilla leader Avinash. The piece started with my meeting with the survivors, Kundan and Suchitra. It was read and shared widely on social media. Longreads also linked the story on their website. But then things took a turn that called everything into question."

While my colleagues ate their dinner, I stuck to my drink and recounted for everyone at my table the following story about the two surrendered militants I had met in Hatta Camp. It is a story that has haunted me and is one of the reasons I'm writing *Enemies of the People*. And, as I offered this account, I felt in the focused attention of my colleagues a desire to find a path to terra firma. Or that is what I felt but didn't seek to confirm because I knew I would only disappoint.

Six months after the publication of my *Granta* piece, in the spring of 2019, a habeas corpus petition was filed by a human rights lawyer on behalf of Kundan's father. Suchitra was also mentioned in the petition. The petitioner demanded that his son as well as Suchitra (the petition claimed that they had got married to each other in the police camp) be produced in court. I learned of this only because Professor Ghosh sent me a message on WhatsApp and having informed me in one sentence about the petition urged me to phone the lawyer. I wrote to the lawyer and asked her if I could call her from the town where I live in America. Yes, she said, and gave me the time for the call.

"I don't understand, what has happened?" I asked.

The lawyer's voice didn't have any warmth in it. She asked if it was true that Vishal Kishore was my friend. I said yes, he was a schoolmate of mine from Patna. But something in her voice made me declare that Vishal and I hadn't been close. Then she asked if Ravi Shankar was my friend too. I said that I met him when I was doing the story.

She said that there had been a tip-off. Recently, an internal police investigation had combed all the electronic surveillance data from the day of the explosion that had injured Ravi Shankar more than a year ago. The data revealed that a call had been made from inside Hatta when Ravi Shankar's convoy had gone out from there on a patrol. The phone used had the same number as the phone that Ravi Shankar had given to Kundan. The police analysts had concluded that Kundan had given advance information to the Naxals about the movement of the convoy and this had given them time to set up the IED just in time before the advance patrol arrived to guard the road and the culverts.

Kundan's father had learned about his son's interrogation from Suchitra; she had called someone else in the village who had a phone. When Kundan's father came to the Hatta Camp, he was told that there was no Kundan there and also no one named Suchitra. A few villagers had then contacted Professor Ghosh. He hadn't believed that he could call his former student; instead, he had contacted a human rights lawyer who had filed a habeas corpus petition. The lawyer's name was Madhabi Chatterji. It was Chatterji that I was now talking to and she informed me that the police had told the court they had no knowledge of Kundan or Suchitra.

The state had shown itself to be a far more powerful writer of fiction than I can ever be. But the lawyer had used my article as part of the evidence she had submitted in court. These individuals were real and I had met them at Hatta Camp. Chatterji asked if I was willing to testify. I told her yes, and that it was the least I could do. Her voice didn't change. "It will be dangerous, if you come here, but they will not harm you, I think, because you will be traveling from the United States. Do you carry a U.S. passport?"

I stopped her. I said, "Let me call you back in ten minutes."

After hanging up, I called Vishal's number. There was no response. Then I called the number I had for Ravi Shankar's home. There too the phone rang for a long time. I called again and again for the next two hours. And then at a different time the next day and then again the day after that. Still, no response. At last I had to call the lawyer and say that I had wanted to talk to her after I had contacted Vishal Kishore or Ravi Shankar but I had failed. They were not answering my calls. She said she wanted me to know that Kundan's father had been very clear about something—his son had indeed called him, on more than one occasion, when Ravi Shankar would come on visits to their village or other adjoining villages. He was a great believer, Ravi Shankar was, in outreach programs. He had organized the Jal Mahal sports tournament. Kundan would ask his parents to give Ravi Shankar's staff, his driver, for instance, the items that he needed back in Hatta Camp. He would ask for clothes or, on more than one occasion, a specific cassette of Bengali songs, and even food prepared by his mother. Why was this one call taken as evidence of anything?

I asked the lawyer what I could do. She said that Kundan and Suchitra had vanished from the surface of the earth. Would I want to write about it? What was the truth of the case? A piece that would make people ask questions or give support.

I wanted to say yes but didn't know what I could really say. In the silence, the lawyer said that Kundan's father had visited her that morning. The father had told her that when Kundan was a boy, right up till he was eleven or twelve, he used to sleep beside him in the hut. The boy would get scared in his sleep, unable to come out of his bad dreams, and the father would need to comfort him. He was a very sweet boy, with a good heart, and with a sensitivity toward others. Still, the father had been surprised when Kundan showed the courage to become a rebel. The father himself, while politically active, had never taken up arms. He wanted to know what the police had done to his boy. Did they cut him into pieces to force him to say something? He had said to the lawyer that if the police had killed him, even if they had eaten his flesh, they should at least give him his bones so that he could perform his funeral properly. The father had traveled by bus to see the lawyer in Kolkata that morning because Kundan would come to him in his dreams. He was standing outside their hut in the rain asking his parents to open the door.

CHAPTER 5

THE NATURE OF LOVE

Love is a girl with dark hair.

I am about a hundred pages into *1984*. Winston Smith has been catching sight of the girl with dark hair and has suspicions that she is a spy. He feels guilty because, among other things, he is keeping a diary. Once he found the girl with dark hair looking at him intently and wondered if she worked for the Thought Police. His guilt is mixed with desire. One night, when he was dreaming in his sleep, he saw her coming toward him across a field. "With what seemed a single movement she tore off her clothes and flung them disdainfully aside." Orwell, for reasons that puzzle me, is at pains to give Smith traits that are misogynistic, but Smith also wants love.. The reader has suspected that these tense passing encounters with the girl with dark hair will lead to something meaningful. And, on p. 108, it happened. The girl, still nameless, surreptitiously passed a note into Smith's hand. *"I love you."* When I came to that line, I was filled with excitement. Love calling out to love.

Vaani left Delhi for her graduate studies at Johns Hopkins a week before the attacks of September 11. She was trying to get away from a bad marriage. Her husband was a rising star in television and, so many years later, is now one of India's most famous news anchors. Vaani jokes that the reason I have been writing about fake news is that I want to take revenge on the man who tormented her. I'm sure there is some truth in that, but I also believe that her ex, Gautam Sikdar, is a vomitous colostomy bag bursting with the fecal fluid of bad faith. If I had the expertise, I would make him the subject of a psychological case study. What I've never said to Vaani is that, of course, her own work is also an assault on what her despicable ex represents.

A writer-friend of mine once described Gautam Sikdar's channel as "TV with rabies." Sikdar is familiar to people all over India as the news anchor who harangues his guests on TV. Every evening at nine, for years now, he has been following an identical routine: he shouts at the panel of guests on his show, throwing at them accusations of deficient nationalism and other sins that might be broad and varied in nature but always returning to the fatal flaw, which in Sikdar's mind is the absence of an adequate patriotic zeal. (Shrill electronic music and short blasts of trumpets amid the wheezings of an accordion make way for the anchor's name on the screen before being replaced by the flashing words master debater. I don't know anyone who hasn't pronounced those words in a way that makes you think of Sikdar as TV's Masturbator.) If you haven't watched him on your screen till now, then don't—spare yourself the spectacle. I say this because rational, well-balanced adults have confessed to being reduced to the figure in Edvard Munch's *The Scream* after only ten minutes of Sikdar. He is a schoolyard bully with a microphone turned up high, dressed in a cheap suit, eyes full of reproach under black-framed glasses, black hair swept back, nostrils distended, curled lips hurling abuse. Did the god of television, before letting out his last breath and dying in front of the cameras, whisper in this man's ear that anger, dispute, the stoking of sectarian fires in homes each night is the only way to keep the medium alive? In living rooms across the nation, his rabid rhetoric threatens to crack the walls and wreck the furniture. Each unhinged tirade of this grotesque monster-child is punctuated by, and always concludes with, a threat repeated in a loud, theatrical baritone: "You can run but you cannot hide! You can run but you cannot hide!"

When Vaani first met him in Delhi, Sikdar, still an undergraduate like her at Hindu College, attracted her because he was also from Jharkhand. He had grown up in Dhanbad, close to her own hometown. Dhanbad was where Vaani's uncles worked in the transport business and she had gone there during the holidays. Sikdar was from a Bengali family and he tried to impress Vaani by saying that his ancestor was the first man to measure the height of Mt. Everest.

Vaani said, "Oh, he was a mountaineer."

"No, a mathematician."

Vaani looked at the skinny man with shiny black hair and oversize glasses and it made sense: he himself looked more like a mathematician than like a mountaineer.

Sikdar explained that his ancestor worked for the Great Trigonometrical Survey; his official title was that of Computer. In the mid-nineteenth century, when the British still ruled India, Radhanath Sikdar had used his mathematical skills to compute the height of the world's tallest peak, which he named after his first boss, the surveyor general of India, George Everest. When Gautam Sikdar told this story, shrugging modestly to admit that he himself wasn't much of either a mathematician or a mountaineer, one of his friends said unkindly, "No, but you are calculating."

Ever since then, the name for the computer's descendant (unverified: not fact-checked) in his circle of friends became the Calculator.

Vaani was born in Ranchi, her father a pilot in the air force and her mother an amateur musician fond of playing the sitar at cultural festivals. All through her childhood, she attended government schools in different parts of India. Then Vaani came to Delhi for her undergraduate studies. Her first teacher was a young PhD named Supriya Nair, a student of E. O. Wilson's at Harvard and interested in "biopoetics." Nair was running psychological studies on children at an orphanage in Kalkaji. Her specific interest was in understanding the ways in which classical Indian music affected the brains of children. The head of that department was a different kind of psychologist. He had studied two decades earlier in Chicago, conducting experiments about stressors and dietary changes among rhesus monkeys that happened to be imported from India. The head's name was Rajinder Bhatia. In Professor Bhatia's lab in Delhi, Vaani first learned to kill rats. Bhatia's psychological experiment involved studying aspects of fasting and feeding: he wanted a scientific explanation for overeating and its relation to the availability of food. Did a rat that had not eaten any food for a day eat more and for longer than a rat that had been fed only six hours ago? Did a rat that was given food irregularly develop a desire to store food in its body? Did that rat in any other way demonstrate a new anxiety about food if subjected to such a regimen? What happened if a rat was turned into a diabetic? Bhatia was working on a theory about the poor in India and their eating habits. (He was dead five years later, from a heart attack, while he was walking with his wife from a restaurant. This was a sad event—he was only forty-three years old—but it didn't stop some students from cruelly remarking that Bhatia should have been studying his own habits of feasting on butter chicken and beer.)

Vaani was on a roster of students who learned to observe and take notes for Bhatia. They monitored the rodents and cleaned their cages. After a group of rats had been used in one set of experiments, Bhatia insisted on using a new group of rats because one of his biggest fears was contamination of data. He didn't want rats learning from any experience in the lab and acting differently. This meant that Vaani and another student, named Bhushan, were tasked with killing the rats during that whole year. Wearing oversize goggles and masks, the students sedated the animals with a dab of chloroform and then snipped off the heads with medical scissors. It was horrible, this exercise, in particular because when the drugged rats felt the scissors closing over their necks, they opened their eyes and turned their bodies rigid. More than once, the poor rat's blood would spurt onto Vaani's plastic goggles.

When Vaani shared her woes with Professor Nair, tears falling precariously close to the cup of chai in her hand, her teacher told her to conduct research instead on the kids at the orphanage where she had herself been working. The academic year was coming to an end. The May heat in Delhi was unbearable. Vaani wanted release from the heat, she wanted the rains to come. The monsoons were still weeks away, but she now had an escape route from Bhatia's lab. Professor Nair's research was on music; Vaani settled on literature and learned to devise tests involving psychological responses to fictional stories.

Vaani adapted a Hindi story by Premchand. It was a story about an orphan boy named Hamid, who visits a fair for the Eid festival. Instead of using his single coin to get something to eat or enjoying a ride or buying a useless toy like his friends, he brings back a gift for his grandmother Ameena, who takes care of him: a pair of iron tongs so that Ameena will no longer burn her fingers when making rotis. For the test, Vaani divided the sixty kids into three groups. The test involved questions. One small group of kids at the orphanage read the story aloud in class and then answered some six to eight questions after being shown pictures. (When you hear about the preparations for Eid, do you also feel happy and excited? Is Hamid like you? Was it right for him to buy a chimta for his daadi instead of getting sweets?) Another small group read only a summary of the story, offered in a detached way and with maximum objectivity or distance, and answered the same set of questions after being shown identical pictures. (Additional questions included Were the other boys really Hamid's friends? Was it easy to understand why Hamid's grandmother was angry when her grandson came back with a pair of iron tongs?) A third group did not read the story nor did it receive a summary; instead, the children in this group were offered an account, seemingly from a newspaper, describing the atmosphere at an Eid fair in a small northern Indian town. They were shown the same pictures but the difference lay in the narrative: there was no real drama in this newspaper report, no sense of temptation or a basic confrontation with an ethical dilemma. (Has anyone ever given you money for a festival? What would you like to buy at an Eid fair? Do you have friends you could share your toys with?)

These tests laid the groundwork for the research that Vaani conducted over the next year, demonstrating in her master's thesis that imaginative literature, as opposed to dry journalistic accounts or detached summaries, promoted engagement among readers. Her further claim was that the complex exploration of emotional conflict ought to be an essential part of any child's education. But the real result of this research, in my humble opinion, was that it allowed the principal researcher, Vaani, to develop an empathy for a stranger she had just met; namely, me. She had till then been married to Sikdar for three years, and I came into her life when I reported a story about her husband.

Gautam Sikdar was only a TV reporter at that time. He hadn't become the loudmouthed, bullying anchor or the human megaphone that he is now. But you could see the signs. Vajpayee was the prime minister. If the recent history of India is a downward plunge into violent, mad, essentially diabolical right-wing delusion, then let's just say the descent had begun. We were picking up speed at that time. I'm talking now of the year 1999. Sikdar was on the margins—the cheering spectator on the road—heckling anyone he saw as a critic of the government. He was the kind of presence in the crowd that knew the camera was looking for him, and he did everything to draw its attention.

A girl named Seema had killed herself in a women's college on Delhi's August Kranti Marg. She was found hanging from the ceiling fan in her room in the hostel. Seema had been alone because her roommate had gone to Ludhiana to celebrate a birth in the family. The dead girl left no note. And the answer to the question that everyone asks, was she pregnant, also came back negative. Then a small news item appeared in *Dainik Bhaskar* saying that two other students in the hostel had said that Seema had been having an affair with a legislator from Uttar Pradesh. For the past several months, whenever this man visited Delhi from Gorakhpur, a car would come for Seema. The journalist, who remained anonymous, had done his job with care. He pointed out that these were only allegations. That the girls had mentioned the name of the man but it would not be right to make it public. He had added that he stood behind his story because both girls had independently offered details about the three or four visits this politician from the ruling party had made to the college campus recently, and he, the journalist, had fact-checked some of these details and found them to be true.

The police did not take note of the story—or, if they did, this fact wasn't made public—but a Hindi TV news channel featured the report on air. A small, curly-haired commentator named Ashish Ahuja—his serious face and glasses conveying the air of a man who was part professor, part poet—asked the viewers to consider a simple question: Were there any learned sociologists or anthropologists among his audience who would know why politicians preyed on young women across this country's campuses? And why, among all the different occupations that men took up to earn their living, why was it that politicians developed a taste for vulnerable female flesh? Was it written somewhere in the Constitution of India, the document by which any politician swore when assuming office, that you must turn girls' hostels and even orphanages into brothels?

This brief piece of commentary ignited a storm, first in Hindi newspapers and then, reaching the offices and the living rooms of the elite, it became a subject of conversation in the English press. Enter Gautam Sikdar from stage right. The commentator Ashish Ahuja had not named the politician, but he had mentioned his ruling party affiliation. This was enough for Sikdar, who acted like a rabid dog whose tail has been set on fire.

He appeared on TV, microphone in hand, standing in front of the offices of his own channel. Looking directly at the camera, he said that if you were watching him you were doing so only as a bystander. He said that he was directly addressing only one person, a man whom he had never met and who worked as a journalist and commentator on a different TV channel. This report, he declaimed, was a personal testimony on the profession of journalism. Sikdar said that journalists can be sleeping at their job, they can be asleep and dreaming, and when they are woken up, because there is a deadline or they are about to be fired, they blithely and irresponsibly usher us into their nightmares. He briefly recited the facts of the case: A young woman had been found dead. No note; no incriminating evidence unearthed during a postmortem. Without checking with the police, a journalist had decided, Sikdar said, on the basis of information that had not been verified by others, that a politician from the ruling party was involved in the woman's death. Were there any learned sociologists or anthropologists among his audience who would know why politicians from the ruling party were the chosen targets of lazy journalists? If journalism was the profession committed to bringing truth to the public, why had it fallen prey to propaganda? And why were innocent and perhaps troubled young women, their lives but also their lamentable deaths, made victims once again by so-called journalists who were perhaps getting money from rival politicians?

Within an hour of the live broadcast of Sikdar's rant, a mob made up of supporters of the ruling party had gathered outside the New Delhi office in Greater Kailash of the rival TV channel. They were waving flags and shouting slogans. Following a time-honored tradition, a fat bundle of straw with an old shirt around it, and with Ashish Ahuja's name written in large letters on a piece of cardboard, was produced from somewhere and with a fair amount of further shouting this effigy was burnt at the gate of the building. No stone throwing was allowed, but the temptation posed by the fire was too much for a couple of excitable youth. To protest the fact that their sensibilities had been so grievously hurt, they burnt one of the vehicles belonging to the TV station. The police arrived and dispersed the mob with what would be described in the next day's papers as a mild lathi charge. That wasn't the end of the story.

The same mob, or a different group of young men who had experienced the same sense of hurt and had then been similarly roused by Sikdar's eloquent defense of a more ethical journalism, then descended outside Ahuja's home in Siddharth Nagar. At first they only chanted slogans about the man's mother being a whore. But then the discovery of one truth led to another. The new slogans pointed out that Ahuja was a pimp. He was paid by the politicians in the opposition. Unfortunately, Ahuja himself wasn't home. His wife was inside the apartment, however, and she telephoned the police when her windows were broken. None of the neighbors stepped out to defend corrupt journalism, and that was understandable, but what this also meant was that, when the hoodlums broke down the front door, Ahuja's wife was all alone. The police hadn't bothered to show up yet. Ahuja's wife begged for mercy and the boys were indeed merciful with the middle-aged woman and didn't rape her. One snatched away the gold chain at her neck, and another devoted his careful, oddly lethargic, attention to her breasts. A third, with paan in his mouth, slapped her a few times and then they were called away by a man in a white kurta who had stopped outside in a small red car.

I had been working at my paper for only three months when this happened, but I was sent out to cover it. At Ahuja's home, I saw the smashed door and the broken windows but there wasn't anyone I could talk to. By now a policeman was seated outside on a stool and he said that no one was allowed inside. I was afraid the editor would be angry if I returned without a story. So I got back on my motorcycle and went to the college where the suicide had taken place. I was young then, and, to be honest, I liked talking to girls. I easily found both those girls who had spoken about Seema to the journalist: they were eating momos in the canteen when I was led to them. At first, they were hesitant. They were afraid and, like many others in their position, they were sitting on information they hadn't shared before. One of them was from Uttar Pradesh, just like the suicide, and the other was from Kerala. Both girls knew Seema and often shared notes from their lectures with her. In half an hour I had learned that the legislator who would show up at the hostel was owed money by Seema's father. There had been trouble in the dead girl's family. Her elder brother had sunk the family fortune, and Seema's father then sought help from the legislator, who was from the same caste. Later, through a further series of misfortunes, the elder brother had been put in jail. This brother had probably also misbehaved with the legislator's wife—or at least said something about her in public that was offensive. The legislator felt it was his right to tell Seema that her father had put her in a very difficult position. He took Seema to the government guesthouse where he frequently stayed during his Delhi visits. Lately, these visits had increased. Seema would be taken to the guesthouse for dinner and was brought back to the college in the morning. She had called her parents when this happened the first time, and told them that the legislator had called her on her phone and asked her to meet with him. What did he want? she had asked. Her father had said only a few words. "I don't know, my child. Go and see what he wants. I am helpless. May God save us."

I took these notes to my editor, who then asked me to catch the next train to Gorakhpur. The next day, I met Seema's parents. The story I had been told by the girls was more or less correct. Seema's brother and the legislator had been named together in several criminal cases; they had been partners and then there had been a falling-out. Do you have any idea why Seema would have taken her own life? The mother sat paralyzed and didn't seem to have heard my unfair question. The father, in his dirty white vest and dhoti, met my gaze and then studied his feet. After he had shaken his head a few times, I thanked them for their time and left. My report made the front page, and in the days that followed both Sikdar and I, for good or for bad, I think mostly for bad, became the news instead of the dead girl and her rapist. We were both interviewed by half a dozen media outlets, and during one of these interviews I noticed that Sikdar had a beautiful woman with him. She introduced herself as Vaani and said very simply that she had liked my story.

A pause.

"You made us think about the girl, and the terrible situation she had been put in. Thank you."

"No, thank you. Thank you for reading it with an open heart."

When this exchange took place, I couldn't see Sikdar because, although he was barely four feet away from me in the small green room, the makeup man was standing between us and busily applying powder on the fool's face.

Does Sikdar know that he is a fool?

Allow me a brief digression.

In the early weeks of the Trump administration, I saw the following hashtag on Twitter: #DunningKruger. As in "One difference is when Obama was wrong he knew it. Trump never has, in his mind, been wrong. #DunningKruger"

David Dunning, a psychology professor at Cornell, and Justin Kruger, his graduate student at that time, conducted a series of experiments and published a study in 1999 which concluded that those most lacking in knowledge and skills are least able to appreciate that lack. This observation would come to be known as the Dunning-Kruger effect. To read the Dunning-Kruger 1999 study, "Unskilled and Unaware of It: How Difficulties in Recognizing One's Own Incompetence Lead to Inflated Self-Assessments," is a therapeutic, nearly cathartic exercise today. This is perhaps because the Dunning-Kruger effect has become a meme. You and I read lines like the following and we have the satisfaction of understanding the limitations of Donald Trump's mind: "People tend to hold overly favorable views of their abilities in many social and intellectual domains. The authors suggest that this overestimation occurs, in part, because people who are unskilled in these domains suffer a dual burden: Not only do these people reach erroneous conclusions and make unfortunate choices, but their incompetence robs them of the metacognitive ability to realize it."

The emergence of Donald Trump on the world stage has brought to light many psychological insights that we can use to explain the actions of fools worldwide.

But Orwell is useful here too. Early in *1984,* this is what we learn about doublethink: To know and not to know, to be conscious of complete truthfulness while telling carefully constructed lies, to hold simultaneously two opinions which cancel each other out, knowing them to be contradictory and believing in both of them, to use logic against logic, *"to repudiate morality while laying claim to it,"* et cetera, et cetera (emphasis mine). Later in the novel, Orwell writes: "to tell deliberate lies while genuinely believing in them, to forget any fact that has become inconvenient, and then, when it becomes necessary again, to draw it back from oblivion for just so long as it is needed, to deny the existence of objective reality and all the while to take account of the reality which one denies—all this is indispensably necessary. Even in using the word *doublethink* it is necessary to exercise *doublethink*" (emphasis in original). Has Sikdar read *1984*? I doubt it. If he were to read it he would find evidence there of his own behavior, but he would also tell himself that Orwell's book is really only about Stalinism.

End of digression.

When Vaani's father was in the air force, he went on bombing raids across the border. But Vaani's father, instead of being a jerk about Pakistan, regarded that country as a competitor, as if they were playing cricket with guns. It was still a game with rules and a code of sportsmanship. This was one reason that the father hated his daughter's first husband. Sikdar was never anything more than a spectator in this game of war and yet kept insisting from our television screens every night that we ought to destroy Pakistan. If you were not spewing hate, you were anti-Indian. What the squadron leader could never forgive was how Sikdar had used the bogeyman of Pakistan to create this idea of the enemy even within India. After Vaani and I came together and visited him, her father never spoke to me about Sikdar but once, when we were drinking late into the night, he said cryptically, "When Vaani told me about you, I said to her that before she found out about your parents or even your friends, she should find out who you regarded as your enemies. No better introduction to a man."

Vaani's father had moved from one base to another in different towns and cities in India. Having had friends from many parts of the country, kids of all faiths and classes attending the government schools she found herself in, Vaani had enjoyed a childhood that was in many ways open and liberal. That happiness lasted for several years before her mother's illness blighted the family's sense of time and the world. Vaani's mother died of cancer when Vaani's little sister, Shikha, was only five. But, even then, there had been the great consolation for Vaani of discovering that her surviving parent was equal to the task of providing love. He was a caregiver and a good cook, but he was also an adventurer and a bit of a daredevil. Vaani herself had more of the sobriety and seriousness of her mother; the father's traits were inherited by Shikha, who grew into an athlete and was often caught in little dramas of rebellion against the authority of her teachers. One story I heard early about Shikha was of an incident during her last year of high school. Just outside the metal gates of the school, a young man a little older than she brought his motorcycle, its engine revving, up to a foot or two in front of her. She stopped, stepped aside, and, after looking him straight in the eye for a second, proceeded to the school gate. This happened a second time a day or two later, the young fellow (a good-looking guy, clean shaven, with a grin on his face that spoke of a cockiness born of privilege or power) pretended to topple onto her. This time too, wordlessly, Shikha moved away. But, when this happened again the following day, she pulled him down swiftly. As soon as he was down, a part of his leg still caught under his machine, she stomped several times on his hands, taking care not to spoil his carefully combed hair.

At parties, like the ones at air bases, Shikha would take the microphone and sing with such abandon that people stopped what they were doing in order to watch her. At a Christmas party at the base—this was after Vaani and I had been married for a year or so and were visiting India during our winter break—I stepped close to Shikha to applaud her and she put her arm around me and planted the microphone close to my lips so that I had to join in, crooning. My courage rose after a couple of lines. I was also drunk. I sang with greater freedom, holding on to Shikha, my hip pressed against hers. Everyone was laughing and clapping, we had a lot of fun, but this didn't please Vaani, who said at dinner the following night, "You should have married my sister instead." For a moment I thought I should protest but I quickly apologized.

I'm saying all this to explain my relationship with Vaani. Or what she could call our context. I liked spending time with her family. I was glad to have in Vaani's father a person I could both admire and share some affection with.

When Vaani came to study at Johns Hopkins in September 2001, I was still working in Delhi, and, as far as I remember, I hadn't seen her again in Delhi after our meeting in the TV studio. She claims she read my reports in the paper. And that, when she had been in Baltimore only a few months, she read online my report about the terrorist attack on the Indian Parliament. There was a strong possibility of war with Pakistan, and I even went to the border in a convoy of army trucks. Vaani read the stories I filed, prose untouched by jingoism and honest about the cost of war, and felt that mine was a voice she could trust. While reporting on the firing of the Bofors guns by the soldiers of the 8 Mountain Artillery Brigade, I had hardly imagined that one day in the future that smell of gunpowder would come back to me when I was walking with Vaani beside the Potomac River under branches laden with fragrant pink cherry blossoms.

The attacks of September 11 had made the Americans alert to other places, other populations. In March the following year I got an email from the journalism department at Georgetown inviting an application for a fellowship given to journalists in troubled spots all over the world. I sent off a rushed proposal. And that is how it came to be that during the midst of pujo festivities organized by the Bengali Association of Maryland, I glanced up from my plate of milky sweets and saw Vaani looking at me. I didn't remember her name, but of course I knew who she was.

Such joy to see a face that was familiar to you from that previous life! I remembered that she was married, so I was guarded in expressing my happiness. She was so open and warm that I felt she was greeting me like an old friend. Her serious and beautiful face was lit up with joy. She was smiling, it seemed, because she had remembered a joke someone had told her about life. During that first meeting we only exchanged information about what each of us was doing in America—there was no rush to say anything more because it was clear that there would be time in this new future that had opened up.

Before I left that party, I said, "I wasn't sure I wanted to come here tonight. But such good luck—I met you!"

Vaani kissed me on the cheek then, which surprised and thrilled me, and said with a smile, "I hope your luck holds and we see each other again soon."

How many chance encounters in the weeks that followed, how many planned meetings, first the lunches and then the home-cooked meals, how many days after my reading aloud to her, her face framed by the oval of light from her lamp, Jhumpa Lahiri's story "When Mr. Pirzada Came to Dine," how many trips to the Mondawmin Mall to buy necessary items for the new apartment when she moved again the following fall, how many conversations about her ongoing arguments with Sikdar over their divorce, how many tears (and then kisses) later, did we come to that evening at the Eisenhower Library where we watched, as a part of Vaani's course work, a documentary called *The Nature of Love*? The film showed infant monkeys that were being studied in an experiment. The monkeys were bred in isolation and their only contact was with two mechanical mothers devised by the psychologist Harry Harlow. One mother was nothing but a stark figure made with wire, a plastic head with eyes, and a feeding bottle with milk in it. The other mother was nearly identical but the wire in this model was covered with a piece of cloth that provided a feeling of warmth and comfort. The purpose of the experiment was to test which mother would be the one chosen by the infant monkey, the mother that provided food or the one that provided security. In every instance, the baby monkey was moved by hunger to take nourishment from the wire mother but again, in every instance, it hurried back quickly to spend up to fifteen or even twenty-two hours each day clinging to the cloth mother. When the monkeys were frightened, they ran to the cloth mother. The wire surrogate excited no affection in the monkeys.

I made a remark about love. Vaani was a private person but she put the documentary on pause and said about Sikdar, "You know, he never touched me except during sex."

I didn't say anything. Did I instinctively take her hand in mine? I don't remember. I loved touching Vaani; monkey-like, I enjoyed contact. We could be sitting in public having lunch but I would put one arm around her. Often, at the risk of making her feel uncomfortable, I kissed Vaani on the street. On that night in the library, I remember putting a question to her, a question that had come to me before too. "What did you like about him, what drew you to Sikdar?"

"His ambition," she said. "We were young. We were both from small towns. He knew what he wanted to do in life. I didn't."

After a while, she added, "When I was in high school, I knew these two girls who were good runners and one of them was also excellent at long jump. This will sound ridiculous, but I used to wonder: Who had told them that they could run or jump? How did they know? No one had told me what I could do and I was lost. But here was Gautam, a young man from a background similar to mine, and he was serious and fully confident about his success. It fascinated me. Plus, he claimed to be in love with me. I liked that. He was possessive about me too. It didn't disturb me at the time. It only made me believe in him more."

Monkeys, but also little children, deprived of loving touch showed abnormal behavior: they rocked their heads back and forth. They didn't like contact when they grew up, they were hypersensitive to touch. The impairment of their brains shared properties shown by the brains of schizophrenics.

The film we were watching about Harry Harlow's research went on to talk about the psychologist's own life. At the same time that he was teaching American mothers to love their babies, thereby resisting earlier theories that infants should be allowed to grow independently without too much fuss or fondling, Harlow's own private life was falling apart. His first marriage had failed, and the second marriage wasn't a great success either. Harlow was a distant father. He worked long hours and he was an alcoholic and a depressive. More disturbing, as his life took a downward turn, his research also became darker.

One of the experiments Harlow designed was called "pit of despair." He separated baby monkeys from their mothers at birth and bred them in isolation to see what would happen. This experiment didn't just induce depression in the infant monkeys—after thirty days, the test drove the monkeys insane. They bit themselves and pulled out their hair. After a longer period of isolation, stretching to a year, they became incapable of any social interaction, unable to move or speak. In some cases, they starved themselves to death. Harlow also built something that he called, with customary bluntness, a "rape rack," on which female monkeys were forced to mate against their will. Why did he do it? While pondering this, Vaani said something that made me think of the monkeys in a new way and gave me a sense of intimacy with them. She said that all these monkeys, the rhesus macaques, used in such experiments by Harlow and other researchers, had been imported from India. Even as early as the 1960s, more than a million. When I heard this, it is possible that I was falling prey to self-pity. I began to think of the monkeys as our fellow immigrants, imprisoned in a lab in a foreign land.

Vaani was especially distressed by Harlow's experiments with the infant monkeys, pointing out that the baby monkey's brain is similar to the brain of a five-month-old human baby. Vaani was busy at that time with her dissertation. We weren't thinking of having a child during those years. I never said this to her, but sometimes I feared that Vaani's research was the cause of her depression. In my own work, I often reported about terrible things, and about injustice, but I always found a sense of release, even discovered camaraderie, through my writing. Vaani had no such outlet. But maybe that was just my ignorance. Because the truth was that Vaani was always asking questions. The cloth mother provided succor to the infant monkey but it didn't teach the infant monkey social intelligence. Vaani contemplated the conditions that produced stability and safety in the animal community. Such questions in her course work or her research were all from a human perspective; she wanted to understand how we lived with others. In the same way that I had heard Vaani talk about the lab animals and their "induced helplessness," I heard from her about the experiments that prompted "learned optimism." Not the optimism induced through doses of serotonin (think of Prozac, Zoloft, or Paxil injected into the monkeys) but the designing of experiments that promoted social learning; for example, groups of monkeys released into areas outside their cages for playdates. The infant monkeys with surrogate cloth moms, when brought out for regular playdates, grew up socially adept and outgoing. When I received such reports from Vaani, the thought crossed my mind that she and I were monkeys in isolation, removed from our families and from our natural habitat, but that we were creatures whose friendship, as demonstrated by science, would help overcome most of life's deficits.

A year passed, then three. Then, more. We had been married for five years when the phone rang one night.

It was late September 2010. The call came around 2:00 a.m., the landline in the dining-cum-kitchen area ringing in the silence of the night. I answered. It was Vaani's sister, Shikha. She said my name and then nothing. I had a moment of lucidity and understood, of course, that something bad had happened.

Shikha said, "Papa…"

"Is he unwell?" This is how you build barriers against the truly bad.

She spoke calmly, "Satya, you'll have to tell her." A pause. "Or do you want me to?"

I said, "No, I will. But she'll want to know what happened."

She said, "The gardener comes on Thursdays. He needed money. It was he who discovered the body by looking through a window. Heart attack."

"Oh."

"I don't know how you will tell her this, but he had been dead two days. We can't keep the body. We are going to cremate him this afternoon."

I said quietly, "You are going to have to tell her that right now. Let me wake her up."

When I went to the bed in the next room and touched Vaani's shoulder, I felt her shudder. She was sobbing.

During the days that followed, I wanted to be there for Vaani, supportive and sharing in her grief, but I sensed that she wanted to be alone. She mourned in silence. In a month, Thanksgiving came. Vaani said she didn't want to go to dinner at anyone's house or invite anyone to our home. More surprising, she said she wanted us to drive to Niagara Falls. I didn't question or argue. We drove in the cold, past fields and frozen lakes, arriving there in the late evening. From the highway, we saw the lights ringed around the white frozen water and in the middle the cascading falls. Vaani wanted us to head straight for the motel where we had booked a room. Above the reception desk in the motel, there was a sign, NIAGARA FALLS: THE WORLD'S TOP HONEYMOON DESTINATION. I nudged Vaani and pointed to the sign with my chin. She smiled a strained smile. That night during dinner at a nearby Applebee's, she told me that when her father was a trainee in the air force, he was sent for three weeks to the Niagara Falls Air Reserve Station. She had wanted to feel a connection with him. I nodded my head. I was glad that we had come, but the revelation also caught me by surprise. It made me think that we don't know everything there is to know about someone we love and are living with. Oddly, I thought of the plastic mask that our neighbor had worn a month earlier for Halloween. The mask's features were immobile, the mouth slightly agape, and what was scary was that we couldn't know whether that expression was one of wonder or pain or panic.

Work had always absorbed Vaani. She plunged back into her regular routine. Home, lab, library, home. She walked to the grocery store some afternoons to get the provisions we needed at home. One evening she returned home looking shaken. She had seen someone who, from the back, looked just like her father. He was holding the hand of a child, clearly a grandchild. Vaani had followed the two as they walked away from her. Then she speeded up to get a good look at the man. He had her father's erect back and sense of style. She heard him speak a few words to the child. The language sounded like Arabic. I got up from the chair I was sitting in. I wanted to comfort her. She let me hold her and with her face near my ear she said, "Let's make a baby." So, from that sorrow also came, a little less than a year later, our daughter. And yet, a different thought also took hold of me and I've never let go of it. As long as Vaani's father was living, I had thought my relative youth would save me. I was going to win. But now I lost hope. I could never win against a ghost.

I wrote these words at an eerie hour, near two in the morning. Outside, it is quiet, no lights on around the villa, only the reflection of a single bulb blinking in the water, on a pier at the far edge of the dark expanse of the lake. In writing about Vaani, I have conjured her ghost. Earlier in the day she had written to tell me that I should stay and work. If everyone followed safety protocols at the villa, I would be okay. Her reasoning was simple: the maximum chance of exposure to contagion would happen if I took the train and then the transatlantic flight back to America. If everyone sheltered in place and washed hands regularly, we would all be safe. She wrote that she would remain in the apartment in Cambridge with Piya. Outside over the lake's dark waters, the wind carries Vaani's voice. She is saying, over and over, "Don't panic, stay calm."

When she was in India and then when she was new in the United States, Vaani claimed to have read my reportage in newspapers. But, over the years, I have found that she has time only for her research. I quite admire her sense of focus. There is nothing in our daily life that she doesn't address as a scientific problem or a puzzle. For instance, when Vaani and I walked on the streets near our home in the summer evenings, a shout or a howl often came from a passing car. Sometimes a honk, followed by laughter. Especially after Trump's election, I found myself flinching. I had my theories. But Vaani wasn't prepared to condemn Americans. She said that research shows that humans everywhere are trained by evolution to trust people who look like themselves and distrust those who are different.

She obviously hadn't read the Psychologist-in-Chief Barack Obama, who, speaking to the press at the White House after the shooting of Trayvon Martin, didn't think this was a universal phenomenon. Trayvon Martin was a teenager armed with a bottle of Arizona fruit juice and a bag of Skittles. Obama told the press: "I think it's important to recognize that the African-American community is looking at this issue through a set of experiences and a history that doesn't go away." He said that there were very few Black men in this country who hadn't had the experience of being followed around in department stores. That includes me, he had added. And that there were very few Black men who hadn't had the experience of walking across the street and hearing the locks click on the doors of the cars they passed. He said that was what usually happened to him. Or getting into an elevator and seeing a woman clutch her purse nervously and hold her breath till she had the chance to get off. *Check, check, check.*

When I mentioned this, briefly, while trying to match her pace during that one particular evening, Vaani said research has shown that conservatives have larger fear centers in their brains than liberals. Therefore, they are more concerned with physical safety than liberals. In fact, the psychologist whose work demonstrated this had found the truth of his research in his own life. After his daughter was born, he felt his neighborhood was growing so dangerous that his family had to move. This is because when people become parents of a tiny, vulnerable baby, they begin to believe that their local crime rate is going up, even if it is falling. Evolution has shaped us to behave in this way.

Vaani's point about evolution drew me onto another path of thought.

"Wait a minute," I said. "Why shouldn't I believe that evolution has primed males to see a beautiful woman like you and loudly signal their mating calls?"

She barely smiled and continued with that walk of hers that said, as it always did, I'm free and I take delight in my body and its movements. Vaani's swift, swinging gait took her away from me, six or ten steps if I wasn't paying attention. I watched her as I followed her, slightly out of breath, and, without wishing to draw attention to myself too much, made small animal noises just loud enough for her to hear. She didn't respond.

The female of the species will keep her distance from the male she doesn't fully trust. Or whom she trusts but wants to convey annoyance or impatience to. Any mistrust she has is heightened in public, where she is exposed to the gaze of others, including other suitors for her attention. She will not easily give herself away. Poor behavior on the part of the male is ignored because evolution has trained her to—is *husband* the word we want?—husband her meager resources in the wild. On occasion, in the face of comical behavior on the part of the male, she will burst into loud laughter, which both surprises and pleases her partner.

Has evolution also trained us to be a couple? I don't know. I'm asking this because the other side of the question about the boot in the face is the question of someone's lips on yours. As I try to calibrate the details in our past that made it possible for us to fall in love, I wonder also about a line I read in a book: "The half-life of love is forever." What is the story those next few years will tell? The truth is that years earlier, when Vaani's divorce came through, I felt that the question of our future had been settled. I gave up the idea of returning to India and applied for a job teaching writing and journalism. My first appointment was at a community college in Rockville, Maryland; my employers sought an H-1B visa for me. Overnight, I discovered a new professional identity as a postcolonial scholar; this new identity was my real passport to America. I was suddenly reading and teaching Jamaica Kincaid, Tayeb Salih, Ngugi wa Thiong'o, V. S. Naipaul, Assia Djebar, Tsitsi Dangarembga, and Arundhati Roy. Vaani continued with her doctoral work on gendered behavior among the rhesus macaques. She was studying the behavior of the alpha males and the hierarchy they imposed. The alpha male would snatch the food it wanted and it also got sex on demand. The passive male that had been courting a female would move away at the approach of the alpha male. And the young monkeys arranged their behavior and picked up cues. What interested Vaani most of all was the question why in such a brutal environment there wasn't more violence. I joked that it was because monkeys didn't have access to guns, but Vaani's inquiry was a serious one: How did power articulate itself through a complex and even subtle *language*? When I asked her about it, Vaani clarified that, though she was investigating power, the idea of language was central to animal life. Language was the complicated web through which any society communicated and exerted control. The monkeys, she was saying to me, were as sophisticated in their response to symbols and signs as the students I was teaching in my classes.

Re: language. Vaani does not use emojis. Actually, she doesn't even like to use her phone and often doesn't respond to my messages until days have passed. ("Can you get milk?" I ask on a Tuesday. On Saturday, I hear back. "When did you send this message?") But then, one day, after I sent her a poem about a hedgehog—a poem by Philip Larkin, possessed of a trademark acid wit but, in it, suddenly tender about the animal he had accidentally killed with his lawn mower—Vaani responded with an emoji. No words, just an emoji that I hadn't seen before, a tiny hedgehog, looking whole and unharmed. Hitherto, she had only used fully formed sentences in her texts, spell-checked, with proper punctuation and words like *hitherto*. What could have occasioned this turn from a grammarian to a vulgarian?

"Emojis?" I texted.

"See email," she responded.

And I found, waiting in my inbox, courtesy of the British Psychological Society, this piece of edifying, if also unsatisfying, information:

> *There is growing evidence about the way emoji are affording emotion and sentiment detection within textual discourse.*
>
> *Researchers within the area of Natural Language Processing (NLP) often use computational models to study social media content containing emoji. These models are becoming increasingly accurate at learning representations of emotion in such content, and it seems that emoji are facilitating this capacity (Felbo, Mislove, Søgaard, Rahwan & Lehmann, 2017; Sari, Ratnasari, Mutrofin & Arifin, 2014).*
>
> *Similarly, emotional hashtags (#) have been found to successfully map onto emotional categories within Twitter content (Mohammad, 2012), and research moving beyond computation models into human inference shows similar findings. Namely that even non-facial emoji play a role in communicating emotion and can disambiguate text messages (Riordan, 2017).* Etc.

I find such language confounding. It is without love—there is no passion, no poetry. I confess that I have more than once, even it seems in the pages of this novel, mocked Vaani's academic language. The coded speech of the psychology professor. You might ask: Has anything given me pause? *Yes!* Have I learned anything? *Yes!* I have learned that it's not that one language reveals and another language hides; instead, what happens is that someone's truth, the searing pain of experience, bursts through, *can* burst through, any tear in conventional language. Here's an example. Piya must have been six or seven then. I had picked her up from school and was sitting in our living room making her a peanut butter and jelly sandwich. Why the living room instead of the kitchen, where I asked her to sit down and wait for me? I was watching the Senate Judiciary Committee hearing on the TV, that's why. Senator Patrick Leahy asked the woman who was testifying about her strongest memory of the sexual assault on her by the Supreme Court nominee. The serious, bespectacled woman who was being asked this question—also a psychology professor, as it happens—was trying to smile instead of crying. She said, "Indelible in the hippocampus is the laughter…" I believed her and that night I wrote a letter of support that I sent to her university address. But at that moment when she was speaking on television, I was trying to hide my tears from my daughter. I wanted to drop the knife and go running out of the door, running down a long street that would take me back to when Vaani was also only fifteen. A morning in March. She had long hair then. The festival of Holi fell on that day. Celebrations were being held all over the country. Her mother was dead and her father had taken the two girls to a relative's house in Roorkee. Why did they even go there? Because it was close by? Two hours on the road the night before Holi. Vaani had an older cousin, she was in that house with her husband. This husband, an electrical engineer, rubbed red and green color into Vaani's hair. Everyone was laughing. Not Vaani. Then the cousin's husband, tall and with a thin sword-shaped mustache, put color on her face. Vaani struggled and turned her face away. Now her face was hidden and only inches from the wall. The man pushed two of his fingers in Vaani's mouth so that she feared she was going to choke. When she freed herself and turned toward the people in the room, fighting to hold back her tears and her rage, someone said, "Oh, these English-medium girls, they haven't played Holi before."

Two summers ago, Koko, the gorilla, died in California. She had been taught sign language by the developmental psychologist Penny Patterson, who had met Koko in the San Francisco Zoo when the gorilla was a year old. By the time the much-loved gorilla died, she was forty-six. I read somewhere that Koko had in her repertoire more than 1,100 signs. She could make signs for food or drink as well as emotions like sad or love or good or sorry. And more complex constructions, like stupid dirty toilet. When I read about Koko, I sent a link to Vaani thinking the story might be useful for her work. But Vaani wasn't very impressed. She said that she wasn't thinking of humans teaching animals. Her focus was on the magic of language in nature. Adult male canaries, she said, learn a new song every year in order to attract mates. We were in the kitchen when she tossed off this observation, but I hurried to my study to write this down in my notebook.

Each year, I promised myself, I would fashion a new song for Vaani.

I wander in the forest of humanity, listening to the sounds released from more than a billion throats.

This song is for Vaani.

After Bev's departure, six more fellows left the villa, including Nikki, who flew back to Newark from Milan Malpensa. I was tempted to join Nikki on that flight, and return home to my family, but Vaani was adamant. "It is clear that flights are the vectors of contagion," et cetera. We were in the third week of February now. There were sixteen cases of patients suffering from the virus in nearby Lombardy, and then, with a speed that seemed astonishing, by the end of the month there were fifty-four new cases. Did I find myself seized at times by fear and panic? I did. Meanwhile, Trump had visited India and there were riots in Delhi with Muslim homes and businesses razed to the ground while police watched. Bigotry was an old virus that had killed more people than whatever was new on the horizon. Neither Trump nor Modi said anything about the impending crisis even though scientists were certain that the disease was going to explode in the coming weeks. In fact, after his return to the United States, as the days passed, Trump had downplayed the threat of the virus. He tweeted that the virus was under control in the United States and that the stock market was looking good to him. On February 26, Vaani called me after watching a press conference where Trump announced he had asked Vice President Pence to lead the Coronavirus Task Force. Vaani was in a rage. She said that the country already had fifty-seven confirmed cases of virus-affected, but Trump had glibly said at the press conference that "we're going to be pretty soon at only five people, and we could be at just one or two people over the next short period of time." She said the virus must already be in the bodies of thousands and the symptoms would appear in two weeks. For my part, I found myself unable to write the fictions I had been writing so far about my past. It was likely that I would leave the villa too, although it was by no means certain. Till the uncertainty ended, I was going to devote myself to the task of scouring my journals and compiling for Vaani a writer's report on news.

I had two insect bites on my left leg that had first turned red and then yellow, but I didn't go down to the town to buy a tube of ointment. Instead, I asked one of the waitstaff to buy me cigarettes. Although I didn't tell Vaani this, I felt I needed to start smoking again. When I gave a few euros to a youth named Armando, and mimicked smoking, he showed he understood me by saying Marlboro, Marlboro. No, no, I said, I wanted to smoke whatever our friend Anna Duranti had smoked while she was still at the villa. Armando, who noticed everything and was attentive about everything, nodded. And, from that day on, this was the new me. Smoking Chiaravalle cigarettes, drinking coffee, and, with a mixture of anxiety and denial, making notes about the news. The reports about the virus were often based on hearsay. This showed that the popular imagination had remained a mix of pedestrian curiosity and familiar prejudice *even in the midst of a pandemic.* In a world of suddenly greater insecurity, this might be oddly reassuring, even if not pleasing, because it offered proof of continuity. For instance, on the morning I left the villa, March 6, these were the top searches at Snopes.com on the subject of the coronavirus:

> Did a Chinese Intelligence Officer Reveal the "Truth About the Coronavirus Outbreak"? [False]
> Did Health Experts "Predict" New Coronavirus Could Kill 65 Million People? [False]
> Did Italy Confirm Almost 200 Deaths in 24 Hours? [True]
> Did Chinese Doctors Confirm African People Are Genetically Resistant to Coronavirus? [False]
> Was COVID-19 Found in Packages of Toilet Paper? [False]

Please read the next chapter for more.

CHAPTER 6

THE VELOCITY OF LIES

Literature is news that stays news. This Ezra Pound quote is routinely invoked at literary festivals—if only by those who denounce novels dealing with the news. For such critics, the real news, the human heart in conflict with itself et cetera, is eternal. But these people are missing the point. I have news for Pound. The frame has shifted. We are surrounded by fake news. Or, to put it more formally, we are living in a world of accelerated and often false media. Literature, in its battle to find out what is real, has to lock horns with how news educates and misleads. Literature can become news by making news. This is because truth doesn't just exist by itself. It takes effort; it is produced. It is an effect of practice.

The villa suddenly feels empty and our lives hollow. Even the lake looks barren. I'm not writing fiction about the past anymore. I feel this urgency about the present, and what to do with the news. Am I right in thinking that by bringing news into literature we make sure that daily news doesn't die a daily death? During these days, it doesn't seem hyperbolic in the least to say that by keeping the news alive, or the truth alive, we also keep ourselves alive. Pound doesn't matter. We are closer here to what William Carlos Williams wrote about poetry and death. Please Google "It is difficult to get the news from poems..."

Here are collected fragments on the construction of facts—and fiction. They are excerpted from the journal entries in my notebooks. Those readers more interested in the story than in news should skip this chapter and go directly to the next one.

1.

Simon, my English friend at the villa, said that what was really frightening about the new disease was the amount of misinformation coming to us.

I thought it was all as expected. For some time now, Walmart has been selling a party game called Fake News. Twenty-four bucks.

I was able to tell Simon this because I had been looking at my journals the previous night. I had noted the preceding fact in my journal on October 22, 2019. On the same day, I had also recorded the following entry: In response to Trump's tweet that the impeachment inquiry against him was a "lynching," Merriam-Webster posted the following tweet: "'Lynch' is our top search today. Even in a metaphorical context, it still evokes a long and painful history of racist violence."

Also re: lynching.

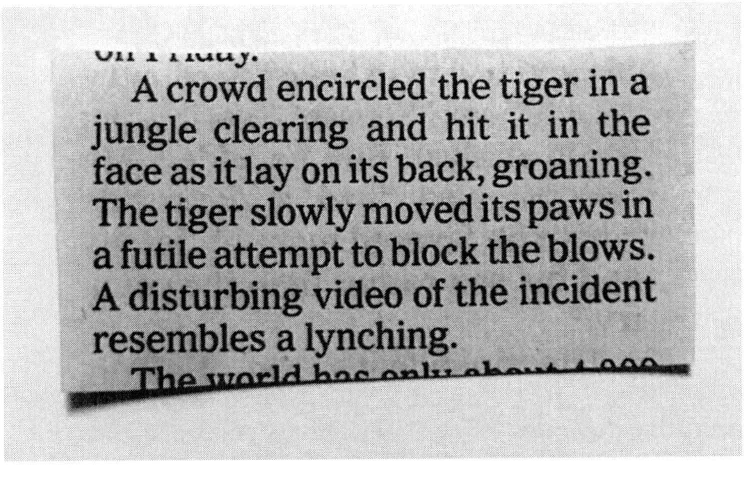
A crowd encircled the tiger in a jungle clearing and hit it in the face as it lay on its back, groaning. The tiger slowly moved its paws in a futile attempt to block the blows. A disturbing video of the incident resembles a lynching.

I had cut out this section from *The New York Times* in late July 2019. The report was about villagers in India killing a tiger with sticks. A detail made me pause. What made the story unusual, and even extraordinary, was that the reporter had made a connection between the animal's killing and what was being done to human beings on India's streets.

2.

Mahatma Gandhi spent more than two decades in South Africa before returning to India to lead the fight against the British empire. While in South Africa, developing his early ideas about satyagraha and nonviolent resistance, Gandhi invested his finances and his energy in a printing press. At that time, publishing was a young business and very much an expression of rapid industrialization. The emphasis was on speed. Gandhi was interested in slow news.

Slow news, said Sue Wallace, a fellow here at the residency. She teaches history at the university in Amherst, Massachusetts, and is writing a book on the politics of print culture. Sue offered that phrase after I told her about this novel. She suggested I read about Gandhi's printing press. At the breakfast table, everyone's ears had pricked up. One could tell without being told that everyone was dealing with the same problem.

In his first ashram, in Phoenix, fourteen miles north of Durban, Gandhi and his satyagrahis (and four Zulu women, whose labor goes somewhat unremarked in the great man's papers) used a hand-operated iron press. The work was demanding and painful. Gandhi: "There came a time when we deliberately gave up the use of the engine and worked with hand-power only. Those were, to my mind, the days of highest moral uplift." This sense of engaged labor extended to the reader too. Gandhi didn't want reading to become an indiscriminate, incoherent, or addictive act. He advocated patience. The form of the periodicals and pamphlets printed at the ashram was essentially discontinuous, pages made up of news clippings and short ethical extracts or condensed summaries of writers like Thoreau, Ruskin, and Tolstoy. The readership that the press catered to was diasporic and spread across the empire: here again, the emphasis wasn't on telegraph-driven or dateline-dominated reporting but, instead, on an undated, more leisurely tempo of reading. News became more like a stream of opinion, idea, and belief, rather than a report on a flow of events. In fact, it was clear that even the idea of an event had come under revision, dissolving into a kaleidoscope of cuttings. Gandhi didn't put faith in copyright. Several of his pamphlets, and his translations into Gujarati of other writers like Tolstoy, he published with the accompanying legend: "No Rights Reserved."

A text made up of clippings could possibly also advance a hasty reading practice instead of a strategy where the reader was forced to connect and make the pieces cohere. In order to make the reader pause and become more self-aware, the periodicals carried didactic quotes like this one from Thoreau: "Read not the Times. Read the Eternities." Gandhi's advice to readers who were bored by his columns was that they try to read the articles again. This advice is appreciated, I suspect, by writers everywhere who are mindful, as I am, of boring their readers because they have failed to provide a feverish plot, a tale full of twists and amazing coincidences, or even something more basic like a tight, continuous structure. Do your duty, Gandhi said. Which reminds me, he wanted readers to be "Thoreaus in miniature," and I haven't, despite our shared love for walking, read a word that Thoreau wrote.

I guess the real question is: How to slow-jam the news?

3.

The following afternoon, I wandered into the dining room with one of my journals. I was looking for fruit. Just the previous day, I had eaten my first quince. The world can be falling apart, people dying in large numbers, and monsters in office only staging photo-ops, you could be getting choked from clichés filling the passageways in your lungs, but you can still taste the sweetness of a fruit for the first time.

Outside the window, seated under a tree, I could see the enormous profile of Jimi Adeola, the doctor from Nigeria. A large quiet man, immensely courteous and thoughtful. Knowledgeable too. I picked up a pear and went out to join Jimi.

"Sah, what is the news?"

"Sah," Jimi said, "in your country, they are ready to call it a pandemic. But not yet."

I thought he meant India, but no, he meant the United States. The CDC had just declared that COVID-19, which is what the disease caused by the new virus was being called, was headed toward becoming a full-on pandemic. The disease needed to meet three conditions. It had already met two: illness resulting in death and sustained person-to-person spread. The third condition was worldwide spread. Jimi said, "That is the report from yesterday, February 25th. All three criteria will be met by next week. Or the week thereafter."

And then, out of his profound courtesy, he asked for my news.

I said, "Have you seen Sue?"

He hadn't.

I was seeking Sue because I wanted to show her a page from my journal. The previous summer, I had made a small painting from a photograph that had appeared in an Indian newspaper. The photograph showed a man kneeling in the dirt, begging for his life. Half of his white vest—and his face—is soaked in blood. He is surrounded by onlookers—we see their legs, not their faces. The man on the ground, who has not been lynched yet but will be soon, is Mohammed Naeem. He is suspected of being a kidnapper. He is asserting his innocence, because that is the truth, but it is already too late for the truth.

A man with red marks on his body

In making a painting from a photograph in the newspaper, I was trying to look at the scene more closely. And perhaps make others do the same. That is also the work that words can do. A caption can change the meaning of what one is looking at. (Think of the clipping I used in the first entry in this chapter. The words that serve as a kind of caption for the video of the tiger being killed also change its meaning.)

The day I had made the painting, my journal revealed, a match between India and New Zealand in the cricket World Cup had been delayed because of rain. Some days earlier, Prime Minister Modi had tweeted his concern for an Indian player who had injured his finger. The prime minister did not have any words, however, about the Muslim victim of a lynch mob near Jamshedpur. Tabrez Ansari, a newly married welder, home for Eid celebrations, was made to chant "Jai Shri Ram" while being tied to a pole and beaten for hours. He later died in police custody.

Mohammed Naeem, whose photograph had moved me to paint him, had also been lynched near Jamshedpur, in Jharkhand. Even earlier than Mohammed Naeem's death, in the same state, Alimuddin Ansari, a Muslim meat trader, had been pulled out of his van and beaten. His van was set on fire. Ansari died on the way to the hospital. One of the main accused in Ansari's killing was the man in charge of the ruling party's media operations. When the eight men arrested for Ansari's killing were released from jail in July 2018, the Harvard-educated politician who was the local representative of the ruling party put marigold garlands around their necks and fed them sweets. I received a WhatsApp message about this from Vaani's sister, Shikha. She was mocking me because when I was in high school in Patna, I was on a tennis team with that politician. He was my classmate at school. At these moments, when this novel takes an autobiographical turn, it is because in this direct way I can comment on the banality of the banality of evil.

The New York Times in its report on Ansari's murder called 2018 "the year of the lynch mob in India." I mentioned this fact to Jimi Adeola. He said he had a great fear of mobs in his country too. The most perplexing phenomenon, Jimi said, was the situation when suddenly a man in a crowd would come to believe that his penis had vanished. And this man accused any other man standing nearby of having stolen his penis.

"Thief, thief."

But is the man believed by the crowd? I wanted to know.

"Yes," Jimi said. "This fear, or call it hysteria, is often commonly shared by others. The accused man can easily be lynched."

I gazed at the lake. How would one paint the fear of the missing penis?

Jimi was saying in his gentle, grave voice, "It is terrible. A tire can be put around a man's neck and then set on fire."

4.

"The American writer in the middle of the 20th century has his hands full in trying to understand, describe and then make credible much of American reality," wrote Philip Roth in an essay in *Commentary* magazine. "It stupefies, it sickens, it infuriates and finally it is even a kind of embarrassment to one's own meager imagination. The actuality is continually outdoing our talents, and the culture tosses up figures almost daily that are the envy of any novelist."

Our leaders produce bewildering fiction. Trump, for example, at a rally in South Carolina referred to the coronavirus as the Democrats' "new hoax." The most enduring lie of his presidency has been the following claim, made in November 2016: "In addition to winning the Electoral College in a landslide, I won the popular vote if you deduct the millions of people who voted illegally." During a speech at a rally in Green Bay, Wisconsin, in April 2019, he made the following egregiously false claim to denounce abortion rights: "The baby is born. The mother meets with the doctor. They take care of the baby. They wrap the baby beautifully. And then the doctor and the mother determine whether or not they will execute the baby." I could list twenty thousand lies uttered by Trump, but there is one that, for some odd reason, puzzles me the most. Trump has claimed more than once that his father, Fred Trump, had been born in Germany. "My father is German, right? Was German, and born in a very beautiful place in Germany." Fred Trump was born in the Bronx in New York City.

In the country of my birth, Prime Minister Modi in a radio address said that the ancient Sanskrit language offered resources to tackle all kinds of challenges in life. He said that the Vedas contained mantras to solve even modern problems like global warming. In 2014, Modi had also said that the worship of the elephant-headed god Ganesha meant that plastic surgery was invented in ancient India, allowing a surgeon to put an elephant's head on the body of a human being.

I was skipping cocktail hour. Not just because the excitement and the ease that had been there had vanished. There was some bad news from home. When I had woken up there was a message from Vaani that Piya had a fever. The email had been sent just before Vaani went to sleep. Around lunchtime I sent a text. Vaani was up now. She texted back that the fever was down by a degree, only 99.5 now, and there was a general lethargy in the child but she was otherwise okay. Nose filled with snot but not having trouble breathing otherwise. That was a relief.

When in my journal I read about the lies uttered by our leaders, did I feel annoyance? No. I felt rage. I wanted to tear the masks of power off their faces. I wanted to humiliate them. Then I remembered that they had been voted into office. And the object of my rage shifted. Who were all those who had voted for these people? I wanted a list of the lies that they had all believed. Later, as I was trying to fall asleep, my thoughts returned to this question and kept me awake. At literary festivals, someone will raise a hand and ask, Do you write in longhand or do you use a computer? Or, Where do your ideas come from? I imagined the audience seated in rows. The silence that follows questions like this. And then the response from the podium. Mic in hand, the writer asking, Actually, sir or madam, the more important question is, Whom did you vote for? Have you done any worthwhile reading? And why was your reading of no use to you at all?

Bitter, bitter.

5.

A brief and random history of rumors: In India, in 250 B.C.E., the *Arthashastra* gave advice about achieving military success by infiltrating the enemy to spread rumors.

During World War II, the British Political Warfare Executive (PWE) formed a Rumour Committee, which would formulate new anti-Nazi stories every two weeks, which would in turn be propagated throughout neutral cities in the hope that they would soon reach Germany. (For example, "Nazis have unusual sexual fetishes," "Hitler intends to flee Germany soon," "A new weapon that can light the sea on fire recently obliterated a German army.") Meanwhile, the Germans spread rumors too. One such false story claimed that an American woman's head had exploded at the hairdresser due to trace amounts of explosive left over after her shift at the factory where she worked.

Steps were taken to curb rumors. In Great Britain, posters of two women speaking, haunted by images of Hitler and Goering: "You never know who's listening! Loose lips sink ships!" A man dressed half as a civilian, half as a German military man: "Talk less... you never know." In America, a poster of a dog mourning his human companion's death: "Because someone talked." A small girl cradling her father's picture: "Don't kill her daddy with careless talk." In France, "Advice to those on leave: a good soldier keeps his lips sealed." Another poster depicting two men, one a soldier, the other a civilian, with a nearby water pitcher containing Hitler's face. Later, during the Cold War, the KGB disseminated rumors that condoms distributed in Africa by Western organizations were responsible for the spread of AIDS.

6.

On September 13, 2016, Wikipedia first reviewed a page called "Fake News."

On December 10, 2016, at 9:11 a.m., @realDonaldTrump tweeted, "Reports by @CNN that I will be working on The Apprentice during my Presidency, even part time, are ridiculous & untrue—FAKE NEWS!"

The Wikipedia page on "Fake News" also carries the following statement: "During and after his presidential campaign and election, Donald Trump began to use the term 'fake news' to describe negative press coverage of his presidency."

During all these years of the Trump presidency, the term *fake news* has been all around us. Trump saw as fake precisely what was real. Good journalists fact-checked him, pointed out his lies. My passion was for something narrower: I felt the need to keep an eye on the real even in the fake. For instance, in Trump's wax figure unveiled at Tussauds just before the inauguration, his hair was "a mixture of human hair and yak hair." I liked the fact that the wax figure's golden coif had required a bit of research: Tussauds called the stylist from *The Apprentice*. The hairstylist said: "It's hairspray and almost like a lacquer." From another news story, this quote also noted in my journal on January 19, 2017: "Getting his tone right was also a challenge for coloring artist Verity Talbot whose palette is full of pink and magenta; an array of tones that she hopes will bring the President-elect to life."

7.

How to respond to rumors?

With strong assertions of truth. Possibly.

But how to find the truth?

Slow news. I now think of it as a performance. How to perform the news so that it reveals its inner self. Or something like that.

The Daily Show curated the "Trump Presidential Twitter Library" like an art gallery exhibition, each tweet presented with the gilt-edged frames that would have belonged in Trump's hotels. Imagine then the broad, ornate, faux-royal frame surrounding the reproduction of Trump's birtherism tweet. There was accompanying commentary. An official-sounding, mocking description, "Masterworks from the Collection," followed by the title "Birth of a Birther"—and then this pitch-perfect and truly hilarious piece of satire, the apotheosis of the language of art criticism:

> Critics may disagree on the greatest of Trump's tweets, but all cite "Birth of a Birther" as his first unquestionable masterpiece. Taken as a standalone work, one can marvel at the audacity of his creative imagination—the delicacy of the halo of the quotations encircling "extremely credible." Yet it is as a preface to Trump's most creative period that "Birth of a Birther" finds its true strength—achieving metaphorical "birthing" of the artist's identity by questioning the literal birth of another. Contradictory forces thus become complementary, as Trump is clearly inspired by the yin and yang first described in ancient China, a known currency manipulator.

8.

Sue is not as troubled as I am by all the falsehood around us. On the path below my window, I saw her walking with LeeAnn, the filmmaker from Connecticut, and I went down to join them. They caught sight of me and LeeAnn cheerfully called out, "Yo, Cronkite." Sue wanted to know how my daughter was doing and I told them that the child had bounced back. She laughed and said, "Did you talk to the waitstaff about all this? Armando is pissed that the soccer matches have been canceled."

LeeAnn was telling a story. Her younger sister is a nurse working the night shift at a hospital in Massachusetts, and LeeAnn had called her to find out how they are preparing for the coming pandemic. But because LeeAnn loves dogs, her sister, the nurse, had a different kind of horror story for her. A couple had come to the hospital the previous night. The man had a bloody arm that he held cradled in his other hand. He was calm; his wife, however, was pretty hysterical. The wife told the nurse that they had been fighting at home and when the husband flipped the coffee table, her dog flew at him and latched on to his arm. The amount of blood he had lost was unbelievable and now here they were in the emergency room. LeeAnn said that her sister tried to calm the woman, telling her that the surgeon on call was the best they had and her husband was going to be okay. But the woman sobbed, inconsolable. "I'm crying for my dog," she said. "My husband now has his excuse to put him down."

"Oh no, that's terrible," Sue said.

I waited for LeeAnn to say something about her sister and her fears regarding COVID. But Sue wanted to know where the sister lived and then the two women began talking about a town off Highway 84.

"Sue," I said, a bit abruptly when there was a pause in their conversation, "I thought of you today when I came across a note in my scrapbook where I had asked if things have come to such a sorry pass because we are distracted."

"It's not a new problem," Sue said. "It was actually noted first two thousand five hundred years ago but now it's even worse. Plato, the Stoics, Epicurus, the Abhidhamma, Kama Sutra, the Zhuangzi—all worry about our relationship to pleasure and how it can make us unhappy. The new technology amplifies this."

"The note in my scrapbook had a clipping attached to it," I said. "Do you know the name George Monbiot? He argues that the media is to be blamed if our attention is diverted. Also, that the greatest environmental threat isn't oil. It is the media. It misdirects us. Every day it tells us that issues of mind-numbing irrelevance are more important than the collapse of our life support systems."

Unfazed, Sue said simply, "It comes with the territory. You cannot, on the one hand, give people the democratic right to have blogs and websites but, on the other hand, expect everyone to publish scientifically vetted truth."

As we walked, she talked in detail about the rise of print culture in America, how, between the years 1700 and 1765, 75 percent of the printers brought out newspapers. Did they only publish the objective truth that one of those printers, none other than Benjamin Franklin himself, claimed? No. But without these printers doing what they did there would have been no idea of the nation.

"This is a necessary conversation," Sue said.

Okay, Sue, I said to myself when I was back in my room. My novel is in that fight then.

9.

In his *Paris Review* interview, Gabriel García Márquez has this to say about facts: "In journalism just one fact that is false prejudices the entire work. In contrast, in fiction one single fact that is true gives legitimacy to the entire work."

Márquez probably did not have in mind bad fiction or fake news but the same principle holds. A single fact provides a tenuous bridge over a gaping abyss of misinformation. But that flimsy bridge is all that is needed by the army of online trolls.

10.

Trump's rise has given birth to so many memes about fiction. Red hats, resembling MAGA hats, but with the legend Make Orwell Fiction Again. A book display at a store, with titles like *The Plot Against America,* under the sign "alternative facts" or what we like to call fiction. And post-apocalyptic fiction moved to our current affairs section. I do not know in which category the book that I'm writing will be put. This is a part of the confusion of our times.

Talking of Orwell, though, I am now halfway through *1984*. Winston Smith and the girl with dark hair, her name is Julia, have slept together, which Smith understands as a blow struck against the Party and, therefore, a political act. Julia is resourceful and pleasure seeking; in contrast, Smith appears pedantic and a bit dull. Julia is street-smart and finds ways to subvert the dictates of the Party. Smith is more timid, but he is also alert to larger questions, like that of the falsification of the past. He remembers the past, which has been obliterated. A time outside this time. Is that why readers went looking for *1984* after Trump was elected? Literature as an expression of a tiny will to freedom.

P.S. Two or three days after I had made the previous notation I came upon a section in *1984* where Orwell fearlessly plants a whole essay, although the more accurate word would be a *treatise,* entitled "The Theory and Practice of Oligarchical Collectivism." *It goes on for some thirty-odd pages!* How post-! How meta-! There is a lucid section on the necessity of war for a society to maintain its own oppressive hierarchies—all brilliant in an old-fashioned way, but didn't editors and reviewers tell Orwell he couldn't just insert an essay in the middle of a novel? I had come to *1984* because I had been told it was an iconic work of dystopian fiction about what we now call *fake news,* but I also take heart from Orwell's bold experimentation. I have little doubt that he thought of it also as a political act.

11.

I lie awake at night. This has been happening a lot lately. This villa—but also the act of writing—seems so far away from the real world. In saying this, I'm reporting from a land called despair. In my hometown in India, but this is true not just of that town, the atmosphere outside the jail on the day those accused of murder or rape or rioting are released is like a wedding. These men are guilty of everything they have been accused of, but because they have power or money, they are able to walk free. Their supporters gather outside the prison gates to celebrate. Car horns blare. There is music, also slogans, taunts, insults, and, of course, sweets. The foreheads of the victorious are smeared with red tilak. They raise their arms to quiet the crowd, join palms to show gratitude. If by any bad luck a girl from a minority community happens to be crossing the street, she is offered a sweet, and, if she says no, someone grips her arms while someone else thrusts the sweet inside her mouth before wiping his hands on her chest.

12.

If you are from India, you perhaps share a memory, which is a collective memory, which means you know it even if you didn't experience it. An animal's head is thrown inside a place of worship. By late evening, a part of the city has gone up in flames. The engineering of public violence through the manufacture of rumors.

Bhisham Sahni's *Tamas* opens with the scene of a government official paying an untouchable man to kill a pig. (The upper castes thought of themselves as the only touchables. Many still do.) The animal's head is thrown on the steps of a mosque that evening. The untouchable realizes he has been made an unwitting accomplice to a riot. Sahni is constructing a secular critique of what in the subcontinent we call communal politics.

Nowadays it is all happening on WhatsApp, the Facebook-owned instant-messaging service. About 200 million Indians are WhatsApp subscribers, making India the biggest market for the social media platform. WhatsApp is free and easy to use; it consumes less data than Facebook or Twitter. Journalist Snigdha Poonam has reported that "Indians produce the majority of the 55 billion WhatsApp messages sent every day," covering the gamut from family photos to political propaganda. Poonam adds that while WhatsApp is "the primary source of news for Indians," what is circulated there in the guise of news is often fake. I believe this makes Indians the biggest consumers of rumors or fake news. Poonam's conclusion is more sober: "The consequences can be deadly," she writes. "Rumors spread over the service are killing people in India."

13.

Why must one slow-jam the news? Because all that is new will become normal with astonishing speed. You will go to visit your father and discover that he has pledged himself to the service of the Great Leader. Or you will visit your friend's house and it will take a minute or more to realize that a meeting is under way and now everyone is looking at you with suspicion. You notice one fine day that all the signs on the road have changed. Your town has a new name. Dogs have grown fat on flesh torn from corpses lining the street where you grew up. The beautiful tree outside your window is dead, has been dead for some time, and has, in fact, just now burst into flames.

14.

I'm drawn back momentarily to the novel I had come here to write. I want to think of *Enemies of the People* not just as a dull, didactic act, but also as a performance. Except such an artistic exercise would also be an experiment. An experiment from which you can draw a conclusion.

Marina Abramović, *Rhythm 0,* 1974, Belgrade. In this work, proposed as a "trust exercise," the artist told viewers she would not move for six hours no matter what they did to her. Abramović placed seventy-two objects, everything from flowers and a feather boa to a knife and a loaded pistol on a table near her and invited viewers at this performance to use them as they wished. (A placard on the table said:

"Rhythm 0. INSTRUCTIONS: There are 72 objects on the table that can be used on me as desired. PERFORMANCE: I am the object. During this time I take the full responsibility.")

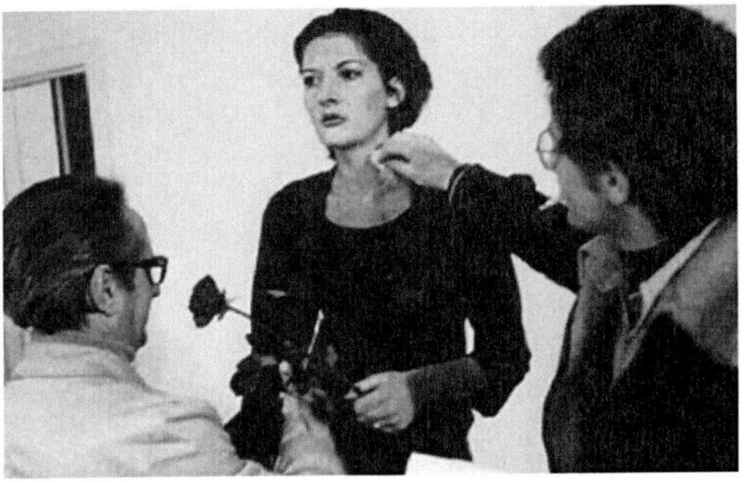

I read a report that said viewers were initially "peaceful and timid, but it escalated to violence quickly." Another report said that "audience members were modest and timid at first" and then they became "more bold" before becoming "aggressive." The list of the audience's actions is both vivid and disturbing: "They poured oil on her head. They pricked her with the thorns of the rose. They cut her clothing. They cut her. One participant actually licked her blood." When I read those words, I thought that what might have motivated Abramović was her curiosity about her audience and its benevolence. Hence, the "trust exercise." I wondered whether the question shifted once she had experienced the violence. ("The experience I learned was that... if you leave decision to the public, you can be killed...") I'm now projecting, of course, but what I think Abramović was left with at the end was a question similar to the one with which I started this book: Will the person standing next to the one who is doing tremendous violence to you step in to put a stop to it? To a small extent, this is exactly what happened during the performance. "They carried her around the room half-naked, then put her on a wooden table and stabbed a knife into the table between her legs. One participant put a bullet in the gun and pointed it at her head, and held it there, until another audience member eventually pushed the gun away." Another account: "In *Rhythm 0*, the audience divided itself into those who sought to harm Abramović (holding the loaded gun to her head) and those who tried to protect her (wiping away her tears)." In fact, according to this source, Abramović hadn't set the performance limit of six hours—it was the protective audience members who insisted that, given the violence on display, the performance be stopped.

Is that the story that her experiment tells—good persons will step in when social harm is being done? No. Let's take note of what happened when, at the end of six hours, the performance was over, and Abramović, tears in her eyes, blood dripping from her neck, walked toward her audience. According to one writer, "The audience scattered. Nobody wanted to confront the active, animated version of the passive figure they had been abusing. For me, this performance art is a powerful demonstration of what happens when people are given the message that it's acceptable to denigrate a human being. Humanity is cruelest when presented with a passive victim, and that's why would-be oppressors first seek to silence their victims."

The artist had wanted to make her spectators also her collaborators. She was successful in that aim. But if one is searching for a story to fit the present moment, it is hard to resist drawing a lesson from what happened when the performance was actually over. The social space will change under the agency of an object turning into a subject.

15.

A clipping in my notebook. This news item is from *The New York Times,* January 29, 2017. Here are the first two paragraphs from the story:

> Type the word refugees into Facebook and some alarming "news" will appear about a refugee rape crisis, a refugee flesh-eating disease epidemic and a refugee-related risk of female genital mutilation—none of it is true.
>
> For the months leading up to the presidential election, and in the days since President Trump took office, ultraconservative websites like Breitbart News and Infowars have published a cycle of eye-popping claims about refugees. And it is beginning to influence public perception, experts say.

16.

In August 2018, *The New York Times* carried a story headlined "Facebook Fueled Anti-Refugee Attacks in Germany, New Research Suggests." The report cited the work of researchers at the University of Warwick who studied one particular detail common to every anti-refugee attack—3,335, over two years—in Germany. "Towns where Facebook use was higher than average... reliably experienced more attacks on refugees." The link was universal, applying to communities of different sizes. A one-standard deviation rise above national average in per person Facebook usage, the research revealed, signaled a rise in attacks on refugees of 50 percent. Concomitantly, when there were power outages in areas with high Facebook usage, the attacks dropped significantly.

17.

In March 2019, I came across this mention of Facebook and mental health. "According to a *Verge* report, Facebook's content moderators get paid $28,000 a year and often end up with PTSD from looking at awful stuff all day."

18.

I just learned that about a week ago, on the evening of February 25, an eighty-five-year-old Muslim woman ("older than our country," someone wrote on Twitter) was burnt alive after a Hindu mob set fire to her house in Gamri Extension, Delhi.

19.

Many of the notes in my journal are about the news. But there are many that are also experiments. It is possible I was thinking of Vaani. Her response to everything that is fake is to design an experiment to clarify what our assumptions are. She stresses that our experiments need not be complicated at all. When I come across a clipping in my scrapbook about a small experiment conducted in an office kitchen at a British university, I think of my dear wife, who is a continent and an ocean away. No word from her so far today. The kitchen experiment went like this: People at the office made tea or coffee for themselves and paid for it on an honor system by dropping money into a box. This had gone on for years. Then, someone put up a picture of a pair of eyes that appeared to be looking directly at the observer. After this was done—the two wide-open eyes staring at the tea or coffee drinkers—the contributions went up three times.

I understand the seductive appeal of stories based on experiments. They appear to us as truth; they are often easy to grasp; and they seem to reveal something crucial about ourselves. I have never consumed these stories without a feeling of guilt. Human behavior is reduced to a formula, the soul exposed as a mechanism, functional and predictable. When the truth is, it is only when I'm surprised, as when I learn how wrong I was about someone I knew, that I know I'm most alive.

Writers are perhaps predisposed to not hold experiments in high regard. In a novel that I was reading last fall, I came across a joke. The joke appealed to me, partly because it was funny but partly because I had started taking an interest in experiments involving animals and was struck by how cruel scientists could be to the animals they were studying. (My own observation, casual, private, has not been tested or peer-reviewed.) Anyway, here's the joke:

A scientist received a grant to study fleas. He would shout "Jump," and measure how far the flea jumped. After a while the exercise got boring for the scientist because the flea always jumped up the same distance. So, the scientist started pulling off the flea's legs, first one and then another. The distance got shorter and shorter, until finally he had pulled off all six legs and the flea didn't jump at all.

"If you remove all six legs," the scientist concluded, "the flea cannot hear."

20.

I took a dislike to a talkative multimedia artist from Mexico named Claudio, who had arrived at the villa a week after me. The unending drama of the self, et cetera. But then I found myself seated across from him at lunch and he told me that he was working on an app that will have information about parents seeking asylum in the United States and their children who have been separated from them. Later, over cocktails in the evening, he asked me if I had a "theory" about Donald Trump. I said that I didn't and tried to focus on my drink. Undeterred, Claudio said he would like to conduct an experimental survey in which at least two thousand people across America would be asked if they thought Trump was one of the following:

1. Unconventional but truthful

2. A liar with something to hide
3. A bullshit artist who didn't care about the truth or lies

What would such a survey reveal? Claudio thought that was a good question. To his mind, it would tell us more about the American people. Claudio said that if most Americans chose the first option, we would know they were immature and lied to themselves. If they chose option two, they showed themselves as mature but with perhaps too rigid a sense of truth and lies. The third option, which Claudio thought was the best answer, would tell us that Americans were not delusional. But, and here he laughed loudly, his goatee pointing up at the sky, this answer would throw up the critical question: If the majority of the voters thought he was a con artist, why the hell did they elect him?

A couple of hours later, an email from Claudio popped up in my inbox. It was an extract from a philosopher's treatise on the nature of bullshit:

> Someone who lies and someone who tells the truth are playing on opposite sides, so to speak, in the same game. Each responds to the facts as he understands them, although the response of the one is guided by the authority of the truth, while the response of the other defies that authority and refuses to meet its demands. The bullshitter ignores these demands altogether. He does not reject the authority of the truth, as the liar does, and oppose himself to it. He pays no attention to it at all. By virtue of this, bullshit is a greater enemy of the truth than lies are.

I saw Claudio again but didn't have much to say to him, and yet the thought that was sparked by his email has never left me. If Trump was only a liar, perhaps the right response would be to be an active archivist, cataloging truths. But what to do with a bullshitter? The point is not to do anything with him at all—or with Modi, for that matter—but to attend to the minds of those who voted for him. What made them so susceptible to bullshit? Or, as Vaani would put it, and in fact does put it, a bit too often, we operate with biases that our rational minds aren't even conscious of. And we do this even, or particularly, when we think we are being most rational. Maybe. But my position is closer to that of a frustrated Hillary Clinton, who said that you could put half of Trump supporters in "the basket of deplorables." I'm quite aware of my biases and I'm also confident that I'm right when I say that Clinton's reading of Trump and this particular half of his supporters was unimpeachable: "They're racist, sexist, homophobic, xenophobic, Islamophobic—you name it. And unfortunately, there are people like that. And he has lifted them up. He has given voice to their websites that used to only have 11,000 people—now have 11 million. He tweets and retweets their offensive hateful mean-spirited rhetoric."

21.

More about bias. This from an article published in *The New Yorker:* "As everyone who's followed the research—or even occasionally picked up a copy of *Psychology Today*—knows, any graduate student with a clipboard can demonstrate that reasonable-seeming people are often totally irrational. Rarely has this insight seemed more relevant than it does right now." The article goes on to present the findings of a psychology experiment conducted at Stanford University. Researchers gave students prompts with opposing views on capital punishment—whether that form of punishment deterred crime or not. Although the experiment was designed with compelling statistics, the data were wholly made up, fictitious. "The students who had originally supported capital punishment rated the prodeterrence data highly credible and the anti-deterrence data unconvincing; the students who'd originally opposed capital punishment did the reverse. At the end of the experiment, the students were asked once again about their views. Those who'd started out pro-capital punishment were now even more in favor of it; those who'd opposed it were even more hostile." Psychologists call this "confirmation bias." For proof of this bias, take a look at the debates on Twitter. My own bias in this matter is that I'm sure studies have been conducted during which participants, after being informed at length about confirmation bias, proceed to behave exactly as before. Novels, then, and the characters in them, appear either real or implausible to the reader depending on the latter's preconceived notions and biases. I'm not writing to change your mind. I cannot change your mind.

22.

In 2010, a psychologist named Amy Cuddy, along with two collaborators, Dana Carney and Andy Yap, published a study on how a person's body postures associated with power affect that person's feelings, hormones, and behaviors. In particular, the researchers claimed that body postures associated with dominant behavior ("power posing") for as little as two minutes can increase testosterone levels, decrease cortisol levels associated with stress, increase appetite for risk, and cause better performance in job interviews. Other researchers, however, found it impossible to replicate these results. One of Cuddy's collaborators, Carney, even disavowed the original results. In fact, this particular experiment is often cited in research circles as a prime example of the replication crisis in psychology. And yet, and yet. A TED talk by Cuddy where she famously preached "Don't fake it till you make it—fake it till you become it" has been watched more than 57 million times. A self-help book authored by Cuddy about these findings was a bestseller and translated into thirty-two languages. What a remarkable feat of *storytelling* this experiment is! How seductive is the theory that all you need to succeed in a job interview is to slip into the bathroom stall for two minutes prior to the meeting and spread your arms out wide and tell yourself that you are powerful!

Tiny tweaks lead to big changes!

Two minutes will change your life!

Sale ends soon!

23.

The "Findings" column in *Harper's Magazine* serves as an introduction to what is fascinating and at the same time risible about experiments and research. Here are some findings from scientific journals published in "Findings":

> Rude sales staff increase the desirability of luxury goods.
>
> Americans who have just ridden an up escalator are twice as likely to donate to charity as those who have just ridden a down escalator.
>
> Scientists do not know why cranes sometimes dance alone.
>
> Rich parents favor firstborn children more than poor parents do.
>
> Doctors found that some American children are prevented from playing outside because their parents dress them too fancily.
>
> Tylenol may reduce existential dread.
>
> Kentucky is the saddest state.

(On the other hand, think of all the novels and their hectic plots. The eager mythologies. In the name of imagination, the many disavowals of authorship and ideology. Not to mention the sentimentalism that, to be honest, also infects the present author.)

In other words, let us not give in to superstition but let us also not fetishize science. Stephen Jay Gould was a famous scientist who died in 2002. In May one year, on his death anniversary, a photograph was posted on Twitter of a slightly heavy man with a mustache (with an unfortunate resemblance to the odious Tom Friedman) standing next to a statue of a dinosaur and the following quote, which is a rebuke to science's hidden assumptions: "I am, somehow, less interested in the weight and convolutions of Einstein's brain than in the near certainty that people of equal talent have lived and died in cotton fields and sweatshops."

24.

Consider for a moment our daughter, the scientist, conducting her experiments even though she was just three at that time. Vaani was a great believer in breastfeeding. And, at three, our daughter received, in addition to regular food, a suckle in the morning and once again at night. Piya would press a hand to her mother's breast and appear to weigh it before applying her mouth and then after a while move to the other breast with the signature remark: "This one not working."

Have I been tempted to conduct an experiment with my daughter? Yes, but only for a moment, and for no longer than that because I cannot tolerate the cruelty of offering a treat and then withholding it. I'm referring to the marshmallow experiment. We have all probably watched the videos on YouTube of little kids who are sitting at a desk with a marshmallow in front of them. The researcher has told them that they can eat the marshmallow when they are left alone but, if they wait for fifteen minutes, they will get a second marshmallow. Two-thirds of the children, we are told, do not wait. (The script applies to a president widely seen as childish. At the time of Trump's inauguration, a cartoon by Paul Noth in *The New Yorker* showed the chief justice administering the oath of office to Trump while holding a plate with a single marshmallow on it. The caption read: "You can eat the one marshmallow right now, or, if you wait fifteen minutes, I'll give you two marshmallows and swear you in as President of the United States.")

25.

Should one come to fiction to escape from the lies? No, literature, too, is seeded with lies. How could it be otherwise? I came across an article by Peter Maass with the following headline: "Peter Handke Won the Nobel Prize After Two Jurors Fell for a Conspiracy Theory About the Bosnia War." The conspiracy theory that the jurors on the Nobel committee were duped by was touted by two obscure German books—which claimed that a small public relations firm in the United States named Ruder Finn Global Public Affairs, working for the Bosnian government, spread propaganda against the Serbs.

Maass calls the conspiracy theory "a vast rewriting of history." (Elsewhere, reporting on Handke's arrival in Stockholm, Maass explained the mantra of the genocide denier: "Throw doubt into the air so that people begin to question the truth.") He details how a French journalist's interview with an executive from the PR firm gave rise to the conspiracy theory. Maass himself had been a reporter for *The Washington Post* during the war in Bosnia. During his visit to one of the concentration camps run by the Serbs, a note was slipped to him by a prisoner. "About 500 people have been killed here with sticks, hammers and knives. Until August 6, there were 2,500 people. We were sleeping on the concrete floor, eating only once a day, in a rush, and we were being beaten while we were eating. We have been here for 75 days. Please help us." This is terrible and moving but what Maass's article also shows us is how difficult it is to erase from the public sphere ("the bowels of the internet") a discredited, dishonest story. Truth might appear pure and incontestable but lies live forever.

Maybe it's because I feel I'm stranded in Europe right now that I feel one shouldn't be stranded without the right sense of history.

26.

There are scientists among the fellows at the villa—there is also a doctor and policy expert in the form of Jimi Adeola—and there is a secret I have kept from them. I'm a writer who writes a mix of essays and literary fiction but I find fascinating the *stories* that researchers tell about science. The story that Jimi told me about stolen penises is the best I have heard here.

From my journal, a near-random example from Vaani's research: Psychologists at Yale found that participants in a study perceived others to be more generous or caring if they, the participants themselves, were holding a warm cup of coffee as opposed to iced coffee.

I once said to Vaani that when I come across a report like this one I marvel at the story line. The researchers seem to have drawn out from the chaos that surrounds us a simple truth about human behavior. Vaani doesn't agree with me entirely; as I have said, she is a believer in data. (Talking of data, she told me in an email two weeks ago that we know that COVID-19 is going to be more dangerous than the SARS outbreak from seventeen years ago because the total number of casualties in China from SARS numbered 774. And in January alone, in China, there were 908 dead from COVID.)

In March 2018, a study published by researchers at MIT said that false news on social media spreads six times faster than news that is true. Robots, the study found, spread truth as well as falsehood at the same rate, but not humans. Which means that human users always spread fake news faster and better than they do the truth. Why does this happen?

The MIT researchers claim that fake news has a higher level of diffusion because it is "novel." This term irked me for professional reasons. I had just published a novel when I read that report. Were the researchers saying that there was something in common between fake news and whatever it was that I was writing?

There was a statement in the report that was particularly bewildering: "We found that false rumors were significantly more novel than the truth across all novelty metrics, displaying significantly higher information uniqueness, divergence, and Bhattacharyya distance." I contacted the researchers and sought clarification. I was told that I could think of novelty "as simply meaning that which you have not seen before."

That was helpful, but I disagree strongly.

Unlike literary fiction, what we call fake news most deeply conforms to a popular prejudice. It is formulaic, often sentimental, and has about it a quality of sickening repetitiveness. For several weeks in 2018, a doctored video showing a kid being kidnapped was circulated in India on WhatsApp. The video ended with corpses of children lined on the floor. Despite wide coverage of the story and police warnings about not believing rumors, the same video led to lynchings of innocent people in one town after another. There is nothing novel in what we witnessed with tragic regularity.

The kidnapping video being circulated was actually from another country: it was shot as an ad for an organization in Karachi, Pakistan, concerned with the safety of children. Now it had been edited in a way to show only an act of abduction. And the image of the children lying dead on the floor? It was from Syria. The children being shown as victims of kidnappings in India were actually victims of a distant war.

At the end of that original video the child is returned to his friends and a banner is unfurled: it contains a warning about how easy it is to abduct children and how we must take care of them. In a BBC interview, the Pakistani adman who created that video, Asrar Alam, responded to the horrific use to which the doctored video has been put. Alam said, "This is very devastating for me. I don't have words. I want to see the face of that man who edited that video for bad purposes."

When I heard Asrar's words, I felt I could identify with them. It is a writer's desire to give a shape and a voice to a character, however villainous. In the age of the Internet, the person you are interacting with online is frequently anonymous; the person threatening you, often in the most graphic and intimate terms, is hiding behind an invented name. Perhaps Alam was saying that he wanted to give evil a face because the idea of a faceless enemy was unbearable to him. Perhaps he was saying that the universe described in the fake video had no feeling, no interiority. In any case, I saw that he was appealing for the presence of something—someone—human. This is the realm of literature.

Genuine surprise, of the sort one finds in a story by, say, Anton Chekhov or Alice Munro, shakes us out of our complacent understanding of the world. It makes us skeptical of what we thought we knew about ourselves and, more than that, about others. But not fake news. It exists to create die-hard believers in an incomplete and intolerant view of the world. Good writing, whether fiction or nonfiction, does not, like a pious police announcement, appeal for calm; instead, it disturbs and challenges beliefs in a way that fake news doesn't and can't.

Against simplicity, complexity. Against judgment, understanding. Against fake news, the radical surprise of real life.

27.

On April 23, 2013, the Associated Press tweeted a piece of breaking news. "Two explosions at the White House and Barack Obama has been injured." The tweet from the AP Twitter handle was fake news, of course, and later a group called Syrian Electronic Army claimed responsibility for it. But, nevertheless, computerized trading algorithms reacted to this tweet, and began trading according to predetermined rules about responses to such crises. What was the result of the fake tweet? The stock market went into a tailspin, wiping out $136.5 billion in equity value. *In just six minutes!* This reveals the terrible danger of fake news—but also, no less clearly, the inherent trap of living in societies whose modes of functioning are governed by automated algorithms. (A smaller truth: it is entirely possible, dear reader, that algorithms devised by those who serve a distant and powerful corporation have determined, based on your previous choices, that this book you are holding in your hands should be brought to your notice. For which I'm thankful but yet resentful of the arbitrariness of the judgment, lacking nuance or any real engagement with you. A few different clicks and, who knows, you would be seeing an ad for a memoir written by Steve Bannon.)

28.

The truth is that the truth is complicated. Here's a story, a terrible story, from the summer of 2017. Eid was around the corner. In Kashmir, on the night the faithful observe Shab-i-Qadr, or the night the first verses of the Quran are believed to have been revealed, an image of a badly beaten man clad only in his underwear began circulating on social media. His name was Mohammed Ayub Pandith. He was fifty-seven. The next day, the police released a statement that Pandith, deputy superintendent of police, had been assaulted and killed outside the Jamia Masjid in Nowhatta. Reading the news, I sensed the reporter's frustration at being unable to parse the truth. Pandith was also a Muslim and a Kashmiri, like the men in the mob who murdered him, and in the end that is the angle that the reporter settled on. "Kashmiris are killing Kashmiris."

But, as I said, truth is more disturbing. According to police, Pandith was tasked with frisking worshippers as they streamed into the mosque in Nowhatta, where a prominent separatist leader was to lead the prayers. One version of events had Pandith getting involved in an altercation with the youth who were shouting anti-India slogans. Pandith was photographing them with his phone. But how would this be possible? asked Pandith's son. His father didn't have a smartphone, only a basic Nokia phone. When he was attacked, Pandith fired three shots from his pistol and injured his attackers. The police chief praised Pandith's action: he had aimed at the legs and not tried to kill those who were about to lynch him. One could say that at least one Kashmiri was not killing Kashmiris.

The incident appears to have happened close to midnight. When the images of Pandith's bruised body were forwarded on social media, all kinds of rumors spread through the valley. There were claims the body was that of a non-Kashmiri who had come to kill the man about to lead the prayers. Another rumor described the dead man as someone from the intelligence bureau spying on the worshippers. A third, more insidious rumor, especially in the context of the Indian subcontinent, was that the man who was lynched was uncircumcised. In so many riots, so many stories, the difference between life and death is as thin as a piece of foreskin. The reporter mentions talk of Pandith being an honest and humble man. He hadn't grown rich like some other police officers.

Last night when I went to bed, I told myself that when I woke up in the morning I would put pen to paper and try to find a way into the report I had kept with me about Pandith's lynching. What kept me awake for a long time was the mention that when Pandith's son went to the police control room to identify his father's body, he fainted. My mind kept going back to the fact that hours after the pictures of Pandith's body first appeared on social media, another photograph was circulated on WhatsApp. It showed Pandith's jaws with no teeth left attached.

So, this is what the human record comes down to.

29.

Fake news leads to lynchings—and then what? Where is the writer to find evidence of life?

Alwar, Rajasthan. July 2018. A twenty-eight-year-old Muslim man taking his cows to his village was beaten up by a mob on the suspicion of his being a cattle smuggler ferrying the cows to an abattoir. By the time the police came and drove the injured man to the hospital, he had already died. It later came to light that the police had first stopped to drop off the cows at a shelter and then had made a second stop for tea. As a writer seeking individual pathos, what I found most moving in the milkman's story was a statement by the man's father; he reportedly said that his son so loved his cows that he would go hungry if there wasn't enough fodder for his animals.

When I read that I thought of a story I had heard in a documentary, *The Men in the Tree,* made by Vaani's friend from college Lalit Vachani. Vachani's documentary is about the members of the Rashtriya Swayamsevak Sangh (RSS), a right-wing Hindu group in India who are so filled with hate that they spread rumors to cause riots in which the Muslims get killed. In the film we hear a former member of the group tell the filmmaker that when he was a young man he posted incendiary pamphlets containing rumors. A riot resulted.

When the man returned home, he found his mother in mourning. Their cowherd Gama had been killed in the riot. And here is the part that rumors relying on vicious stereotypes can never get at. Gama was a Muslim. Gama cared for the cows—cared for them more than the RSS man himself did—and he had been murdered because of the rumors that had been spread to cause the riot.

30.

When Gandhi caught the Spanish flu in the autumn of 1918, he was offered cow's milk to aid in his recovery but he refused. Gandhi was opposed to the practice of "phooka," in which air is blown forcefully into a cow's vagina to induce her to lactate. The sickness was serious: Gandhi was only forty-eight but he wrote that "all interest in living had ceased." Although he felt he had served an "invitation to the angel of death," he continued to live by his principles. He was slow-jamming not just the news but also his recovery. He was still unwell when news came that Germany had been defeated in the war. So far, despite his faith in nonviolence, Gandhi had supported the British in the war. But after the British won, and they still made no concessions to Indians, Gandhi took up the fight for freedom. Although he was still weak he gave the call for satyagraha to be unleashed across the nation. The colonial government had offered little relief when the entire population reeled under the influenza epidemic. To make matters worse, a period of drought followed. An American missionary named Adam Ebey recorded that "people begged water. They fought each other to get water; they stole water." Another report: "In the countryside, cattle died for lack of grass, and bullocks had to be watched lest they leap into wells chasing the scent of damp." In the vacuum created by the state and its inaction now stepped the nationalist groups. Small reformist groups, many of them inspired by Gandhi, provided help to the masses. Medicines, milk, blankets, even help with the cremation of corpses. The slow, patient mobilization of support during the time of the epidemic had a direct result: it allowed the call for freedom to be taken seriously and spread widely. In *Young India,* the newspaper that Gandhi founded, an editorial appeared after the April 13, 1919, massacre of hundreds of peaceful protesters at the hands of the British. Entitled "Public Health," it expressed the popular feeling that a government that allowed 6 million to die of influenza, "like rats without succor," wouldn't mind if a few more died by the bullet.

31.

All the news around us is of the havoc caused by the virus. We should be concerned about that, of course, and I now wash my hands incessantly. But, if I could, what I would shout from the rooftops is that much as we fear the virus, we ought to be worried about the killer inside us.

A video from June 18, 2018: Qasim, a Muslim trader who lived in a one-room apartment with his wife and children, can be seen half-sitting in a dry canal and asking for a drink of water. On both sides of the canal, young men are standing. No one gives him water and he falls over in the dirt, as if settling for sleep in his bed, laying one folded knee neatly atop the other. It was later found that Qasim's body had been pierced with screwdrivers and scraped with sickles. In the video, he is being accused of killing cows and you can hear people baying for his blood. For their part, the police filed a report linking the assault to a motorcycle accident. Qasim's relatives questioned the police narrative, which was further discredited when a journalist carried a hidden camera to a meeting with one of the chief accused in the crime. The man said that people greeted him with loud cheers when he was released from jail on bond. He had never experienced such pride before.

For me, the question remains: What can you write that will make anyone reading you give a dying man a drink of water?

32.

A few basic definitions:

> A *novel coronavirus* (nCOV) is any recently discovered coronavirus of medical significance not yet permanently named. The word *novel* indicates a "new pathogen of a previously known type" (i.e., known family) of virus.
>
> *News* is information about current events. The genre of news as we know it today is closely associated with the newspaper, which originated in China as a court bulletin and spread, with paper and printing press, to Europe.
>
> A *novel* is a relatively long work of narrative fiction, normally written in prose form, and which is typically published as a book. The present English word for a long work of prose fiction derives from the Italian *novella* for "new," "news," or "short story of something new," itself from the Latin *novella,* a singular noun use of the neuter plural of *novellus,* diminutive of *novus,* meaning "new."

In September 1665, at the time of the Great Plague, Daniel Defoe, that early proponent of the English novel, would have been a little over four years old. (By the following year, the plague had killed seventy thousand people in London.) But, trying his luck at the sleight of hand that is autofiction and writing as an eyewitness, Defoe wrote in *A Journal of the Plague Year:* "We had no such thing as printed newspapers in those days to spread rumors and reports of things, and improve them by the invention of men, as I have lived to see practiced since. But such things as those were gathered from the letters of merchants and others who corresponded abroad, and from them was handed about by word of mouth only; so that things did not spread instantly over the whole nation, as they do now." What would Defoe have made of our times? In a report on COVID-19 and the dissemination of fake news, a newspaper stated: "In the age of social media, misinformation spreads a thousand times faster than the virus." The World Health Organization, taking note of the false and often malicious content being spread on social media sites, said that it was confronting an "infodemic."

Not only did Daniel Defoe help popularize the novel form, but he is also credited with producing one of the first examples of modern journalism. A week after his release from prison, he produced an eyewitness report on the great storm of 1703, which killed eight thousand people. If he were living in our times, Daniel Defoe, who apart from having had a career as a spy was also no stranger to the pillory and the humiliating burden of debts, might well have been curious about, and perhaps even written about, the phenomenon described in this news report about the coronavirus pandemic: "Security researchers have even found that hackers were setting up threadbare websites that claimed to have information about the coronavirus. The sites were actually digital traps, aimed at stealing personal data or breaking into the devices of people who landed on them."

In my notebooks I set myself a modest task. In the news reports I read or the postings on my Twitter feed, I looked for stories that wouldn't appear in what used to be called a bourgeois novel. These stories I noted down in my notebook as a personal record of the pandemic. For instance: Leilani Jordan, a twenty-seven-year-old grocery store clerk in Maryland, died from COVID-19. Before her death, she had complained to her mother that her employer, Giant Food, didn't provide masks or gloves. Jordan was forced to bring her own hand sanitizer to work. After the young woman's death, Giant Food gave her mother a certificate for Jordan's six years of service and a paycheck for $20.64.

I also thought of Timothy Snyder's *On Tyranny*, on how to avoid being deceived by fake news:

> *Figure things out for yourself. Spend more time with long articles. Subsidize investigative journalism by subscribing to print media. Realize that some of what is on the internet is there to harm you. Learn about sites that investigate propaganda campaigns (some of which come from abroad). Take responsibility for what you communicate to others.*

Practical advice! Perhaps I should discreetly provide in *Enemies of the People* a list of fact-checking strategies. If earlier fiction helped the reader with facts, how to dress, how to shave, how to take tea, then, in our times, fiction is to help readers recognize what is fictional about all that is touted as fact. In a short chapter on language, Snyder also advocates reading books as an act of resistance. And yes, fiction too. "Any good novel enlivens our ability to think about ambiguous situations and judge the intentions of others." The writing of novels as an essential service.

33.

At the turn of the twentieth century, a psychologist at Indiana University named Norman Triplett found out that when children were asked to execute a simple task (winding line on a fishing rod), they performed better when in the company of other children than when they were alone.

How innocent are these stories about children!

In 1951, the social psychologist Solomon Asch found that people would agree that one drawn line matched the length of another—even if it clearly did not—if others around them all agreed that it did.

I repeat: How innocent are these stories about children. Replace them with adults and you get a mob. I'm suddenly in the scene that Jimi had described for me: the crowd that collects around the man who is shouting that his penis has been stolen.

I fear the mob. A mob is single-minded about its claim to truth.

CHAPTER 7

THE DEATH OF INFORMATION

On the flight back from the residency, I was on edge because, despite the mask on my face and the disinfectant wipes, I was sitting packed in a metal container with four hundred others. We all removed our masks when the flight attendants gave us our hot meals. For some reason, none of the flight attendants wore masks. I heard one of them tell the elderly woman seated behind me that the air inside the plane is as clean as the air inside an operating room. The previous night Vaani had texted me a screenshot from some scientific study: I was supposed to ask for a window seat near the middle of the plane. If I found such a seat, I would have the least exposure to the virus. But I wanted the comfort of easy access to the toilet during a long transatlantic flight. I took an aisle seat and I was nervous. What made me more nervous was that I was reading the last forty or fifty pages of Orwell's *1984*.

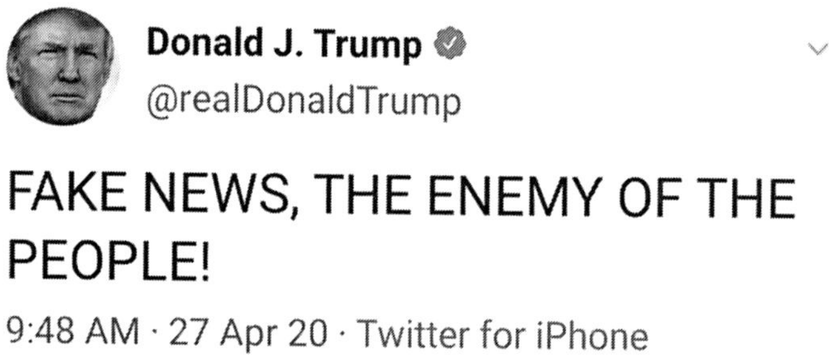
Donald J. Trump
@realDonaldTrump

FAKE NEWS, THE ENEMY OF THE PEOPLE!

9:48 AM · 27 Apr 20 · Twitter for iPhone

Page after page of descriptions of acute privation and torture. All the possibility of pleasure has vanished, and certainly resistance too, except that our protagonist is alive. With a mind filled with so much fear about a barely understood disease, I found myself absorbed by the details of Winston Smith's complete physical breakdown. When Smith is shown his image in the mirror, he finds it difficult to recognize himself. (Lost in that world, I stepped into the small airplane toilet, with my mask on, and saw a stranger in the mirror.) It is not that I was identifying myself with Winston; rather, I felt an enormous pity for him. And the future to which the entire population had been condemned by the totalitarian regime. When the lights were dimmed in the plane's cabin and the air turned cold, then, strapped in my cramped seat, I found that I had more fully entered the novel's bleak landscape.

Smith's torturer says to him: "If you want a picture of the future, imagine a boot stamping on a human face—forever." That line stopped me. I felt those words were addressed to me. I had written a version of this to start my own novel, only weeks earlier. Then, an unexpected turn had brought me to Orwell's novel, even if it was written seventy years ago, which was telling me that "the espionage, the betrayals, the arrests, the tortures, the executions, the disappearances will never cease." All resistance was futile. Was this what I also needed to accept? A few pages later, Smith is asked if there is a single degradation that hasn't happened to him, if he hasn't shed every ounce of humanity in begging for relief from pain, and he says, "I have not betrayed Julia." Okay, I thought, so there's that. There will be the boot in the face, there will be a world pandemic, but there will be love. That will keep us alive.

Just before I left the villa, I had come across a post that mentioned a story about Margaret Mead. Asked what was the earliest sign of civilization, the famous anthropologist said, "A healed femur." A healed femur? In the animal world, you cannot survive with a broken leg. You are a meal for the predators. But a healed femur suggests someone took care of you, they helped bandage your limb, they helped you walk, they brought you food, they protected you. Compassion or caring is the first mark of civilization.

But Orwell wasn't going to be merciful or compassionate. A few more pages in, and Smith has betrayed Julia too. And then soon thereafter, while the map on my screen said that we were flying over Nova Scotia, the novel came to an end. Smith is no longer Smith. He doesn't love Julia; he loves Big Brother. The novel as a cry of depthless despair.

Except that I turned the page and there was an appendix. "The Principles of Newspeak." Ostensibly still a part of the novel, it laid out the principles behind the official language of the imaginary imperial state where the story is set. The reader learns again and again that the diminution of meaning in language through a vast reduction in the vocabulary and nuance is all aimed at excising from the human mind a breadth of imagination and freedom. All the ugly neologisms are there not so much to express meaning as to destroy it. In effect, Orwell's appendix is a political countermanifesto—as well as an appeal on the behalf of art. Save the language—and save the world!

In the end it is very much a writer's call to arms. It says that if you pay attention to words, and fight to be honest on the page, you will survive with your humanity intact. The point is not to serve as a branch of propaganda but to preserve the uncomfortable or disturbing truth against unrelenting and widespread assault.

The plane was in a holding pattern for a long time. I dozed for a while and dreamed that I was talking on my phone and transmitting the virus to whomever I was talking to at the other end. In fact, it became clear that the illness was streaming out of my phone not just to the person speaking to me—who it was,

I couldn't remember—but to everyone who was on my contact list. I was walking on the street in New York City and talking on the phone when this realization hit me, and when I looked up, I saw the police in black uniforms and masks swarming toward me from all directions.

Why did I think that it was I and not the state that had been criminal in its disregard?

I came back to an empty house. On my flight, I was afraid that we would all be quarantined when we landed at JFK, but no one stopped us to even check our temperature. On the train north, a nearly two-hour ride, I encountered a good crowd of passengers, exhausted commuters eyeing each other warily, no one daring to sneeze. There was no stacked mail in our mailbox and I guessed Vaani had made an arrangement with the post office. In my suitcase, there was leftover cheese and I had that before falling into bed.

Waking up early, before dawn, and finding no coffee in the house, I went to the twenty-four-hour gas station nearby and got myself a cup of some undrinkable stuff. Then, the wait for the grocery store to open. The surprise of finding no chicken on the shelves and no canned beans either. And, this baffled me, no tofu. I had in the past barely stopped to pick up a pack of tofu from the stacks in the refrigerated section and now when I wanted just one there was nothing. People around me appeared to be acting in a frenzy and a new fear then entered me: I was afraid less of the sickness finding me and newly fearful that I wouldn't be able to feed my family when they joined me. It seemed prudent to pick up cans of tinned tuna. I had seen bottles of hand sanitizer in the gas station that morning but had decided to buy some later, when I went to get groceries. In this store, the largest in town, there was no hand sanitizer left. No gloves, no wipes. On the way back, I stopped at the gas station to pick up three bottles of hand sanitizer.

Days passed. In the note that the residency director sent all the fellows saying sorry but we would have to leave on account of the crisis, she hoped that we would perhaps hit a more creative stride when we returned to our homes. "When Shakespeare was quarantined because of the plague," she added cheerfully, "he wrote *King Lear*." I wasn't writing *King Lear* at home, I wasn't writing anything. I was a vegetable lying on its side, all its roots focused only on extracting the news. I read that a Pew Research Center poll found that 62 percent of adult Americans believed that the media were exaggerating the effects of the pandemic. The reporter had interviewed the inhabitants of a Texas town who said things like "we just need to trust the Lord to solve this." The man who offered that quote was at church passing out cards that read "C.O.V.I.D. 19" as the acronym for "Christ over viruses & infectious disease" and a comforting Bible verse.

In India, on March 22, in his first acknowledgment of the new coronavirus, Prime Minister Modi addressed the nation on TV. He called for a public curfew from morning to evening the following Sunday, for a total period of fourteen hours. On that day at 5:00 p.m., he said, people were to come to their windows and balconies to display their support for health workers. "We will clap our hands, beat our plates, ring our bells to boost their morale and salute their service." In response, one of the prominent spokespersons for Modi's party tweeted that the ancient Hindu scriptures instruct us that temple bells and blowing into conch shells kill germs—and how profound was Modi's idea of asking 1.2 billion Indians to clap hands, beat plates, and ring bells together. The farce didn't end there. A rumor that gained wide traction soon afterward was that the coronavirus has a life cycle of twelve hours and Modi's fourteen-hour curfew would help break the chain and curb the further spread of the virus. A fact-checking group pointed out that the proposed curfew would help with social distancing but not eliminate the possibility of infection. This is because the coronavirus can survive on surfaces for up to three days and infected individuals can spread the contagion for up to three weeks. And despite such warnings, when the hour came and went, the spread of fake news continued. Posts like the following: "NASA satellite videos LIVE telecast has shown that the coronavirus is retreating in India... The cosmic level sound waves generated have been detected by NASA's SD13 wave detector and a recently-made bio-satellite has shown COVID-19 strain diminishing and weakening. Proud to be an Indian." A few days later, Modi announced that on the following Sunday, every Indian should stand at their doorstep or on their balcony at 9:00 p.m. and hold a candle, diya, flashlight, or even a lighted mobile phone, for nine minutes. Vaani's sister, Shikha, forwarded us a WhatsApp message she had received and appended to it a face-palm emoji: "Corona virus does not survive in hot temperature, as per research by NASA. If 130 candles are lit together, temperature will increase by 9 degrees, as per IIT professor. So, Corona will die at 9.09 PM. Masterstroke by Modi."

After a visit to the bank, I came home to attend an online seminar. The college faculty was being introduced to Zoom. For my virtual background, I chose a photograph I had taken of the villa with the serene expanse of the lake behind it. ("Oh, Satya, where are you?" asked a colleague in computer science whose own dark wall wouldn't give anyone cause for a sudden feeling of fernweh.) For an hour or two that afternoon I felt I was back at the residency and in that new space of quiet I wrote the first piece of fiction I had written in days. Did it belong in *Enemies of the People*? No, it was more a record of the time I was living in. Another way of saying, the world has me in its jaws but I'm still alive.

"WHERE DID YOU GET THE MASK?"

The bank robber wore gloves and a mask.

The teller, a middle-aged woman, had been meaning to buy a mask for herself. There had been reports that they would be needed in a few weeks' time.

This is a bank robbery, the note said. Be quiet. I have a gun. Give me all the cash. I have the coronavirus.

He had underlined *virus*.

Four years earlier, in the bank's branch in a Cleveland suburb, the teller had faced a robbery. Men with real masks and shotguns. Scary stuff.

This guy looked normal—no, safe—in that mask. She was known to have a sharp tongue but she didn't immediately say: "You have the virus? Go to a hospital. This is a bank."

The teller seemed to feel, without knowing this or even thinking about it much, that they were entering a new time. So much was uncertain. Also, there was no long line of impatient customers in the bank, in fact, no line at all.

Still holding his handwritten note, she nodded and then asked a question to delay the inevitable.

A bottle of hand sanitizer sat on her side of the bulletproof glass right next to the red button that would ring the alarm in the police station.

"Sir," she said, setting the note aside and reaching for the bottle, "is it okay if I first disinfect my hands?"

I was back from my residency for two weeks before Vaani and Piya returned home from Cambridge. Although I was on a sabbatical from my college, I received regular updates by email. The students were not going to come back after the spring break. Everyone was to be on Zoom. It was still unclear when the students would be able to return to campus—two weeks? a month? after the summer? And then it was certain that we were in really deep trouble. We had to focus on the immediate need to be safe and stop the spread.

Shikha, Vaani's sister, is an animal lover. She has her sister's compassion, but there is an obsessive quality to her caring. Shikha sent us the news on WhatsApp that a zoo in Germany may begin feeding animals to animals as funds dry up in the pandemic. The administrators there had said they were going to spare the zoo's twelve-foot polar bear, Vitus, till the end but they were prepared to sacrifice the other, presumably less popular, animals. "If you guys in the West cannot feed the creatures in your zoos, what is going to happen to the already malnourished animals in the zoos in India?"

Just that question following the link, nothing else, not even a greeting. As if we had been carrying on a conversation all morning about how to take care of the planet. I turned to Vaani and asked, with just a touch of irritation in my voice, "When did *we* assume control of the West?"

Vaani laughed. The laugh didn't mean she agreed with me. She was laughing with joy, showing love for her sister.

I shouldn't complain about these notes from Shikha. I have a need to know. The news is *my* obsession.

For example: In the *Hindustan Times,* a report about a migrant worker who stole a bicycle from a man in a village in Rajasthan. The Indian government had imposed the most brutal lockdown to control the spread, but this had meant that millions of poor, starving migrant workers and their families had been left to find ways to return to their villages. They were trekking hundreds of miles on highways and train tracks. This particular worker, the bicycle thief, was on his way home to Bareilly in Uttar Pradesh, more than a hundred miles away. The owner of the bicycle found a note, written in Hindi, that the worker had left behind: *Namaste ji. I am taking your cycle. If possible, please forgive me. I have no means. I have a child, who is disabled and cannot walk, and it is for him that I am having to do this. We have to reach Bareilly. Your guilty—A traveler.*

At a press conference in early March, a reporter from NBC asked Trump: "What do you say to Americans watching right now who are scared?" Trump responded: "I say that you are a terrible reporter. I think you had a nasty question." At that same press conference, Trump touted hydroxychloroquine, a malarial drug unproven as a COVID-19 treatment. He said, "Let's see if it works. It might and it might not. I happen to feel good about it, but who knows, I've been right a lot. Let's see what happens." Two days later, he again made a push for hydroxychloroquine, calling it a "game changer."

Even while Dr. Anthony Fauci, the director of the National Institute of Allergy and Infectious Diseases, cautioned against the use of hydroxychloroquine without adequate testing, prescriptions for the drug went up by 200 percent when compared to the same period the previous year. Why were doctors prescribing a drug to fight COVID-19 when its effectiveness had not been proven? Almost half a million prescriptions had been filled. Why? Vaani told me that there had been an experiment from some years earlier in which the researchers told actors to go to doctors and pretend that they had symptoms of depression. Some of the actors were instructed to ask explicitly for drugs while others were not. Patients requesting antidepressants were more than twice as likely to receive them, whether their symptoms called for the drugs or not. In the case of hydroxychloroquine, Trump's active touting had an effect on common citizens who pushed the demand for prescriptions. This was how people behaved, doctors as well as patients. That is what I learned from Vaani. From Shikha I learned something else. "Thanks to you," her WhatsApp message began, "thanks to your President, the officials in Mumbai were going to try out hydroxychloroquine on thousands of people in the Dharavi slums. This would have gone on for fourteen days. The excuse was that social distancing isn't possible in a slum. Sure. But is it not possible to still be scientific and ethical and humane even where social distancing isn't possible? I think we got infected by Trump's foolishness when he came to India in February."

There is a dogwood tree at the end of our street that fills me with joy. The week that it had burst into flower was the week there were the highest number of deaths in this county. More weeks passed. The flowers were gone and yet my small backyard was drenched in green. Vaani and Piya had been back from Cambridge for seven weeks. Everything was now closed there. I had earlier thought I would drive up for the Boston Marathon but of course it was canceled. Vaani liked the green outside our kitchen window here. The yellowwood that she calls the most beautiful tree in the world and, further away, my favorite during the last days of April, the American chestnut with its upturned chandeliers of white.

A reason to live. Give people that and watch the death rate fall. That is what Vaani heard on the radio, and she began to make notes on the top of the newspaper in her kitchen. The reporter said that in the early 1970s, two psychologists performed an experiment in which they got a Connecticut nursing home to give each one of its retired-age residents a plant. Half of the residents were assigned the job of watering their plant and they also attended a lecture on the benefits of taking responsibilities in their lives; the other half had their plants watered for them and attended a lecture on how the staff was responsible for their well-being. After a year and a half, the group that had been encouraged to take more responsibility, even for such a small thing as a plant, proved more active and alert, and appeared to live longer.

A novel titled *Enemies of the People,* its preoccupations tied closely to the present moment, is the plant I have been nurturing in order to stay alive myself. I will live long, unless the virus kills me. This novel and the memory of the residency must be occupying my subconscious. I fell asleep in the afternoon and dreamed that I was in a car with Bev. Were we in India? I remember the desert around us. There had been an accident on the road, and, as I drew closer, I couldn't slow down and our car had plowed into the wreckage. And then I was at the hospital, on a white bed, explaining to Jimi, who might or might not have been the doctor, that I had been exchanged in an experiment on the highway. *Do you know the bystander effect? You can see the video from the 1970s. A person is sitting alone in the room that is filling up with smoke. This lone witness leaves the room to ask for help. The same scenario is repeated with three people. Everyone looks furtively around, expecting someone else to act.* Did Jimi nod and say anything in response? I cannot remember. I would have liked him to say: "Yes, in the case of the penis thief, all the agency is usurped by the accuser. No one questions him. Oddly, by joining the mob, everyone is still displaying the bystander effect. They sacrifice their individuality to join the mob."

"Oh shit, my bai's husband has come down with Covid." This was on WhatsApp from Shikha. Her maid Jamuna had called her to say that her husband had the virus. This put a stop to Jamuna's daily visits. Jamuna and her teenage daughter would now need to be quarantined. This didn't mean much to us—Shikha employed Jamuna to clean the apartment and then cook a meal each morning, so that she had dinner waiting for her when she returned home—until we got the news that Shikha had been threatened with arrest over the matter.

But that happened later. We were trying to find order in our lives. Vaani read somewhere that the coronavirus can last on plastic surfaces for up to seventy-two hours. Groceries and perishables we washed or wiped down with disinfectant but you cannot do that with paper. We laid out in the hallway all our mail as well as our daily newspaper. After three days, we opened our mail, and it was the same with newspapers. I was following the news incessantly on Twitter and online on my computer, but reading the news in print, a childhood habit that I had never given up, meant that I was able to discover how much the world had changed in three days. And how quickly.

Did I feel bad about this? No. I had lost all sense of time. Days blurred into each other.

Besides, everything was falling apart. Things were getting worse. Reading the news in print from three days ago was like going back to better times. Not exactly like being present at the dawn of creation—but close. No, but really, this is what I mean: suppose it was March 24, and I was opening the newspaper, which that day in my house was from March 21, and, on that day, countries like Laos and Myanmar were still free from the virus. It was as if on March 21 they were still safe, in another century, except the reality was that on March 24, when I was reading the March 21 newspaper, both Laos and Myanmar had reported their first confirmed cases. This made all the news I was reading more unreal than usual.

I wasn't writing much, but I reminded myself that even though *Enemies of the People* will be about the lies told by the failed state and the lies we tell ourselves, I also wanted an uncondescending recognition of the power of small people and small lives. Against the lies of the rulers, the unaffected truths of the struggles of the ruled. Also, also, at the end of the day, pitched against fake news, the truth of fiction.

During the Indian lockdown, a fifteen-year-old girl named Jyoti Kumari carried her father, Mohan Paswan, on the rear carrier of a bicycle from Gurugram near Delhi to Darbhanga in Bihar, a distance of around 750 miles. She covered this enormous distance in seven days, getting rides for short distances on the way. The father's leg had been injured in an accident—he was an auto-rickshaw driver. He was unable to work and their landlord asked them to vacate their home. And so, Jyoti bought the used bicycle from a neighbor and set out on her marathon journey.

But truth takes strange forms. Once this story was reported in the news, the Cycling Federation of India asked Jyoti to appear for an all-expenses paid cycling trial. If she succeeded in the tests, she would be provided support and accepted as a trainee at the National Cycling Academy. When I read this new installment in the news, I imagined Jyoti Kumari in her modest home in Darbhanga; she had performed such an amazing feat, but how did the Cycling Academy wish to reproduce the desperation of wanting to reach home during a lockdown? Of saving her father's and her own life? Apparently unmoved by Ivanka Trump's tweet calling her journey "a beautiful feat of endurance," Jyoti Kumari turned down the Cycling Academy's offer. She said that she needed to focus on her studies, which had been disrupted recently, and, besides, she was feeling tired after such a long journey.

After an early dinner one evening in April, I was listening to a radio station in New York City. A man was speaking of his experience as a temporary worker handling corpses of COVID victims in the refrigerated trucks because the hospital morgues were full or overflowing. This man, Erik Frampton, was working in the Bronx, in the trucks that could contain up to 110 bodies. It was "difficult, gruesome work." The hospitals had run out of body bags, the heavy black bags being replaced by thin white ones. These bags ripped easily and there was spillage of bodily fluids. The scene Frampton described was chaotic and messy. When the bags failed, the workers used hospital sheets. Blood and fecal matter leaked out. Frampton and his coworker wore body aprons, two masks layered over each other, and gloves.

They hoped that they were safe. The starting pay was seventy-five dollars an hour. Frampton spoke of how he and his husband were scared, and that they no longer kissed. And then, suddenly, he was speaking of his mourning for the bodies he was handling. He said, "My mournfulness for each body, my respect for each body is a literal imagination of who knows them. Who's calling about them? What person could not visit them when they were, you know, in isolation before they had to go on a respirator and they couldn't talk anymore? Who wants to know where that person is right now?"

I had my ear glued to the radio in my kitchen and I was crying by now, crying for the man who was speaking, crying for the ones who had died or had lost loved ones to the virus, crying for my wife and child sitting at that moment in the next room watching a rerun of an episode of *Friends*. There were reports that parents who were doctors or nurses were shielding their families from the virus by staying away in a separate part of the house if they could afford it. Separate entryways, hastily constructed showers behind the garage, no shared meals. That night, as I was putting Piya to sleep, I took out my notebook to write a short story, which, given the times, I imagined as guerrilla fiction:

SPIDER-MAN

The man was on FaceTime with his kids. The girl was older, seven and a half. Her brother has just turned three.

"How was your day?"

"We made brownies," the girl said. She looked at her mother sitting behind her when she said this.

"Brownies," the boy repeated.

The mother said to the boy, "Do you want to show Dad your drawings?"

The boy held up his drawings in front of the phone—a

variety of irregular shapes in different colors that he confidently identified by names: Dad, Mom, dinosaur.

The man said, "Show me Dad again."

It looked like him a bit. No face, just glasses. That is what he looked like all day, a shapeless mass in the hazmat suit. Only the color was off. His was blue, the boy's figure was orange. Every evening at seven, when he came out of the ICU, he stripped out of the PPE suit and waited for the Uber at the corner of Linden and East Ninety-sixth.

Then came the inevitable question.

Once again, it was the girl. "Dad, when will you come home?"

"Soon."

When this question was asked each night, he would look not at the kids but at his wife's exhausted face.

If he hooked his legs on the lowest rung of the fire escape outside his window, he could easily reach down and tap on the window of the room below, in which his family was already gathered in bed.

The kids would get the surprise of their lives.

But he didn't want to pretend that he had any superpowers. Three dead that day, a bit better than five the day before, a ghostly procession of growing numbers.

We sometimes caught sight of Jamuna hovering in the corner of our screens during our Skype calls with Shikha. This is what happened. In late May, to ease Jamuna's worries about her daughter, who was to sit for her exams in June, and needed to be safe and also to study, Shikha suggested that the girl could move in with her. Purnima, that is the daughter's name, was going to be the first in her family to go to college. Shikha was thinking of Jamuna, small and thin, in her airless room with her sick husband, and the teenage girl trying to study, and she said, "Tell her to wear a mask when she comes. She can stay in the guest room. We will stay out of each other's way for two weeks. She can study all day. I'll give her food and she can eat it in her room."

Jamuna was crying at the other end.

"You don't like the idea? You will miss her too much."

"No, Didi," Jamuna said.

"Warn her, please, that I'm not as good a cook as her mother!"

The girl arrived in the afternoon. Two days later, a little before lunch, a subinspector of police was at the door. Tall man, sunglasses, dark forearms. His badge said KULDEEP RAWAT. He was wearing a mask, although it only covered his mouth and chin. There had been a complaint from the housing society. Tenant rules didn't allow you to keep your domestic help as residents in your flat. It had been reported that Shikha was keeping her maid in her flat. The other disturbing matter that needed to be investigated, the inspector said, was that, in the middle of a pandemic, Shikha had brought into the building someone who was possibly infected by the virus. A police vehicle was waiting downstairs. Both Shikha and the girl would have to come to the police station to answer questions.

"Why not ask me questions here? This teenage girl is not my maid; she is my guest. She is studying for her exams."

Mr. Sudharshan, the Canara Bank manager, had come out of his flat at the end of the short corridor and he was looking at Shikha rather sadly. At the other end, Asha Sud stepped out in her customary housedress. ("That name rings a bell," I said to Shikha later. And she said, "Oh my God, that's so Freudian or something." I searched my memory but, fortunately, it wasn't Freudian at all. Asha Sud's name was familiar to me because Shikha had filmed her beating on a thali with a piece of metal at 5:00 p.m. screaming, "Go, Corona, Go.") None of the neighbors expressed any concern or offered any support. Shikha suspected that there had been a discussion about her on one of the WhatsApp groups. This was a collective thing.

Inside her apartment, Shikha asked Purnima to put on her mask. She called her friend Dushyant, a lawyer, and asked if the cops had any right to summon her to the police station in these circumstances. Dushyant said, "The short answer is yes. Where are they taking you?"

"Sector Twenty."

"I'll be there in half an hour," Dushyant said.

Shikha and Purnima, with Dushyant standing in the heat outside because he needed to smoke, were kept waiting at the police station. That is when she sent us her first message on WhatsApp. There was the scare about the virus. If there was some bizarre arrest made and they were put in detention, they would be risking getting infected from so many people squeezed into small spaces. But Vaani and I, sitting with our breakfast, looking out at the trees in our backyard, had another worry. A white police officer in Minneapolis kept his knee and weight on a Black man's neck for nine minutes and twenty-nine seconds, even after the man on the ground had lost consciousness and then stopped breathing. The dead man's name was George Floyd. Despite the pandemic, the country had exploded in protests. Everyone, or maybe just the white people, was for the first time seeing the police for what they really were. The boot in the face.

Vaani was drinking tea and eating granola (for some reason, always dry granola only, without milk or yogurt). While waiting for news from Shikha, I read out to Vaani a report from that morning about how monkeys in Meerut stole the coronavirus blood samples collected from patients there. I thought she would find that amusing, maybe even feel pride at the mischievous intelligence of the animals with whom she had been working for so long, but she just shook her head. "Stupid bureaucrats."

Then, she broadened her theme. She wanted to address the stupidity of her colleagues. An op-ed in the *Times* had discussed an old social psychology experiment demonstrating the following: If the participants in the study had just washed their hands they had a more positive attitude toward immigration than did those who hadn't. The op-ed, written by a psychologist at an Ivy League institution, argued that with all the hand washing we were currently engaged in, our *moral* outlook would take on a more tolerant, even a more generous, tone. A personal feeling of cleanliness leading to an attitude of altruism.

Vaani imitated Piya's childish, incredulous voice: "Really?"

I was buoyed by her skepticism. Not because one shouldn't trust empirical data but simply because the *evidence* of things being otherwise is there for all to see. A month earlier, in Palghar in Maharashtra, two monks and the driver of their car were beaten to death by villagers who suspected them of being thieves. The monks, one of them seventy years old, were on their way to a funeral. Due to restrictions on travel during the lockdown, the monks and their young driver had taken a rural road. The village mob, armed with axes, stones, and sticks, fell on the strangers because of WhatsApp rumors about thieves on the rampage during the pandemic. In one of the videos of the incident, the older monk is seen coming out of the police building with a policeman. The police are far outnumbered by the villagers. The monk, his head bleeding, pleads for his life—but is quickly dragged away.

So, no, frequent hand washing isn't likely to cure humanity's ills.

After three hours, Shikha was let go. She asked the policemen if the housing society would have filed their stupid complaint and the police would have decided to act on it if Purnima hadn't been a poor tribal girl, an Adivasi. Shikha told Inspector Brij Bhushan Singh that Purnima was suspect in the eyes of her mostly upper-caste neighbors who couldn't imagine an Adivasi staying in a home like Shikha's except as domestic help. Sheer bigotry. Also, this was harassment, especially when a pandemic was raging. At which Inspector Brij Bhushan leered at her and asked, "Madam, why are you complaining? Have we done anything bad to you? Were you molested here? We gave you water to drink while you waited, did we not?"

I asked Shikha on WhatsApp if she was going to address the press and provoke Vaani's ex, Sikdar, into making outrageous statements on his show. She replied, "Shitdar is busy with other things. These days we have locusts coming from the West and Shitdar is on TV each evening screaming that the locusts have been trained as terrorists in Pakistan. Such a pest!"

For her amusement, I then forwarded Shikha a tweet by an economist at Johns Hopkins. His tweet read: "My colleagues @JohnsHopkins have informed me that #CowUrine does not ward off the #Coronavirus. #India needs science as a guide." Beneath the tweet was a photograph of bhakts in saffron, seated in the lotus position, marigold garlands around their necks, holding glasses of amber fluid.

I have always been the one who keeps asking Shikha for news from India, anything to overcome this feeling of distance and alienation that begins to affect me. In recent days, it is Shikha's brief messages, without any hellos and never with any personal news, that greet us when we wake up in the morning. Last week: "We were reading reports here that your doctors and nurses didn't have enough protective masks. But it appears your police has everything it needs."

I resumed the routine I had followed at the villa, of reading pages from my journal and making further notes. A couple of days ago I asked Shikha about the sociology student-activist in

Delhi who was denied bail while the ruling party politicos who incited rioting and arson by Hindu mobs have gone scot-free. In response, Shikha wrote to say that the student was pregnant, and maybe that should not be the part that is emphasized, but celebrities in India had tweeted their shock at the killing of a pregnant elephant but hadn't found it important to protest on behalf of a pregnant activist. Then she sent a link on WhatsApp to a video of an assault on protesters by the LAPD. She first wrote, "We want to know why your cops are simply copying our cops!" and then, an hour later, "Does that country have a law that says the police will beat the shit out of its citizens after the 8 PM curfew? I wonder why our police, on the other hand, thinks of it as a round-the-clock job."

That night, I adopted an academic tone and asked Vaani what she could tell me about the hurried judgment that the men in uniform form about us. A smile crossed her face as if she were an astronomer who had, at last, spotted signs of water on a distant planet. I'm exaggerating and I know Vaani would be annoyed if she were reading this—and yet, the truth is she is never as passionate, as full of joy, even as much *herself,* as she is when discussing social psychology. I apologize to her in advance for these pages, of course. It is necessary for me to report that, as she ate the matar paneer and rice I prepared for our dinner, when I asked Vaani whether her psychology research could shed any light on the sad fate of George Floyd and so many, many others, she said quite easily, "Have you heard the term *Korsakoff syndrome*?"

I hadn't, but a small flower of happiness blossomed in my heart. Imagine a flower of a delicate hue, a pale violet or a selfish blue. For the length of this discourse, I was to be the recipient of Vaani's full and undivided attention. Korsakoff's syndrome is a form of amnesia, she began. A person suffering from this condition is unable to retain any information or form new memories. Vaani was telling me about this because in a study involving patients with Korsakoff's syndrome, psychologists found that those men and women showed the same pattern of likes and dislikes for people and objects as the other participants in this study, who were not suffering from this syndrome. So, for instance, all the participants were shown photographs of a "good guy" (as described in fictional biographical information) and a "bad guy." Twenty days later, the Korsakoff's patients had virtually no memory of the biographical information; nonetheless, nearly 80 percent of them liked the "good guy" in the photos better than the "bad guy." Even in the absence of any conscious memories of the reasons, these patients suffering from chronic amnesia still had appropriate unconsciously generated positive or negative feelings about people and objects they had previously encountered.

"You are saying the police at some deep unconscious level are choosing George Floyd as criminal and inhuman?"

"I'm saying that racism, because of their upbringing, and the media, and sometimes even science, is part of the social unconscious of American citizens. Certainly, cops. They need not even be conscious of the series of choices their brain is making. The one who is Black is obviously the criminal. And a narrative is to be supplied, if not immediately available, to make that true."

"If psychology has located this cause, can it also suggest a cure?"

I was halfway through my question when I knew that Vaani would point to another experiment.

A psychologist at the University of Amsterdam, Reinout Wiers, had asked patients who wanted to stop drinking to come to his lab for two weeks. Wiers asked them to sit at a computer and use a lever to classify photographs. If they saw an alcohol-related photograph (objects like bottles or corkscrews, wineglasses, etc.) they were to push the lever, and if they saw something else (say, a beautiful landscape) they were to pull the lever. The pushing away of alcohol-related objects was intended to increase the avoidance motivation and, Vaani said, Wiers really succeeded in changing the unconscious attitudes of his patients from positive to negative.

Was it as simple as that? I tried to imagine a psychologist asking cops to sit in rows in front of individual computers. The cops would see a certain face and be asked if the person was good or bad. This would be repeated across a range of faces and attitudes. Women in cocktail dresses, for instance. A white man carrying a briefcase. Black youth wearing hoodies. And then, at the end of the test, the psychologist would discuss the results, exposing the biases of the participants. The meeting would break for a simple, healthy lunch funded by the taxpayer. The psychologist would then ask the participants to be seated in front of the computers again. If you see a Black face, please pull the lever toward you. If you see an alligator, push the lever away from you. This repeated exercise would alter in time the unconscious mechanism of the cops' minds.

But isn't that what training should be about? One would think that anyone entering the police force undergoes tests and exercises that foreground popular biases or stereotyping and help officers navigate them. Instead, all the evidence we were seeing everywhere was so disturbing. I had doubts about the particular method that Vaani had described—to be honest, it appeared a bit silly—but I didn't say anything. I helped her clear the dishes.

In India, Shikha was safe, but the poorest were dying by the roadside and on train tracks. And here in America, while we had so far escaped unscathed, Black people were being killed not just by the virus but also by the police. I saw that my friends, especially if they were white, were putting up posts about having contributed to bail funds for the protesters who had been arrested. There was news about an Indian man in Washington, D.C., stylish, intellectual-looking, who had given shelter to scores of young protesters corralled by the police after the start of curfew. Not only had he done that, but he had the fine sense to deliver succinct lines to the press. "I'm not a hero, I opened a door."

I was quite ashamed, to be honest, for having done nothing. All I had done was take care of my child and my wife. My child who, by the way, seemed to be regressing to an earlier childhood, sucking on her thumb, wanting to be held through the night. For several days now, I hadn't thought about *Enemies of the People*. All I had done was make journal entries about rumors and lies. (The problems that the pandemic had brought to the fore! From Ghaziabad, in Uttar Pradesh, came a story with the headline "Mother Sends Son to Buy Groceries, He Returns with Wife." The mother had complained to the police, the police had complained to the press.) All my journal entries about the bad faith of the politicians and the beliefs and experiences of people during lockdown. How was that going to benefit anyone? Oh yes, the future historian looking for evidence not of what those in authority recorded but, instead, ordinary people with ordinary anxieties living through a pandemic, was going to find in my journals a record of a writer who had returned from a residency and exchanged WhatsApp messages with his sister-in-law, who, at least, was courageous enough and generous enough to court danger.

Vaani, on the other hand, wasn't fretting over any of this. No agonizing over the obscure place we occupied in history. After hearing my complaints, she once even asked whether it wasn't enough that we were able to survive during a pandemic. In our own town, where we had voted strongly for a Black congressman in 2016, a peaceful protest was announced. Everyone was to wear masks and try to stay distant. There were instructions to bring posters saying Black Lives Matter. I liked that a protest was taking place but immediately offered to stay back home and take care of Piya. Without complaint, Vaani left. When she returned in the evening, she said that there were so many young people, all of them marching and singing and dancing, she had stopped outside a pizzeria and bought four large pizzas to give to the kids. I was glad.

Her serenity had been challenged over the last few days. Alison, a researcher she had become close to at Radcliffe, was sick and close to dying. Or that is what it felt like, Alison's husband said, for at least two days. It was unclear whether she became infected in Massachusetts, in which case Vaani would also have been exposed, or back at her home in Jackson Heights, Queens, where she developed the symptoms. Alison had been spending the year at Harvard on the same fellowship as Vaani. Alison's husband, a radio journalist at WNYC, did a moving report on his wife's illness, their self-quarantine, their hopes and fears. Sitting in our kitchen, safe from the ravages of the world, at least for the moment, we listened to the report.

David said that while he was recording his story, his four-year-old son was asleep on the couch. David recounted their conversation (*Dad, is Mom dying? Will you also get sick? Will I die?*) and Vaani sobbed next to me. We had heard frightened questions from Piya, and perhaps Vaani was thinking of our daughter, who, at that moment, was in the bedroom watching a kids' show on TV. There wasn't a day, or some recent days it seemed, not a single hour, when Vaani wasn't thinking of Alison and her family.

I liked David's honesty—and Alison's tired voice as she answered her husband's questions on the phone even though he was in the next room—and also his modesty. At one point, David said that he was aware how lucky he and Alison were—they had a secure income, a home, food, and they also had each other. He said he knew a young Latino man whom he had interviewed in Astoria just the previous week. His name was Ángel and, sick with COVID-19, he was living in his pickup truck. Ángel didn't want to infect his young family, who were living in the small room that they shared. David revealed that he had been calling Ángel for the past few days but no one answered the phone.

David and Alison were lucky. We were luckier still. In a world made so unlucky by our lying and incompetent leaders, we were so lucky. The world was reeling from the pandemic, but Kashmir had been in the longest lockdown, since August the previous year. It was a strange thing for me to remember this during the pandemic. At first there had been no news from the valley. A friend here in the math department has aged parents living in Srinagar: for weeks, he couldn't reach them. A man traveling to Delhi was given a phone number to call. A stranger's phone number. He was to call that number and simply say: "Tell Yusuf that Amma-Abbu are fine. Do not worry." Yusuf is a small man, dark for a Kashmiri, always smartly dressed and dignified in his speech. When I ran into him last year at the cheese shop, I could see that he had half-moons of worry under his eyes. The only news Yusuf had received from Srinagar was what he found in *The New York Times:* more troops brought in; complete lockdown; no communication, no Internet or phone service. In a world flooded with information, the death of information. He heard that there was a little movement allowed during curfew to get essentials like milk or medicines. Then came a trickle of news. About arrests in the middle of the night, men being flown away to prisons in other parts of India. Love was also in lockdown: as during earlier crises, in the classifieds section of the newspaper

Greater Kashmir, the pages were covered with all the wedding cancellations. All the notices beginning with the same set of words: "Due to the prevailing situation in the valley..."

INVITATION CANCELLED

Marriage ceremony of my daughter which was scheduled on 15th & 16th of July 2016 shall be performed with utmost simplicity and the invitations extended to relatives nears & dears on 15th & 16th July Stands Cancelled in view of prevailing circumstances. In convince is highly regretted.

Mehraj ud Din Misgar : 09815901538
Bashir Ahmad Misgar : 09815906048
Mohd Amin Misgar : 9622428960

INVITATION CANCELLED

This is to inform that the marriage ceremony of my son, Mr. Suhaib Muhammad Khan of Syed Colony, Kanitar Sadrabal, Srinagar which was scheduled on 17th July 2016 has been cancelled due to prevailing situations.

Mr. Muhammad Ashraf Khan
Syed Colony, Kanitar, Sadrabal, Srinagar
Cell No: 9906868147

Cancellation of Dawat-e-Waleema by Muqeem's of Chrarisharief

Due to prevailing circumstances, Daawat-e-Walima being organised on Sunday, the 17th of July 2016 on the eve of Marriage Ceremony of Nayeem Rizwan Muqeem S/o Mohd Yousuf Muqeem being solemnized by Muqeem's of Chrar-i-Sharief is being cancelled.

Haji Mohd Yousuf Muqeem, his Family and all relatives regret the inconvenience so caused. The Baraat will proceed simply and the function will conclude with extreme austerity.

Khawani will be held.
BREAVED FAMILY

INVITATION CANCELLED

Due to the unavoidable circumstances the Walima function stands cancelled, however Nikah ceremony of my son Shakir Hussain Jan will be performed as per schedule.

Mrs. Haji Mohd Shafi Jan
275-Govt. Housing Colony Bagh-e-Mehtab, Srinagar
Phone No: 0194-2430260

INVITATION CANCELLED

We regret to inform that due to prevailing circumstances the marriage ceremony of our daughters which was scheduled to be held on 16th & 17th July 2016 is hereby cancelled. However Nikah ceremony will be held as per programme, in a simple manner.

Mrs & Mr Abdul Majid Mir
Gulshanabad Chrarisharief
Cell: 9858364427

INVITATION CANCELLED

This is to inform that the marriage ceremony of my son, Mr. Amir Ashraf Mir of Wanbal Rawalpora which was scheduled on 15,16 & 17th July 2016 has been cancelled due to prevailing situations. However the other formalities will be solemnized as per programme.

Mr. Mohammad Ashraf Mir
Wanbal Rawalpora (9906993719)

INVITATION CANCELLED

This is to inform that the marriage ceremony of my daughter which was scheduled on 11 & 12 July 2016 has been cancelled due to prevailing situations. However Nikah Ceremony shall be performed as per schedule.

CARCHOICE SANATNAGAR
Noor Muhammad Yatoo
S/o Late Haji Abdul Aziz Yatoo
R/o Masjid Bagh Sanat Nagar Srinagar

R/O Madhu Bagh Nowshera Srinagar
Mobile No. 9797119207, 9419000033

INVITATION CANCELLED

This is to inform that the marriage ceremony of my son, Mr. Muneer Ahmad Bhat of Fateh Kadal, Srinagar which was scheduled on 15 & 16 July 2016 has been cancelled due to prevailing situations. However the other formalities will be solemnized as per programme.

Mr. Ali Muhammad Bhat
Fateh Kadal, Sgr (8494010809, 9906957924)

INVITATION CANCELLED

It is informed that the invitation of marriage ceremony of our son, Muhammad Jibran Gul which was scheduled on 11th and 12th July is cancelled because of the unfortunate prevailing circumstances. However, the Nikkah will be as per schedule. Inconvenience is highly regretted.

Mr. & Mrs Gul Muhammad Wani
Khalid Colony Soura Near Govt. Boys Hr. Sec.
9797701901, 9906704708, 9469390007

INVITATION CANCELLED

In view of the prevailing circumstances in the valley, we have decided to cancel the Marriage Function of our daughter. However the Nikah Khwani will be performed on 15th of July with utmost simplicity.

SALAM-UD-DIN MAKHDOOMI
GOUSIA MOHALLA, UMER COLONY, LAL BAZAR.
9419443390, 9469077999

INVITATION CANCELLED

It is informed that the invitation of marriage ceremony of our son, Muhammad Jibran Gul which was scheduled on 11th and 12th July is cancelled because of the unfortunate prevailing circumstances. However, the Nikkah will be as per schedule. Inconvenience is highly regretted.

Mr. & Mrs Gul Muhammad Wani
Khalid Colony Soura Near Govt. Boys Hr. Sec.
9797701901, 9906704708, 9469390007

H No 129 Shadab Lane Usmania Colony,
Bagh Mahtab Srinagar
Cell No: 9419007183, 9858822737

INVITATION CANCELLED

We regret to inform that due to prevailing circumstances the marriage ceremony of our daughter which was scheduled to be held on 13th & 14th July 2016 is hereby cancelled. However Nikah ceremony will be held as per programme, in a simple manner.

Mrs & Mr Master Ghulam Hussain
Doonipora Alamgaribazar Sgr.
Cell: 9419080250

INVITATION CANCELLED

In the wake of the unrest in valley, the invitation of marriage ceremony of my son which was scheduled on 15th at Nigeen Club of stands cancelled.

Syed Nisar Ahmed Shah Hamdani
R/o Budshah Colony Sanatnagar
(9796111500, 01942439627)

INVITATION CANCELLED

Due to the ongoing unrest in valley, the invitation for marriage ceremony of my son Lateef Maqbool Mir, scheduled on 14th and 15th July 2016 stands cancelled. The nikkah ceremony shall however be held in a simple manner.

FROM
Mohd Maqbool Mir, Firdous Colony,
Illahi Bagh Road Buchhpora

INVITATION CANCELLED

This is to inform that the marriage ceremony of my daughter which was scheduled on 15 & 16 July 2016 has been cancelled due to prevailing situations. However Nikah Ceremony shall be performed as per schedule.

Mrs. Abdul Hamid Bazaz
R/o Umarhair Buchpora Srinagar
(9906547775, 9622331514)

But is there singing in the dark times? Yes, one day in the news I came across this report of love during the time of curfew:

A young Kashmiri man from Shopian traveled more than fifty miles with a friend to a village to catch a glimpse of the girl he was in love with. This was during the lockdown. The two youths had cooked up a story. In the girl's village, they asked for Majid sahib, a fruit dealer, an imaginary name. A local man named Kaysir accosted the boys after seeing them return to the same lane three times within the hour. Who were these strangers in his village, he wanted to know, especially when movement was restricted? The boys gave up their secret. Kaysir knew the family of the girl, and he adopted the boys' ruse and decided to help. Kaysir knocked on the door of the house in which the girl's family lived. Her father opened the door. Kaysir said that the youth were from out of town and looking for a Majid sahib, a fruit dealer. The check he had given them had bounced. The father confirmed that there was no one of that name in the village. Perhaps he felt bad for the boys because he then offered them tea. The boys politely said no. At that moment, one floor above them, a window opened and a girl looked out with surprise on her face. The two youths left with Kaysir.

On the deserted village road, Kaysir asked the boy, "Saw the girl?"

The boy said, "I saw the crescent of Eid."

I mulled the news about the boys from Shopian. The boys had filled my heart with cheer. With my renewed commitment to the idea of novel writing as an essential service, I sat down and quickly wrote a very short story:

> ESSENTIAL SERVICES
>
> Every day that week a line formed outside the liquor store by noon. Those in line stood six feet apart, checking their phones, or reading a book, or looking up at the trees. Twelve people were allowed at a time into the liquor store.
>
> A man and woman, wearing masks and gloves, arrived from different directions. The man, who might have been in his twenties and whose mask was blue colored, made a flourish with a gloved hand and let the woman take the place ahead of him. For a moment, he studied the back of the woman's head. She had blond streaks in her hair.
>
> "You weren't answering the phone last night," the young woman said to him, turning. "Do you think it is easy for me to step out like this?"

Her companion hadn't stopped smiling under his mask ever since she arrived.

He now said, "I've heard that the wait is longer in the line outside the CVS on South Hill Road. Your father must need his medicine. Let's meet there tomorrow."

CHAPTER 8

HAVE YOU SEEN THE SEA?

So that is the world we are living in. We are scared of the future, we are angry at those in power who have disregarded the common good, and we are filled with guilt from the knowledge that there are so many in the world who have so little to protect them. That last thing—the feeling of complicitous guilt—has helped me reach a conclusion. Don't trust anyone who claims they have clean hands. Yes, I mean that metaphorically. Mostly.

It is unbearable to watch Trump assure himself and the members of the press corps that he has done a great job. It is no less tiresome to hear Modi bloviate about what can be achieved if we stand united—while he and his followers do everything to divide the country and profit from divisions. Not just the leaders. The dull bureaucrats cherry-picking data to assure people that everything is fine and that they are doing their job. All the kowtowing journalists in Delhi and Mumbai, the conspiracy theorists in the studios of Fox News in New York and Washington, D.C. The imbecilic political illiterates in MAGA hats and Modi masks in the two countries I know best. Each one of those political illiterates who believes that the weak or the vulnerable do not need access to fundamental rights, that science is mere hogwash, that staying at home during the coronavirus crisis is a ploy to steal the election from Trump, that enough has already been done and even that was an unnecessary indulgence—such people are examples of what you must not allow yourself or your children or your students to ever resemble. *Do not become lackeys of the state.*

That's where one starts. The stance to adopt, like a batsman taking guard at the crease. But, beyond that, what? These crises unfolding so quickly in our world today, they demand a response. In each instance, we witness such a diminution of the human body—not diminution, *annihilation*—at the hands of power. It would appear logical that we put our bodies on the street in protest. Except that it is precisely a mass protest that the coronavirus has made inadvisable. I remember the protest in Delhi where the human rights lawyer had urged her audience "Keep a record. Don't trust the state." Well, that kind of agitation against unjust citizenship laws was one of the first victims of the pandemic. It was disbanded to prevent the spread of COVID-19 through crowding. And yet, and this was hopeful, despite the rules of social distancing, in Minneapolis and other cities of America, after the murder of George Floyd, huge protests rose up. People in long processions, all wearing masks. It is a powerful statement. A part of me belongs to that movement of people in large numbers. A minority turning into a majority. But there is always another part of me, I don't know whether I should call it my younger or my older self, that wants to stay true only to an activism of the word. To believe primarily in recording words on the page. Against the brutal sentence of the law, a sentence filled with the truth of witness. *God gave Noah the rainbow sign, No more water, the fire next time!* This belief isn't something new called forth by the events of recent days, it has been with me for a long time, certainly from the time I set to work on this project.

Now it is June 2020. I heard a protester with "Black Lives Matter" written on her T-shirt warn in a video posted on Twitter, "Target will reopen. The stores will reopen. That's assured. What is not assured is our safety and real justice." In India, a poet celebrated for his political verse was sent to the hospital after he fell unconscious in prison; he is eighty-one years old. Here, in upstate New York, during my hurried and far-between trips to the grocery store, I have been surprised to see some of our students. They are unable to return home because of the pandemic. I was away the whole semester on my sabbatical, but I suddenly find myself in the grocery store in the produce section standing across from someone who was in my Literature of 9/11 class two semesters ago. It is difficult to talk through the masks. The spray of mist on the lettuce and broccoli only makes me think of aerosolized virus. Time to leave. "Email me if I can be of any help."

The email that arrived, instead, was from the college president. It was addressed to the whole college community. One of our students was Tasered and shot by the police the previous night. He is a well-known figure on campus because he is a basketball player. Akwasi Jones. Akwasi is fighting for his life. The president's note mentioned that Akwasi's parents and sister have arrived and are with him.

The president's email doesn't mention it, but the three officers involved in the shooting are all white. What happened was that Akwasi had locked himself out of his car and was trying to open the door on the passenger side with a wire hanger. A patrol car pulled up. Akwasi saw it and went on with his work. The cop who approached Akwasi already had his gun drawn.

Akwasi was asked to spread his hands on his car, and the cop patted him down. When he was asked for identification, Akwasi explained to the officer that his wallet was inside the locked car. The officer wanted to handcuff him first. This led to an argument. All this happened on a residential street, but there was a video recorded on a phone by a woman watching from a second-floor window. (Was she the same person who had called the police?) Did Akwasi tell the cop that his apartment was only two blocks away and that his roommate would testify to his identity? Perhaps he did and the cop didn't care. The cop wanted Akwasi to stop arguing, to submit, and the cop was also ready with the handcuffs.

Did Akwasi resist arrest? It is possible that he objected to being handcuffed because he had committed no crime. The cop called for backup; he can be seen on the camera, his face swiveling to the side to speak into the radio on his chest. When the new cops arrived, they didn't hesitate. In the video that has been circulating, you hear the woman holding the phone gasp. Because the phone shakes, the woman's attention drawn by the scene instead of remaining focused on her screen, we cannot see what has happened. It is still light outside, the phone screen filled with the glow of the orange sky and dark green leaves close by. For another fleeting moment, the phone stays still on a blue curtain. Then we are back on the street.

Akwasi has fallen down on his stomach and is convulsing, light wires connecting him to a yellow object held by one cop while another, his knee on the fallen body, wields a set of handcuffs. If you watch the video again, you might notice this time the soles of Akwasi's shoes, black Air Jordans, black soles with white circles in them. That's all that is visible of him. Mostly what you see are the uniformed shoulders, the white arm of a cop, and in the corner of the frame the wheel of Akwasi's car. The woman holding the phone has seen something that the camera in her phone hasn't, because she makes another sound like a gasp. A second later, the explosion of sound that is gunfire in quick succession.

It has happened so many times, and yet it doesn't fail to shock. The brutal repetitiveness of it. The indelible script in which the history of race is written in this country. You think of the marches, the sit-ins, the speeches, Jackie Robinson, MLK Day, Michelle Obama, the Black Panther, hell, all those stamps commemorating the Harlem Renaissance that you bought only the month before the pandemic hit—and then the police come and leave all that history—no, a living body that might still have breath in it—bleeding on the street.

Of course, a protest rally was announced for the next day.

A student in my class, Ishaan Prahi, sent this news to me. Ishaan is from Delhi. He and two others in my Immigrant Literature class from a few semesters ago were going to join the protest. A group on Facebook was handling the logistics. The email sent by the organizers stressed the need for safety and nonviolence. Not just because of the pandemic but also because of a statement made by the local sheriff, who has been aggressive in his defense of police tactics. The cop who shot Akwasi, it has come out, had a smiling photograph of himself on Facebook with the caption, which can be seen as premeditated intent to shoot first and ask questions later: "I'd rather be judged by 12 than carried by 6." When asked about this, the sheriff said, "Look, we won't be defined by political correctness. We cannot put our officers in danger. All lives matter."

After Ishaan and his classmates went to the rally, the march proceeding from a public park in the inner city named Sojourner Truth Park, past the police precinct and the post office to the city court office, where there is a large square, they found out that a right-wing group had organized a counterrally, and it was winding its own way through town, a large crowd made up of white men and women, most of them without masks and many holding burning torches.

The counterprotest, by all accounts, was awful. It became clear very quickly to my students that it was unabashedly and brazenly a white power rally. I received an email from Ishaan, who was a part of a small group of protesters sending out tweets through the night: "This is what it must have been like to witness the KKK. Except that none of these people are wearing white hoods." And, "No masks. This is the face of white supremacy." The students started posting screenshots from the Facebook page of the group that had organized the counterprotest. They were filled with hate, these posts, showing Black people with monkey faces and representing them as looters and convicts. It turned out, and this information too was made available through screenshots, that people had reported the page to Facebook. There were more than thirty complaints from people in the community saying that this was spreading hate and dividing the community. But the page had not been taken down.

The next day I read online that the crowd wore MAGA hats and carried posters saying WE SUPPORT OUR POLICE and BLUE LIVES. This sentiment was interspersed with other slogans like KEEP AMERICA GREAT. There were two thousand people at the rally. The police surrounding the white supremacy crowd, some of them helmeted and on horses, appeared to my students more like a phalanx of protectors.

The following day Ishaan and I talked on Zoom. He was in his messy dorm room while I sat in our kitchen with a virtual background of a starry sky behind me. After the protest, Ishaan; his girlfriend, Sarah, who is white; and her best friend, Jasmyn, half-Black, half-Asian, walked into an outdoor seating area outside a local bar. They were charged up and also a bit tired and wanted to relax. Beer seemed a good idea. Two men drinking at another table, both middle-aged and white, came up to the students. Ishaan told me that he thought at first the men were interested in the young women. But the first man just pointed his bottle at them and asked them if they had been out there at the march. The kids looked at each other and then at the men. The men weren't aggressive or hostile, just a bit odd and unwelcome.

Sarah said, "We were there, yes. Protesting."

The first man said, "You all go to college here? You too?" He pointed now at Ishaan.

The students nodded. Ishaan said that the men were keeping a safe distance, but barely.

The man said, "It is an expensive college. It is, isn't it? Tell me any one thing they taught you right. Any one thing."

Now the students felt this was turning out to be a conversation they would later enjoy recounting on Snapchat or under the tents outside their dorms.

Jasmyn said, "Well, last semester, before the college closed, I learned that 95 percent of climate researchers say that humans are causing global warming but there are apparently others who think otherwise. What do you think?"

The men thought what Jasmyn had said was funny. I was told they laughed.

The second man had less of the openness than the first. His face turned into a scowl when he addressed Jasmyn.

"Don't you think Americans"—and a slight pause here—"you are an American, right? Don't you think Americans have more reason to fear being killed by drug dealers than by a stupid sunburn?" (When I was told this, I didn't need to wonder where such arguments come from.)

Jasmyn, her face reddening, said something like "Dude, when the waters rise, and the levels are already rising, or don't they report this on Fox News, it will affect the whole damned planet. Just because you're American won't keep you safe from heat waves or hurricanes. What do you think is happening right now with the coronavirus?"

In response to which, both men said in one voice, "Chinese virus."

My students just looked at each other instead of at the men. But they were not done yet.

The first fellow, who still retained his smile, now addressed Jasmyn. "Okay, so you are a science major or something, right? Tell me, do they teach you real science at your school? I'm guessing there's some Black in you. You are here for some bullshit protest for a Black guy who had pot in his pocket. Did you know that the reason why Blacks commit more crime is that they have a higher testosterone level than the average human being? I'm right now talking of Black males. Our prisons are full of them."

My students were stunned by this man's bigotry, and his ignorance, and their faces must have given away this feeling of shock. And where had this detail about Akwasi having pot in his pocket emerged from?

The guy smirked and said, "You didn't know that, did you?"

Sarah asked the man, "Does your brand of science also say that God created dark people for life in the tropics while white people were created for living in the temperate zones?"

"Well, that's just common sense, isn't it?" the man asked. He was wrong about the science, but my students also now knew that their complacency about being right wasn't going to save the world.

Jasmyn hadn't let go of the image of Akwasi's father, a tall, dignified man who looked a bit like Patrick Ewing, speaking at the protest of his immense pain. The sorrow that had now engulfed the family. His wife and daughter had stood next to him, tears coursing down the young girl's face. The father said he had worked two jobs, as a line cook and a janitor at a computer firm, for two decades. He had put Akwasi through school and was delighted when his son was awarded a scholarship at our college. The previous day, he said, a reporter had asked him whether he regretted sending his son to college. What kind of question was that? Akwasi's father had a hurt but also amused tone in his voice. He repeated that line and waited. He said that he had told the white reporter that what he regretted was that the police, with complete disregard for his son's life, had nearly murdered him.

The argument went on for a bit longer while around them people at their socially distanced tables ordered their drinks or talked or ate their chicken wings. No one was hurt. When the story was being narrated to me, I quite easily imagined an assault in an alley outside. However, nothing of that sort happened.

As he told me this story, Ishaan's face on my screen would grow light and then darken again as the curtain in his dorm room lifted in the breeze. He leaned closer and said that he had learned more from that conversation at the bar than he had done from many of the classes he had attended at our college. I felt somewhat insulted when he said this. Hadn't my classes—with readings from Aimé Césaire, Frantz Fanon, Bessie Head, Nawal El Saadawi, Anita Desai, all the way down to Zadie Smith—taught him more? Ishaan had his reasons. He felt he had stepped out of the bubble. He had encountered opposition in the real world. More important, he realized that he could not rely on reason alone. Reason was a dumb mule that could carry the load of any ideology or any fool with his eye on power. In the past, and perhaps even now, scientific discourse had also served as that dumb beast of burden. The man outside the bar was appealing to science, a false science, to make a dubious and dangerous claim. After saying all this, Ishaan stopped for a moment. He then said, "I kept quiet at the bar. I wondered whether my friends thought I was a coward for not speaking up. But I knew that if I didn't get killed that night, I'd write about what was happening. Not as science, but as a report on our times."

I told Ishaan that he should write about his experience at the white supremacy rally and its aftermath. He nodded. Then he told me a story.

In the late eighties, Ishaan's father was a university student in Delhi and took part in street plays. On January 1, 1989, they were performing a play in an industrial township outside Delhi. A winter morning, not too cold, perfect for playing cricket but also for street theater. The performance was part of an election campaign for a communist leader. Soon after the actors had started the play, a group of men came armed with sticks and iron rods. They were shouting slogans for the ruling party candidate. Ishaan's father was a junior member of the troupe; their leader was a talented and charming young man named Safdar. Safdar tried to talk to the men, telling them that in five minutes the performance would be over. Perhaps, he suggested to them, you too can enjoy the play. But the men hadn't come to do anything like that. They first attacked Safdar, hitting him in the head with iron rods more than twenty times. He fell down, his blood flowing on the road. The actors, chased by the goons, ran and hid in the small quarters in which the workers lived. For a long time, walking up and down the streets, the men searched for the actors. They took out guns and fired in the air. On finding a door open, they forced themselves inside and fired at a Nepali laborer home from work. He was newly married and had a small child. The worker died, and a few hours later, in a Delhi hospital, Safdar was declared dead too.

The play that had been interrupted is now performed all over India on Safdar's death anniversary. That play is called *Halla Bol.* It asks you to "raise hell." Ishaan said that he always thought his father told him this story because he wanted him to be careful and not expose himself to danger. The real lesson, Ishaan now said, after he had come back safe from the rally, was that he was going to talk to Sarah and Jasmyn about working on a project together. He was going to raise his voice, raise hell.

I was looking at Ishaan's face, thin, narrow, a somber look in his eyes. Now and then, for a tiny fraction of a second, his image froze on my screen, as if Ishaan was reaching for a kind of stillness. There is always talk of the innocence of youth and their smiles; I find their unexpected gravity more touching. Perhaps they are one and the same thing.

Ishaan said of Sarah and Jasmyn, "They were so brave and articulate."

"Yes," I said, "yes." How could I not encourage him? The possibility of a young person opening himself up to the world, learning from the example of others. I also felt challenged as a teacher. I said that perhaps Sarah and Jasmyn and he could continue to meet with me after the pandemic was over. A reading group would be a good start, and then perhaps sessions to plot a future course of action. The young, I thought, could find allies elsewhere too.

The breeze again lifted the curtain at the window in Ishaan's room and I saw that he had put a thick hardcover volume of *War and Peace* on the windowsill to keep his window from banging shut. We were coming to the end of our meeting. I told Ishaan that I had been working on a book called *Enemies of the People*. He asked me what it was about. I said I had started with a simple question: How many among your neighbors will look the other way when a figure of authority comes to your door and puts a boot in your face? When I began, I had imagined a near-literal boot in the face. Because don't all the videos of lynchings testify to that fact? And you would think the same if you were looking at protesters, especially if they were Black, being beaten on the streets of America by the police in absurdly futuristic military gear. The point was to ask who among us would look the other way when they came for you with their guns or knives or warrants. What I had not considered, but what was becoming increasingly clear to me, is that the boots in the face are just the barefaced lies uttered by our leaders and believed by their followers. I saw Ishaan nodding his head when I said that in what I was writing, I was trying to record the drama of this battle between what was true and what wasn't.

Ishaan said that it had been nice to talk, even if it was only on Zoom, and that it would be good to chat again sometime soon. When he said that, I asked him to stick around for a bit longer. I said, "Before you leave, can you take out your notebook and write something? Write one true sentence. Write the truest sentence that you know."

He bent over and picked up a notebook. He looked up at the camera on his screen.

"What?" I said.

"You should write a true sentence too," he said, so softly, so seriously, that I couldn't refuse.

In my small black notebook with its blank pages I began writing with a pencil that needed sharpening. Ishaan, his head bowed in the rectangle on my screen, was already writing. I felt he had a lot to say, and I too set myself to the task. I wrote quickly, without stopping, trying to get to the heart of what I was thinking at that time, and had been thinking about, in fact, for a long time.

A lot of life is left in a man being killed.

He does not at first foresee the end. He knows, of course, that anything can happen. When it begins, his only worry is that he will be unable to work. At the very least, he thinks, he will be unable to lift heavy loads. He has used his hands all his life. They are his tools. He had himself made the door of his room from which they dragged him.

Then it settles in as disappointment. There is so much more work to be done in the unfinished house. The iron rods striking him are raising dust from a ground sown with regret.

He knows he can list the names of the men, whose voices he recognizes in the dark. A few from the dinner in his house only two nights ago. He will repeat the names to the police, he tells himself, before losing consciousness for a minute.

Or more.

He comes back to life when he hears a child's voice asking if the man is dead. Is he? One man's voice, and then another's, sending the child back inside. The child is a stranger, but the man being killed would like him to know that he is alive. It has been a long time since he made a sound. He tries to speak without scaring the kid, without crying. It comes out like a moan, and immediately a boot, no, a brick, smashes into his face.

He tries to focus elsewhere. His chest is home to an excruciating pain and he suspects broken ribs. His pain keeps him in the present. Death, or the possibility of his dying, comes to him when he notices that, despite the pain and the wild commotion, he has slipped into a dream.

He remembers being in the classroom when he was ten. They had read a poem. The teacher was newly married. He can see her now, a fresh flower every day in her hair. The poem was about a warrior dying, dreaming of his homeland on the alien battlefield. The teacher had liked him. She stopped coming to school when she was going to have a baby.

Unlike the warrior, he is dying in the dark lane outside his house.

A friend of his had died five years ago from dengue. During his final hours, the friend had thought his mother was still alive, sitting with him in the shabby hospital ward. Mother, he called out, I want water.

The reason he thinks of his friend just now is that he is thirsty. His uncle used to keep a pot of water under the neem tree. He wants a small drink. As a child, he would look up after taking a sip and see parakeets bursting out from under the canopy of green leaves.

He thinks of a nephew, dead at thirteen, killed by a bus when on his way to school. Compared to that poor boy, he has lived a full life. Despite all the fears that parents are prone to, his children grew up into adulthood. If they survive tonight—his daughter was left cowering in the room upstairs, his son left for dead with his head split open—they will be able to fend for themselves even if he is absent from their lives.

They have stopped hitting him, or maybe he can't feel anything anymore. His eyes are swollen shut. Is it still night? He wants it to end.

He has stopped telling them they are wrong. Now his tongue is like a small animal running in one direction and then another.

A sudden new pain like a million ants crawling up his leg. He thinks the men are setting him on fire.

Out of great weariness comes a new change. He feels he is walking away, able to cover a vast distance, without any real effort of his limbs. In the shadow of a boulder that blots out the hot sun, there is silence.

The man being killed has never seen the sea. But he hears its wide sound now in his ear, and this would be magical if it were not so real. So real that he can taste the salt of the soft waves.

BIBLIOGRAPHY

The writing of this novel spanned a four-year period which coincided with an era of chaos that a report on Donald Trump in *The New York Times* characterized thus: "A presidency born in a lie about Barack Obama's birthplace." And ended on a lie in the words of Trump himself:

As a report partly on news, this book cites frequently from mainstream media, and acknowledgment is offered where stylistically necessary, but I would like to more explicitly thank those outlets and individuals fighting fake news, in particular, Media Matters, Democracy Now!, and, in India, Pratik Sinha's Alt News and Ravish Kumar's *Prime Time*. Where the book plunges into news from the further reaches of the human heart, the sources are more varied and untraceable.

Also see: Glenn Kessler, Salvador Rizzo and Meg Kelly,

"President Trump has made more than 20,000 false or misleading claims", *The Washington Post*, July 13, 2020; Amit Bhatt, "Declare cow the national animal of India: Rajasthan High Court", *DNA*, June 1, 2017; Aakar Patel, "Bhakts in denial: If Narendra Modi could improve things, he would have done it by now", *National Herald*, June 14, 2020; "Cows exhale oxygen, absorb cosmic energy, home to gods: Rajasthan HC judge", *Hindustan Times*, June 19, 2017; Chetan Bhagat, "How blind bhakts can actually hurt India's democracy", *Times of India*, January 10, 2017; "Why Narendra Modi's Heart Bleeds For Cricket Star Shikhar Dhawan", *Outlook*, June 21, 2019; Sumedha Kirti, "'Pained': In Rajya Sabha Address, PM Modi Condemns Jharkhand Lynching But Says Wrong to Blame State", *News18*, June 26, 2019; "Tabrez Ansari Lynching: Police Drop Murder Charge Against 11 Accused", *The Wire*, September 10, 2019; Abeera Dubey, "Judgment Primer: Alimuddin Ansari lynching case," *CJP*, August 7, 2018; 'Union minister Jayant Sinha garlands 8 convicted for Ramgarh mob lynching", *India Today*, July 6, 2018; "Sanskrit can even tackle climate change: PM Modi", *United News of India*, August 26, 2018; Maseeh Rahman, "Indian prime minister claims genetic science existed in ancient times", *Guardian*, October 28, 2014; Aakar Patel, "Bhakts in denial: If Narendra Modi could improve things, he would have done it by now", *National Herald*, June 14, 2020; Harsha Kumari Singh, "Before Taking Mob Victim To Hospital, Rajasthan Cops Arranged Cow Shelter", *NDTV*, July 23, 2018; "Hindutva: The Growth of Violent Hindu Nationalism", *Outlook*, November 20, 2002; Vaibhav Tiwari, "Clapping, Beating Utensils—How India Thanked Covid-19 Fighters", *NDTV*, March 22, 2020; Shaina NC, [Twitter post], 2.25 p.m., March 20, 2020; Himanshi Dahiya, "Burning Candles Kills Coronavirus? PM's Message Given False Spin", *The Quint*, April 3, 2020; Peter Baker, "In Trump's Marathon Briefings, the Answers and the Messages Are Often Contradictory", *New York*

Times, April 8, 2020; Anuja, "Unity is power, strength, progress and empowerment: PM Modi", *Live Mint*, October 25, 2020; and Andrew Adonis, "Narendra Modi Is Everything Apart From What He Seems", *The Wire*, April 8, 2021.

For descriptions of psychological experiments, major thanks to Daniel Kahneman's *Thinking, Fast and Slow* and John Bargh's *Before You Know It*. On children lying, *NurtureShock: New Thinking About Children*, by Po Bronson and Ashley Merryman; also, Kim B. Serota et al., "The Prevalence of Lying in America: Three Studies of Self-Reported Lies." Elizabeth Kolbert, "Why Facts Don't Change Our Minds," *The New Yorker*, February 19, 2017. Susan Dominus, "When the Revolution Came for Amy Cuddy," *The New York Times Magazine*, October 18, 2017. I made a note of Cressida Leyshon, "Callan Wink on Fiction in the Age of 'Alternative Facts,'" *New Yorker.com*, August 13, 2018. I have quoted from Junot Díaz's *This Is How You Lose Her* and Harry G. Frankfurt's *On Bullshit*. A discussion about the psychologist Harry Harlow on the radio show *This American Life* brought me to Deborah Blum's biography of Harlow entitled *Love at Goon Park*. Other sources include Lucas Mann's "Trump Wants to Make Reality TV, But Now the Cast Is Ignoring His Directions," *The Washington Post*, October 20, 2019; Graham Rayman, "The Alarming Record of the F.B.I. Informant in the Bronx Bomb Plot," *The Village Voice*, July 8, 2009; Aleksandar Hemon, "Stop Making Sense, or How to Write in the Age of Trump," *The Village Voice*, January 17, 2017; Luke O'Neil, "Lies, Damned Lies and Donald Trump: The Pick of the President's Untruths," *The Guardian*, April 29, 2019. Giorgio Riello, *Back in Fashion: Western Fashion from the Middle Ages to the Present*, for information on the production of cotton shirts. The joke about fleas is taken from Elif Batuman's *The Idiot*. On the coronavirus pandemic, I have quoted from Sheera Frenkel, Davey Alba, and Raymond Zhong, "Surge of Virus Misinformation Stumps

Facebook and Twitter," *The New York Times,* March 8, 2020, and Annie Gowen, "Coronavirus Deniers and Hoaxers Persist Despite Dire Warnings, Claiming 'It's Mass Hysteria,'" *The Washington Post,* March 19, 2020; Andrew Liu, "'Chinese Virus,' World Market," *n+1 Online,* March 20, 2020; Richard L. Kravitz, "When Trump Pushed Hydroxychloroquine to Treat COVID-19, Hundreds of Thousands of Prescriptions Followed Despite Little Evidence That It Worked," *The Conversation,* July 9, 2020; and *This American Life,* "The Test," March 27, 2020. On Gandhi and the Spanish flu, I have liberally quoted from Laura Spinney, *Pale Rider: The Spanish Flu of 1918 and How It Changed the World.* Thanks to Sumita Chatterjee for recommending *Gandhi's Printing Press: Experiments in Slow Reading*—I'm greatly indebted to the book's author, Isabel Hofmeyr, for the fascinating study of Gandhi and slow news. Thanks to Joanna Slater and Niha Masih for the report "In Delhi's Worst Violence in Decades, a Man Watched His Brother Burn," *The Washington Post,* March 6, 2020. Thanks to Arun Venugopal's report "One Worker's Experience on the Morgue Overflow Shift," WNYC, April 16, 2020. Peter Baker and Maggie Haberman, "In Torrent of Falsehoods, Trump Claims Election Is Rigged," *The New York Times,* November 5, 2020. For other details from India, a testimony entitled *Memories of a Father* by T. V. Eachara Warrier and a journalist's report, *Shoshan, Sangharsh, aur Shahadat* (Oppression, Struggle, and Martyrdom) by Anuj Sinha. Soutik Biswas, Chinki Sinha, and Shuddhabrata Sengupta are my reliable sources in matters of what could be called people's media in India. I thank them all, on behalf of my novel's narrator.

ACKNOWLEDGMENTS

In a 2017 article on behavioral science in *The New Yorker,* I read that grocers had learned that they could sell double the amount of soup if they placed a sign above their cans reading "limit of 12 per person." There is some cunning there, but also a certain magic. I don't know anything about selling books but I do understand a thing or two about writing them. If there is any magic in it, it is in the discovery that one doesn't write a book alone. Thank you to the Rockefeller Center at Bellagio, the Yaddo Corporation, the MacDowell Colony, and the Lannan Foundation for supporting my work. Thank you to David Davidar, who has been the first reader for my last four or five books. Thank you to Nicole Winstanley, who sent me unbelievable hope just when I was leaving for a residency, and then, once I had come back with a new draft, provided me the most generous, thoughtful feedback that shaped the novel you are holding in your hands. Thank you to Ravi Mirchandani for fulfilling a long-held dream of mine to publish with Picador UK. Thank you to my editor at Knopf, Timothy O'Connell, for supporting this project from the start and, gradually, with serene patience, helping find its true form and leading it into the light. Thank you to David Godwin, Susanna Lea, Lisette Verhagen, and my agent Jay Mandel at WME. Thank you to Erin Edmison, Bill Hoynes, Ian Jack, Martha Jessup, Tim Johnson, Liz Johnston, Lucas Mann, David Means, Michael Ondaatje, Jordan Pavlin, Rob Shapiro, and Hansda Sowvendra Shekhar for critical help and advice. Thank you to Sophia

Florida, Faith Hill, Sumana Roy, and Elena Schultz for helping me during my research. Thank you to the following friends whose conversations with me about art and writing helped me while I was working on this book: Josh Begley, Anna Bertucci, Teju Cole, Kiran Desai, Navid Hafez, Emilie Houssart, Hua Hsu, Emmanuel Iduma, Josh Kun, Ben Lerner, Suzanne Lettieri, Yiyun Li, Stephen Miller, Leah Mirakhor, Jenny Offill, Dushko Petrovich, Mark Sarvas, Shane Slattery-Quintanilla, Linda Spalding, Pat Wallace, and Xinran Yuan. Thank you to my family for taking naps and staying woke.